Land Victoria Houston's
first Loon Lake Fishing Mystery . . .

Dead Angler

Praise for *Dead Angler* . . .

"As exciting as fishing a tournament."
—Norb Wallock,
North American Walleye Anglers' 1997 Angler of the Year

"Houston introduces us to a cast of characters with whom we quickly bond—as fly fishers and as good citizens—in the first of what I hope will be a long series."
—Joan Wulff,
world-class fly caster, and cofounder of the Wulff School of Fly Fishing

"A compelling thriller . . . populated with three-dimensional characters who reveal some of their secrets of trout fishing the dark waters of the northern forests."
—Tom Wiench,
dedicated fly fisherman and member of Trout Unlimited

MORE MYSTERIES FROM THE
BERKLEY PUBLISHING GROUP...

THE HERON CARVIC MISS SEETON MYSTERIES: Retired art teacher Miss Seeton steps in where Scotland Yard stumbles. "A most beguiling protagonist!" —*New York Times*

by Heron Carvic
MISS SEETON SINGS
MISS SEETON DRAWS THE LINE
WITCH MISS SEETON
PICTURE MISS SEETON
ODDS ON MISS SEETON

by Hampton Charles
ADVANTAGE MISS SEETON
MISS SEETON AT THE HELM
MISS SEETON, BY APPOINTMENT

by Hamilton Crane
HANDS UP, MISS SEETON
MISS SEETON CRACKS THE CASE

MISS SEETON PAINTS THE TOWN
MISS SEETON BY MOONLIGHT
MISS SEETON ROCKS THE CRADLE
MISS SEETON GOES TO BAT
MISS SEETON PLANTS SUSPICION
STARRING MISS SEETON
MISS SEETON UNDERCOVER
MISS SEETON RULES
SOLD TO MISS SEETON
SWEET MISS SEETON
BONJOUR, MISS SEETON
MISS SEETON'S FINEST HOUR

KATE SHUGAK MYSTERIES: A former D.A. solves crimes in the far Alaska north ...

by Dana Stabenow
A COLD DAY FOR MURDER
DEAD IN THE WATER
A FATAL THAW
BREAKUP

A COLD-BLOODED BUSINESS
PLAY WITH FIRE
BLOOD WILL TELL
KILLING GROUNDS
HUNTER'S MOON

CASS JAMESON MYSTERIES: Lawyer Cass Jameson seeks justice in the criminal courts of New York City in this highly acclaimed series ... "A witty, gritty heroine." —*New York Post*

by Carolyn Wheat
FRESH KILLS
MEAN STREAK
TROUBLED WATERS

DEAD MAN'S THOUGHTS
WHERE NOBODY DIES
SWORN TO DEFEND

JACK McMORROW MYSTERIES: The highly acclaimed series set in a Maine mill town and starring a newspaperman with a knack for crime solving ... "Gerry Boyle is the genuine article."—Robert B. Parker

by Gerry Boyle
DEADLINE
LIFELINE
BORDERLINE

BLOODLINE
POTSHOT
COVER STORY

Dead Creek

VICTORIA HOUSTON

BERKLEY PRIME CRIME, NEW YORK

DEAD CREEK

A Berkley Prime Crime Book / published by arrangement with
the author

PRINTING HISTORY
Berkley Prime Crime edition / November 2000

All rights reserved.
Copyright © 2000 by Victoria Houston.
This book may not be reproduced in whole or in part,
by mimeograph or any other means, without permission.
For information address: The Berkley Publishing Group,
a division of Penguin Putnam Inc.,
375 Hudson Street, New York, New York 10014.

The Penguin Putnam Inc. World Wide Web site address is
http://www.penguinputnam.com

ISBN: 0-425-17703-3

Berkley Prime Crime Books are published
by The Berkley Publishing Group,
a division of Penguin Putnam Inc.,
375 Hudson Street, New York, New York 10014.
The name BERKLEY PRIME CRIME and the BERKLEY PRIME CRIME
design are trademarks belonging to Penguin Putnam Inc.

PRINTED IN THE UNITED STATES OF AMERICA

10 9 8 7 6 5 4 3

one

To fish in trouble waters.

Mathew Henry: *Commentaties*, Psalm LX

Dr. Osborne's brand-new Mercury 9.9 outboard propelled his trusty Alumacraft so smoothly over the gentle waves glittering in the late-afternoon sun that he almost missed the hidden entrance to the brook. Loon Lake had many such fingers reaching deep into the tamarack forest, but this one was special. And at last the ice was gone and the winds had calmed and he could begin his search again.

Nearly seven months had passed since he'd been able to fish for its sinister treasure: the old, long, dangerous muskie that had rocked his boat when Osborne tantalized him last summer with his favorite lure: the surface mud puppy. He'd spent the winter calling the fish "my shark of the north" and vowing to his buddies that "that son of a bitch" would grace the mantel above his fireplace someday—across from the big picture window where Osborne watched the sun set over the big lake every night. He might be more tentative about rough water in his old age, but a big fish could still stir him.

It was a perfect day for fishing. The tamarack outlined

the shore, still spindly but glistening neon green with bud-
ding needles. The air was sharp and cold like a knife
against his skin. He inhaled deeply. It was the kind of
day, thought Osborne, when it's a gift just to breathe.

Osborne throttled the new motor way back. The engine
responded like silk under his hand, slowing the boat to a
silent glide. He leaned against the handle, nudging the
boat into the center of the stream, carefully steering clear
of submerged rocks. He knew the location of each small
boulder intimately, and they looked like old friends as he
drifted over. The dog curled up in the front of the boat
raised a questioning eye.

"I have a plan, Mike." The sixty-three-year-old retired
dentist spoke in a level tone to his black Lab as though
the dog had inquired about a two-year treatment of gum
disease. "We may miss today, and we may miss tomorrow—but sometime this year—you, me, and our friend,
we're gonna have that come-to-Jesus meeting, oh, yes we
are."

Osborne checked quickly to be sure the heavy gaff and
his net were correctly positioned near his feet in case he
was lucky sooner rather than later. He undid the latch to
the livewell so he could swing it up and open with ease.
Fishing alone made him doubly careful he wouldn't end
up with a nasty, thrashing fish loose in the boat with just
himself and the dog.

Osborne let the motor hum, selected the brown rod with
the old Ambassador Garcia reel and, flipping his right
wrist expertly, twice lofted the wooden lure. Seconds
passed as the lure soared, then plunked softly, first to his
right, then to his left. He was reeling before it landed,
tipping his head back slightly so a sliver of the late spring
sun could warm his face and forehead.

"Life is perfect, Mike," he said with quiet authority.
"Life is perfect." Mike leaped to his feet then, wagging
his tail and staring mournfully at his master, indicating
nature's call.

"Life *was* perfect, Mike." Osborne shook his head. The dog had a real knack for needing to piss at all the wrong times. "Okay, boy, cool it while I find us a spot to pull in. Sit . . . wait . . . good dog." Carefully, he hooked the lure on the rod and laid the rod down across the seats.

Osborne scanned the edges of the brook for a firm hillock. Much of the area was swamp and wetland, and the shadows from the towering firs made it hard to see. He spotted a good, wide, firm clump and revved the motor toward it.

Suddenly a sickening, grinding noise from under the boat caught him off guard. He switched off the motor, unhappy to hear the grinding continue until the propeller blades had stopped.

"Oh boy," he said, dreading the sight of a broken blade on his brand-new motor. Gently, Osborne moved his fishing rod so he could lean forward onto his knees to peer over the left edge of the boat.

He froze, so stunned he couldn't breathe, then he lurched back, almost tipping himself out of the boat. Desperate, he grabbed for both gunwales, terrified he was going to fall out and right into the horror beneath him.

The boat steadied, and Osborne looked up at the crystal blue sky. Not a sound did he hear except his own harsh breathing. Even the dog sat silent, watching him, his head cocked inquiringly. Osborne got himself up straight on the boat seat and reached for both oars. Arms shaking, he finally got them into the oar locks and, barely dipping the oars below the surface of the water so as not to touch anything under him, turned the boat around and gunned his motor out of the hidden brook.

Mike, looking back, started to bark loudly.

"Goddamn it, piss in the boat," said Osborne. He had to get to a phone. He had to get the sight out of his head. Never in his lifetime of cleaning fish, gutting deer, drilling root canals had he ever seen anything like it.

The sparkling clear water had magnified what he saw:

a black wire cage about ten feet long and four feet wide with bodies floating in it. The photographic imprint in his mind was so sharp he could still see the blue denim jeans, the sodden dark woolen shirts. But what he really couldn't forget was the one face staring up at him, its mouth a black hole with a tongue protruding and cloudy eyes bulging directly at him. Instinct told him it was dead, but his pounding heart made him feel like it was rising up out of the water, lumbering after him.

two

Angling is somewhat like poetry, men are born to be so.

Izaak Walton, *The Compleat Angler*

Osborne pulled the boat up at the public landing by Keane's resort and, forgetting to leash the dog, ran through the door of the bar, just as a battered blue pickup drove up to a big log that marked a parking area.

A lanky, deeply tanned man with a head of rich, reddish auburn curly hair and a chest-length, very curly, auburn but graying beard unwound his long frame from behind his steering wheel as he watched Osborne slam through the front door of the bar. He reached for his hat, a large stuffed trout perched on top of an old, fur-lined leather cap with ear flaps that hung down loosely.

The head and tail of the fish protruded on opposite sides over his ears. Draped across the breast of the fish, like a jeweled necklace, was an old wood and metal fishing lure, its silver disks glinting in the sunlight. Carefully, he set it at a jaunty angle, checking it out twice in the side mirror, before sauntering into the bar.

Osborne spotted his neighbor's belt buckle first. Under

normal circumstances, just watching the guy enter a room was worth at least one chuckle. Vertically challenged by the average doorway, six-foot-six Ray Pradt moved like an accordian tipped sideways, with a loopy walk so disjointed his close friends kidded that his lower torso rolled into a room a full hour ahead of the rest of his body. That bothered Ray. He liked to think he made his first impression with his hat.

"Nah," the good dentist had told him one day, "Anticlimactic." Hence Ray had invested in a sterling silver belt buckle that featured a walleye in the act of striking, a fish suspended in midair as it leaped from his belt toward the eyes of the beholder. The darn thing got snagged on every jacket and shirt he wore, but Ray didn't mind, he liked to make an entrance.

Osborne waved to Ray as he finished shouting into the phone, which was connected to a stunned switchboard operator at the Loon Lake Police Station. At that moment, Osborne could tell, it was also connected to the three elderly party-line eavesdroppers who'd long refused to give up their shared phone line and rotary dial phones simply because the antique system tied them so effectively into their neighbors' lives. Osborne had heard multiple gasps along the line as he relayed his gruesome news. He certainly understood why; his own hands were still shaking so badly it was hard to keep the phone to his ear.

"Thank God, that's done." He set the receiver back in its cradle next to the cash register and sank onto a nearby stool. Except for Osborne and Ray, Keane's Bar was empty. Osborne felt his shoulders relax ever so slightly with the release of the tension: The horror was now someone else's problem.

"I never thought this place could look so good," he said, waving his hand at the genteelly shabby little resort bar with its red vinyl chairs and knotty pine tabletops. The place hadn't seen redecorating in forty years or more. Because Keane kept a refrigerator stocked with staples like milk and bread, and a paper cup nearby for customers to pay on the honor system, it wasn't unusual for the folks living along the lake road to stop by on a late afternoon, avoid the rush at a local grocery store, and get a beer with their bread. A beer and gossip.

Ray slipped onto the stool alongside Osborne, brushing a friendly arm across the elderly dentist's shoulders as he did so. He examined the polished knotty pine surface of the antique bar for moist water rings before removing his hat and setting it down in front of him. Then he spoke.

"What . . ." He paused. Ray had his own deliberate cadence he used when he wanted to make a point. "The hell . . . is going on, Doc? And why did I hear you ask for 'the man with no laugh'? Where's your friend . . . Lewellyn?" He spoke in a low, jocular tone, but Osborne could see in the mirror behind the bar that Pradt was watching him closely, his eyes dark and serious.

"Out of town," said Osborne. "Bad timing."

Very bad timing. The one selfish thought he had had as his boat burned its way across the lake was that this grisly discovery was just the excuse he needed to spend more time with Lewelleyn Ferris, Loon Lake's chief of police.

Just one year into the position, Lew was the first female police chief in the history of the little Northwoods town. She was also the first woman Osborne had ever known who loved to fish as much as he did. Loved it and was better at it in some ways. She beat him hands down at fly-fishing. But he knew she would be hard set to challenge his bait-fishing technique, especially when it came to muskie fishing. And right now was the absolute best time to display his finesse as June, which was just around the corner, was his lucky season for hooking one of the monsters.

In fact, his trip up the creek had been somewhat of a covert operation. He was scouting, hoping to confirm that his "shark of the north" had survived the brutal winter and still controlled the territory. If so, his plan was to lure Lew into his boat—no fly lines this time but casting with a surface lure. Twelve-pound test—no heavier. A demonstration of fishing for trophy muskellunge the way *he* liked it. She was likely to disagree with his approach, he knew, so he was anxious to get her on the water while conditions were ideal. But muskie fishing took hours, and it was tough for Lew to find that kind of time in her schedule. On the other hand, if they had to work a case together . . .

Mentally, Osborne crossed his fingers. He had a point to prove, and he knew that nothing would impress that spirited, opinionated woman more than his landing a fierce fifty-incher right at her feet. Of course, being a realist at heart, he knew that was too much to hope for, so he would be happy just to raise the damn fish. To see a flash of the hard, evil head through the dark water, to hear the long, mean body swirl and circle the boat. Envisioning the moment in his mind, already he could hear Lew's gasp. The gasp of the expert fisherman who recognizes not only the skill it takes to raise such a fish but the talent and exquisite touch demanded to land such a prize. He knew he had the skill, he prayed he had the talent.

Osborne was still amazed that Lew had entered his life. More than once he had thanked the fishing gods for engineering their meeting. Had to be divine intervention— the circumstances were just too unusual. Late the previous summer, she had volunteered to help a friend of a friend sharpen his long-unused fly-fishing technique. That friend once removed turned out to be Osborne, who had been more than a little taken aback to find himself relearning the arcane sport from a woman.

Then, just hours into that first lesson, their roles as teacher and student were reversed by death: the discovery of a body wedged under rocks in the river where they were fishing. Osborne's equally unused but sharper skills at forensic dentistry had helped the police chief rapidly determine she was dealing not with a drowning, not with an accident, but a murder.

Grateful for help from a qualified professional, assistance hard to come by in the backwaters of northern Wisconsin, Lew had deputized Osborne that night. The alliance worked for both: she boosted her profile among her law enforcement colleagues, he discovered what he least expected to find in a woman—a fishing buddy.

Over the summer and into the fall their friendship had flourished as Lew sharpened his casting technique and schooled him in the wizardry of trout flies. But soon the curse of winter descended, ice and snow putting a rude end to their angling. Errant snowmobilers and a rash of drug arrests squeezed Lew's time for their coffee breaks.

Right now she was up on the New York/Canadian border, a witness in a lawsuit involving the Oneida Indians who had requested her testimony in a dispute regarding land they owned in the state of New York.

Osborne was more than a little chagrined at how happy Lew had been to go, especially when he learned the real reason for her delight. She would be close enough to the famed Wulff School of Fly Fishing on the legendary BeaverKill to fit in a long weekend refresher course on the techniques of fly casting. Much as Osborne tried to be happy for his new friend, in his heart he had to face the truth: This would give her an unassailable edge. Never could he compete in the trout stream.

Lew had been gone two long weeks now, forcing him to recognize yet another reality: he missed her. He really missed her. He hadn't had such a crush on a woman since third grade.

three

Of course, folk fish for different reasons. There are enough aspects of angling to satisfy the aspirations of people remarkably unalike.

Maurice Wiggin

"Yep," said Ray, nodding in sympathy from his bar stool. "With Lew out East still, you got ol' cement-face to deal with, huh? What's he—acting chief until she's back?"

"Unfortunately," said Osborne, grimacing.

The natives of Loon Lake had a standing joke. John Sloan, Lew's predecessor, who'd arrested many of them in their wild and woolly teen years, had never, ever been known to crack a smile. Not in the forty-five years that most had known him. A forced "heh, heh" might escape through stiffly spaced lips from time to time, but even that was just enough to fuel roaring guffaws. It had reached a point that all the regulars at McDonald's, an informal men's club of early risers that included Pradt and Osborne, made up what sounded like a good old Indian moniker, "the man with no laugh," to kid Sloan—behind his back, of course.

"So what . . ." said Ray, reaching for a toothpick from a small glass sitting on the bar, " . . . the doggone heck . . . is up, Doc?"

Osborne crossed his arms on the bar and looked at Ray. His hands had calmed down since he made the phone call. Ray's perspective on the nightmare was going to be interesting and one Osborne was anxious to hear.

Until two years ago, Osborne had viewed his neighbor through the eyes of his late wife and Mary Lee and had no use for the man. The very mention of his name would prompt one of her rare expressions of profanity as in, "That son of a bitch!"

The two first clashed when Ray, in Mary Lee's opinion, "stole" the lakefront acreage next door to their new house. An exceptional parcel of land with the best view on the Loon Lake chain, the lot was one that Mary Lee had coveted to buffer their own property, which she liked to call "our lake estate."

Ray turned that dream into a nightmare. Alerted to the land's sudden availability through his own secret grapevine, he made an immediate bid at the asking price, paying cash for the total before anyone in Loon Lake even knew it was for sale.

"Paul!" Mary Lee had gone ballistic when she heard the news, shrilling, "I will not live next door to a grave digger! You better do something about this."

If Osborne thought that was rough, the morning Mary Lee discovered Ray had positioned his beat-up mobile home in full view of her living room window was worse.

"My vista!" she had shrieked. Osborne had never seen his wife in such a frenzy. He stood by in silence as she rampaged up and down the rutted drive that led to Ray's trailer, shouting for their new neighbor to move his "goddamn trash heap" before she called the cops. Ray didn't move a thing, not even when Mary Lee got John Sloan, police chief at the time, to drive out and view the situation. Hands in the air as if to duck her anger, Sloan told her, as had her husband, there was nothing anyone could do. The transaction was legal, money had changed hands, and Ray could park whatever and wherever he wanted on his own property.

So Mary Lee made it her mission to torture Ray. Almost daily she could be seen running toward his minnowing truck, a battered blue pickup with the door dented in on the driver's side, as it slowed to make the turn into his drive, waving an angry hand and snapping at him about this and that.

Osborne didn't appreciate the view of Ray's trailer either, especially after the money Mary Lee had insisted on sinking into the new house with its expensive landscaping. But, unlike Mary Lee, he wasn't scornful of Ray, he just wondered about the man. He knew Ray's family, and they weren't bad people. The father was a family physician in Rhinelander. Ray's older sister was one of Chicago's top litigators, and his younger brother a hand surgeon over at the Mayo Clinic. His mother was a founding member of the Rhinelander Garden Club, an invitation-only clique that Mary Lee had hungered to join.

Initially, Ray appeared to be like any other bright middle-class kid with athletic talent. In high school he was a star basketball player, and Osborne, like the other parents, expected to see him hit the fast track: an athletic scholarship to Marquette University likely to be followed by a little pro or semipro ball and on to a career in insurance or banking, maybe stocks and bonds. But life yanked early at Ray. When a tournament game blew both his knees out, he lost the college scholarship. Though his father could certainly afford to send him anywhere he wanted to go, Ray decided against college.

Choosing the water and the woods over books, he spent his first year out of high school bushwhacking his way through the swamps and forests, living off the land. Before he turned twenty, he had become one of the Northwoods' most sought-after fishing and hunting guides. When the brutal winters would force his wealthy clientele from Chicago, Minneapolis, and Milwaukee to flee south or west, Ray would augment his income by shoveling snow and digging graves.

To Osborne and his other buddies at McDonald's, Ray might live from dollar to dollar, but he seemed a happy man. A fellow whose early-morning grin signaled the fish were biting. An optimist who took his coffee black and had a storehouse of bad jokes: "So what's the epitaph for old man Spencer, that crazy Packer fan? G-o-o Deep!"

But Mary Lee was uncompromising. Vistas, not fish, counted in her world. The day came when her unreasonable, unrelenting crabbing at Ray—even though she took care to avoid another shouting match—forced Osborne to betray her.

One balmy summer night, while she was out with her bridge group, Osborne ambled down the rutted, leaf-strewn drive with a six-pack of Leinenkugel in hand. Joining Ray where he sat on the wooden bench that anchored the end of his new dock, the two men had gazed west, drinking the beers and talking weed beds and muskie lures while the sun set in glorious streaks of violet and bronze. The next morning, a string of fresh bluegills, cleaned and ready for the frying pan, appeared on Osborne's back porch and, later that same day, the offending trailer was moved a critical twenty feet.

Mary Lee still ranted, of course. Osborne knew better than to tell his wife to shut up. He did, however, give her a dim eye. She got the message and toned it down, but she never gave up, muttering a never-ending list of complaints against the bearded, classless interloper. These she was wise enough to voice in the confines of her own home.

Several months later, as the first blizzard of the season raged through the Northwoods, Mary Lee's lingering bronchitis turned deadly, her fever ratcheting up to 104,

and her breath rasping in her chest. The windchill was 50
degrees below zero with blowing snow four to five feet
deep in drifts across their driveway. Desperate to get his
wife to the hospital, Osborne phoned his neighbor, the
only man with a snowplow along Loon Lake Road.
Within minutes, Ray had mounted the plow on the front
of his pickup and was pushing through the bitter blackness
for a woman who had done her best to make his life
miserable.

"If you go off the road, Doc, you'll need help," was all
he said when he insisted on accompanying Osborne to the
hospital. He stayed the long two hours that the trauma
team worked on Mary Lee, and he was there when the
young surgeon emerged to tell Osborne he lost her on the
table. Ray waited as he signed a few papers, then drove
Osborne in silence to his daughter's home. On the way,
Osborne tried to apologize for Mary Lee, but Ray stopped
him short. "No," he said, "I don't want to hear it. Doesn't
matter, Doc; never did."

He also had the good sense to wait a few months before
he gave Osborne his suggestion for Mary Lee's headstone:
"I told you I was sick."

And so it was that seduced by bluegills and Ray's un-
failing good nature, Osborne found himself looking forward to their daily chats. Soon they were fishing together:
an odd couple.

Ray was the opposite of the reserved, soft-spoken dentist
who was old enough to be his father. A natural-born sto-
ryteller whose greatest pleasure was holding court among
friends and strangers, Ray loved people. He loved com-
miserating in taverns, on boat landings, in bait shops, or
in diners, sharing tales of the big buck that got away, the
deceased farmer who was so large he had to be buried in
a septic tank—"They just don't make grave liners that
big"—and other variations on the grim and hilarious lives
lived deep in the backwoods. He amazed Osborne with

his ability to turn any story into an epic filled with the
humor of human error. But even as he was famous for
telling a good story, he was equally famed for his inability
to end it. Almost always his audience had to scream for
the punchline. Still, they loved him.

Osborne observed early in their friendship that he
wasn't the only one to appreciate Ray. The man seemed
to know everyone in a fifty-mile radius of Loon Lake:
male, female, young, old, well-heeled, or homeless. He
knew them and vice versa: everyone waved back at Ray.

Right now, he was the one man Osborne was happy to
have on the chair next to him. He could pull answers from
places where few thought to go.

"You eyeing the Wild Turkey?" asked Ray after Osborne
unloaded his tale. With the thumb and index finger of his
right hand, he pulled at his beard absentmindedly, thinking over Osborne's story. The two men stared at the rows
of bottles that ran along the wall at the back of the darkening bar.

"No," said Osborne. "I'm checking out the Bushmills.
Care to join me?"

"Wouldn't blame you if you did." Ray's voice stayed
even. Osborne swung his stool slightly to glance at Ray.
The two men had shared more than a few hours in the
room at the top of the stairs behind the door with the AA
coffeepot on its window. Ray had his own demons, and
Mary Lee's death had been a little unsettling for Osborne.
However irritating she might have been, the woman had
filled his life to the edges and left a huge hole when she
died. But he was dry eighteen months now.

Just as he decided to go for a ginger ale, the door to
the bar swung open.

"Well, folks," he heard Ray say just a little too loudly,
"he-e-re's Johnnie!"

"Dr. Osborne." John Sloan nodded at Osborne with the

special deference he granted to all professional men, important men like himself.

Ray he acknowledged with a lesser tilt of his head as he shoved his hands into the pockets of his navy blue down parka.

"Did Lucy tell you I'm standing in for Chief Ferris till she's gets back Sunday night?"

"She did," said Osborne. "Sorry about this."

"You're sorry? I've got a bigger problem. Pecore is sicker 'n a dog."

"You gotta be kiddin'," said Ray, swinging around on his bar stool, "you got murder and the coroner's got the flu? Doncha think he can drag himself outta bed for this one? From what Doc's told me, we're not lookin' at dead crayfish here."

"Well, he can't," said Sloan, as he stood a little sheepishly in front of the two men. It was clear he'd already tried, threats and all.

"He's that sick," said Osborne.

"He's hugging the throne."

"That may not be all bad, John," said Ray dryly. "At least his dogs won't be licking up your evidence." Osborne took note of an authoritative tone in Ray's voice. It surprised him. Sloan looked a little taken aback, too.

On the other hand, Pecore was not exactly respected in town. A pathologist of questionable skill, he had irritated the townspeople when they discovered he let his two golden retreivers roam unrestricted in his lab. Truth was, the dogs probably minded their own business, but Loon Lake residents were appalled. Since county law dictated that every death in the community had to be run by Pecore, many families had taken to accompanying the bodies of loved ones through the entire process just to be sure the canines didn't lick Grandma.

"I don't know what to do," said Sloan. "I put a call in to Wausau, but none of the state men can get up here until tomorrow morning, if then. They're all strung out over a designer drug bust outside of Stevens Point. They got paperwork up the wazoo to do for the feds yesterday."

"Gosh, John," said Osborne, "how long can you put off any investigation?"

"Well . . . not too long, y'know. But I do not want to touch or move anything wthout being able to photograph and ID the bodies at the site."

"John, my call went in on this damned party line," said Osborne. "I hate to say it, but you're gonna have every goombah with a boat that floats over there eyeballing that situation very shortly."

The chief just raised his hands and shook his head in complete frustration. "I know, I know. I've got two men and a boat with me. . . ."

"I've got my thirty-five-millimeter in my truck," said Ray, who also made a few bucks on the side selling wildlife photos to local calendar printers. "You're welcome to use it, or I'll shoot some for you."

"That's a thought," said Osborne to Sloan.

"Yeah, that's possible. The boat's got a nice wide deck and plenty of floods on board to make it easy to light the scene. Hell, Pecore just uses his twenty-year-old Polaroid. They sure can't hold me responsible for doing the damn IDs underwater now, can they? I mean, if we get a quick-and-dirty check and shoot those bodies down to Wausau first thing in the morning. That should work, don't ya think?"

Sloan looked away from the two men for a moment, then he said, "Yeah, let's do it. Just you make sure I get all the negatives. I don't need official records being shown around to all your drinking buddies, Pradt."

"C'mon, I can make ten bucks apiece on those mothers," Ray teased Sloan but quickly stopped when he saw the man start to glower. "Of course not. I'll give you the camera and let you take the film out yourself."

"Oh shit," said Sloan. "That's a problem. How'm I gonna get the photos processed? The photo shop's closed.

I suppose I could take the film over to the newspaper, but then I'll have the paper all over me to give them some photos, and that's the last thing I need."

Right then, Osborne could see that John Sloan had never handled a case like this, and he was afraid he was going to screw it up. Retiring just about a year ago after thirty-five years on the force, Sloan had taken pride in the smooth running of his small department that serviced a town of less than three thousand people. Now he was considering a run for mayor. He didn't need to look like an idiot when the high-tech cops from the big city came in to review his police work.

"I'll do that, too, if you want," volunteered Ray. "I do my own processing. Why don't you wait until we're at the scene and decide? You may be fine waiting till to-morrow on 'em. Otherwise, my place is just down the road right next door to the Doc's. It'll take less than an hour to get you some eight-by-ten black-and-white prints, even color. You tell me, I can do both."

"Color." Sloan turned to Osborne, "Doc, can you do a dental ID?"

"He sure can. Let's go!" said Ray, jumping off his stool and heading for the door.

Osborne turned to his buddy with a look of astonishment on his face.

"What are you talking about?" he demanded.

"What's your problem, Doc? You did a great job for Lew on that body in the river."

"That was one body," said Osborne, "and I knew the victim. She was a patient. This is different."

"C'mon, Doc," urged Ray. "Chief Sloan, the good dentist here told me he ID'd corpses during the Korean War."

"That's right, I did—for about two days," said Osborne, shooting Ray a dirty look. "I did bodies in bad shape, too. But today they use DNA. . . ."

"Pecore?" Ray snorted. "You kidding? He uses Braille with his gloves on."

"What do you say, Doctor?" Sloan's eyes looked brighter. "If you could just log the basics, that gives me enough. Here's all I got to do: Get enough of an ID so we can match each body later with what we see tonight. My men can pack them carefully for the morgue, then the state boys take over in the morning and do a complete forensic analysis. But we've got to get over there before I've got the whole town on the scene and before anybody fools around and moves a thing."

"C'mon, John, they aren't going to touch those bodies." Osborne found himself very leery to get close to the nightmare.

"They're sure as hell going to trample all over any evidence on the ground and they're going to grind up any marks you might have on some of those submerged boulders," said Pradt quietly. Both men looked at him. He was right.

"Sure," said Osborne suddenly, bluntly. "I'll do the dental ID. John, I'll do the best I can. In the war, I did a full-mouth exam on site and later, when I assisted on reconstructive surgery for some of the men who'd had their faces blown to hell, I did some bone work that might help here. If you want, I can sketch the muscle and bone profile for each jaw. . . ."

"He'll knock the socks off the Wausau boys," said Pradt.

"I don't know about that." Osborne stood up from the bar stool. It'd been three years since his retirement, and he was finding it felt good to be an expert again. He'd handled dead bodies before and managed. With the cold water as a preservative this might not be as bad as some he'd worked on.

"John, can you give me a ride down to my house so I can get my dog squared away and pick up my instruments?" Since helping Lew six months ago, he had kept his black bag just inside the linen closet, hoping he might have the chance to use it again. Too bad she was out of town. That made the job grim and only grim.

As he started to walk out behind Sloan, Osborne glanced into the mirror behind the bar. He saw himself looking quite normal, which surprised him, given how tense he felt. As usual, he was in his fishing khakis with his favorite dark green fishing hat clamped down tight to protect his bald pate. His deeply tanned face looked the same, too. The high cheekbones inherited from his mother's family stretched his skin so he still looked younger, he always thought, than his sixty-three years.

He glanced back at Ray, slouching along behind him. Ray's eyes caught and held his in the mirror. As he plopped his trout hat back on his head, the younger man raised his eyebrows in speculation. Osborne figured they were both thinking the exact same thing: Just where was this little ride going to take them?

four

Only dead fish swim with the stream.

Malcolm Muggeridge

Loon Lake was black under the big police boat. An icy froth sprayed their faces as the boat turned sharply from Keane's to fly on a diagonal across the lake. A north wind blasted Osborne full in the face. Though it was still light, the sun had dipped below the tree line on the shore they were approaching, casting lengthy shadows out across the water.

"Slow down," he shouted after five minutes had passed and the boat neared the shoreline. He could feel his face turning wooden in the cold as he hollered over the roar of the engine. "There's a rock just under the surface along here that I use as a marker. You hit it and that's the end of your propeller."

Sloan cut the engines and guided the boat in sudden silence along the shore. Osborne rose from his seat, legs wide apart to steady himself in the flat-bottomed cruiser and raked the beam of a large floodlight through the water beneath them until he spotted the huge rock. "Hold up, we got it. Okay, sharp right." He moved from the left side of the boat to the center. He did not want to be the first to touch base this time.

"No lights," said Sloan. "I don't want anyone following us in here until I'm ready." They had spotted a few fishing boats at a distance, but none seemed concerned about them. The entry to the creek was well disguised by a peninsula of tamarack that jutted out and curved to hide the inlet.

Ray stood in the back of the boat, his camera hanging from a strap around his neck. He, too, spread his legs for balance as he scanned the woods while the boat nosed its way up the creek.

The boat drifted forward. The only sound now was everyone in the boat breathing. Sloan stood beside Osborne with two deputies leaning, one on each side, against the sides of the boat, their eyes raking the water. Osborne didn't know the younger one well. Lew had hired him the week before she left for the East Coast. But Roger, a mild-tempered man who'd failed in the real estate business, was a former patient. A bland soul in Osborne's book, Roger struck him as quite out of place in law enforcement, but then, thought Osborne, maybe his agreeable nature made it work. After all, his job tonight was to do the dirty physical work so Sloan could stand by with his hands in his pockets and look important.

Ray kept vigil in the back of the boat. A cloud cover was hastening nightfall. Matte blackness moved in from behind. Dense brush closed in on all sides as the boat, which suddenly seemed smaller, drifted forward.

"Maybe we missed it?" Sloan's voice cracked hoarsely. A barred owl hooted from a few feet into the brush, and everyone jerked around.

Suddenly, a soft grinding sound came from right beneath their feet.

"Bull's-eye," said Osborne and pointed to his right. "There's a knoll over there where you can pull up. Be careful, this is all swamp back in here, you can slip and go up to your shoulders."

The boat swung to the side and away from the hazard in the shallow creek. Dusk had definitely settled, and the surface was opaque.

"How deep?" Sloan grunted.

"Four maybe five feet," said Ray. "I had some leech traps back in here a couple years ago. Looks a little deeper now with the ice melt. I think the beavers moved things around, too." As Ray talked, Sloan took the floodlight from its perch and turned it onto the water.

"Holy shit!" he jumped back. He quickly recovered and moved back, training the light so everyone else could see. Osborne stepped aside. Examining what someone else had touched and moved would be one thing; seeing this vision again was quite another.

Osborne listened to Sloan and the deputies exclaim or suck in their breath. Then he watched Ray, who looked hard in silence, then moved closer, bracing his long arms against the gunwales. He hung over the boat for a long couple of minutes, studying the bodies in the cage. Several times he looked up to study the Norway pines, the tamarack, and the dense brush that crowded the creek. Spring air and sunlight hadn't penetrated all of the forest yet, and clumps of snow still guarded sections of the slowly thawing ground.

"I'll tell ya what," he said. "Let's get those floods hard on this, then let me shoot that knoll before anyone gets out of the boat. Just in case we've got some tracks over there. Okay? I don't think they brought this in by boat."

"Sure, Ray," said Sloan, "take your time." As Ray slipped a lens and flash onto his camera, Sloan motioned to the deputies to follow Ray's instructions.

Ray propped his right leg up on the bow of the boat and leaned forward, his motor drive whirring. Then he swung off to the right and aimed toward the woods. "Interesting," he said. The motor drive whirred. Then he lowered his camera and stepped up onto the edge of the knoll.

He looked around, paused, and waved the camera toward the ground, gesturing with it as he talked. "Now this is *real* interesting, folks. Someone drove in through the brush . . . on a snowmobile. You got tracks in the snow cover back under that brush. Great definition. I'll shoot some macro so you'll have close-ups. Sure looks like an Arctic Cat with one rider to me."

"C'mon, Ray, how the hell?" asked Roger, the doubt clear in the deputy's voice.

"How do I know it's an Arctic Cat? I own one. These are the tracks my machine makes," said Ray. "Now shut up while I shoot."

"Yeah, well, we've got five thousand snowmobiles coming through here some weekends," said Sloan. "This'll be like trying to identify a Nike shoe print—every goombah in the county owns one."

"Look for one with blue paint scratched off the sides," said Ray, focusing his lens on the trees. "They scraped past a couple a Norways to get to the water. Take a look. And they were in a hurry, ripping those branches back. See that paint on the tree trunks?"

Sloan and the two deputies were silent. Osborne remembered the McDonald's crew talking about Ray one morning when he wasn't there: "That razzbonya can track a snake over a rock," somebody'd said. It probably ate his shorts, but Sloan had to know that, too.

"Yeah, we're lucky to be here tonight, too, because that thaw we're supposed to get tomorrow will melt this stuff. These tracks will be slush in a couple of days," said Ray.

"Anything else?" Sloan asked gruffly, not a little irritated to be so beholden to Ray. Roger was still shaking his head, if not in doubt then in surprise.

Osborne, on the other hand, wasn't surprised at all. The hours he had spent fishing with Ray had made him aware of two simple truths about the man: One, he could be trusted. Two, the wearing of the stuffed trout hat was a ploy. An invitation not to take him seriously. But anyone who fell for that made a serious error, which most people did. Osborne was one of the few who knew Ray Pradt was easy to underestimate. Ray knew it: he banked on it.

Why was that, anyway? It was a question Osborne couldn't answer. He wasn't sure he wanted to. Instead, after fishing with his friend, he would indulge in a pleasant little pastime he had come to call his "Ray Ramble"—a meditative polka set to the tune of Ray's rhythms.

After stowing his fishing gear, Osborne would settle in on the wide front porch overlooking Loon Lake, a newspaper on his lap and a cup of coffee in hand, as he watched the winds stroking the waves. Before lifting the paper to read it, he would reflect on the hours he had just spent with his neighbor, usually with a smile on his face.

Seldom was there a time, watching or listening, when he hadn't learned something from the man. Something sensible, practical, yet leavened with a goofy grin or self-deprecating remark as if humor would mask the value of the insight, protect Ray from a world designed to take him too seriously, to demand commitment. Osborne knew, as did just a few other Loon Lake residents, that behind the grins and guffaws was a man of serious talent. No one could read the shadows on the water or the shudders of the forest like Ray. He had the vision of an eagle scanning for prey. Nor could anyone else hear the voices that haunted the woods as acutely as Ray, except, perhaps, a deer.

The men worked swiftly in the dark cold. The boat was rigged to drag for drownings, so it took only moments to hook the submerged crate and pull it up to hang vertically from the winch at the front end of the boat. Sloan had relaxed about anyone seeing their lights since they were more than enough upstream to hide the spill from the floods.

Osborne stood back, watching the deputies work. From

high above and behind them, the distinctive call of the great horned owl who owned that side of the lake signaled that the forest was watching. Osborne couldn't help but wonder what the magnificent old bird might be thinking.

The sky was clear, so from his perch under the bright half-moon and a million stars he would be looking down on the brilliant circle of light thrown by Sloan's flood-lights onto the boat deck and the brushy shores of the creek. He would see a rusted metal cage, not unlike a dog crate, pulled up and tipped forward, its contents ready to be emptied onto the deck and pried one from the other. Leathery clothing stuck to limbs, and features were frozen by the icy water. Working around them would be five live men who would avoid thinking too hard about what they were doing.

"Wait a minute! I've seen a crate like that before," exclaimed Ray from his vantage point on the hillock. He squatted to shoot several frames. Then he stood and studied the suspended crate.

"Geez—now where did I see that? Boy, I can't remember. . . ." He twisted his fingers in his beard, then he shrugged and gave up. "I'll think of it." He shot more photos as Sloan and the deputies struggled to separate the bodies, which had been looped over and around one another. As neatly wedged, thought Osborne, as a fresh can of King Oscar sardines.

One by one, they set each on a tarp laid across the bottom of the boat. Osborne stepped carefully over each body, looking hard at the faces before jotting notes on each. "No oxygen means no decay," he said as an aside to no one in particular. "Facial detail is well preserved, these faces are remarkably unblemished. I don't believe the expressions will get in the way of any relatives identifying the victims."

"You know what's weird?" said Ray, as he followed behind Osborne, shooting close-ups, "they all look like they're sleeping. They don't look like they were terrorized or anything. . . ."

"I'm not so sure . . . at least not a relaxed sleep," interrupted Osborne with an edge to his voice.

"How do you know that?" asked Sloan, stepping forward to study the faces more closely himself.

"I don't—more a sense maybe—maybe . . ." Then Osborne stood up straight and sighed heavily. His back hurt from leaning over so long. "Maybe the tightness in the jaws . . . on each one. I don't know, John. I'm probably wrong, it's been years since I did this."

"Yeah," said Ray, nodding and ruminating, twisting his fingers in his beard. "You never think about it, you know, but the look on your face when you die is how a lotta folks will remember you. . . ."

"That's enough, Ray," said Roger, giving him a look of friendly disgust. "Not that most of us get to *plan* how we'll look. . . ."

"These guys might have." Ray ignored the snide tone in the remarks. "They look so damn peaceful, y'know?"

"Guys!" snorted Roger. "Can't you tell a woman when you see one?"

Silence settled over the boat as the five live people studied the faces of the four dead ones. Roger was right; they were looking at three men and a woman, all dressed for cold weather fishing except for hats. Only the woman wore one, an oilcloth drover's hat pulled down far enough that only a few strands of white-blond hair escaped to frame a squarish face obviously softer and more feminine than the others.

"Could be worse," said Sloan.

"You've seen a lot more than I have," said Osborne. He shrugged. This speculation was going nowhere, and a cold wind was picking up. "Peaceful, maybe, but they don't look happy to be doing whatever it was they were doing. Does that make sense?"

No one answered.

Sloan nodded to himself as if he agreed with Osborne. "Okay, Doc, what do we do next here?"

Osborne leaned in over the first body. "If you'll hold this one to the side like this," he said to Roger as he deftly pulled the jaw open. "Fine, good." The adrenaline rush worked well to keep his hands and fingers warm in their thin rubber gloves. He ran an index finger across the ridges of the tooth surfaces, back behind the molars; he set both hands to each side of the jaw, measuring from ear to chin; then he quickly sketched on a small pad notes detailing fillings, caps, crowns.

The second jaw held a partial denture.

"Jackpot," Osborne said softly and looked up at Sloan. "This denture will have a registration number on it you can trace to the lab where it was made."

As he had with the first, he made a rapid sketch of the jaw and skull configuration. The act of sketching took him back to his youth, a time when he thought he could choose between being a concert pianist or a sculptor. Reality set in later, of course; dentistry paid the bills. But even in dental school, he had loved studying skeletal structure, the sculptor in him admiring of the aesthetics that made the difference between male and female.

Male skulls, like the ones he was examining, aside from their differing overlay of flesh were, in fact, very similar: robust, knobby, and larger than female skulls, with more pronounced jaws and heavier brows.

As Osborne worked, he numbered the pages in the corners, then took one piece of paper, put only a number on it and set it on the body for Ray to shoot so notes and bodies could be easily matched.

Sloan stood alongside, making notes of the clothing and other details of each body to bolster the ID as a backup, should any of Ray's photos not turn out. As Osborne finished, Sloan had Roger confirm the sex of each victim while the younger deputy tried to peg hair color and Ray shot close-ups of everything.

"No wounds that I can see," said Roger, huffing a little as he heaved the bodies through the process.

Osborne's hands moved deftly. The ice had preserved the bodies well, and no exposure to air meant no odor.

"I feel like I'm working on statues," he said, before leaning into the last mouth. "This isn't nearly as bad as my war work. You may want to mention in your notes, John, that these are mature adults, and they are likely to be fairly well-to-do. So far, each one has had good dental care, *expensive* dental care. In my opinion, these are people who certainly cared about their appearance. Professionals, perhaps?" He looked down at the fourth and final victim. He had saved the woman for last.

Osborne loved the female skull, so smooth and gracile, as if it had been spun into life on a potter's wheel, shaped by caressing hands. This one was no exception, all its edges planed and beveled beneath the flesh.

Osborne ran his index finger matter-of-factly along the ridges of this last set of teeth, then dipped it back behind and forward again. He stopped. He peered in. This time he ran two fingers through and paused at three spots.

"Gold inlays," he said in mild surprise, "haven't seen those in a while."

He reached for another instrument and started to tap along the teeth. He stopped suddenly, "John, can you bring that light in a little closer?" He leaned forward and studied the interior closely. He closed his eyes as his fingers slipped back and forth over the surfaces beneath them. He knew those slopes and curves as intimately as he'd known his wife's body.

Osborne pulled his hands from the corpse's mouth. Then he sat back and looked down at his hands. He looked off to the left, away from the men. He had to take a deep breath before he spoke. "This is my work," he said softly. "I did these inlays. They are gold, they were done many years ago—but I did them. I must know this person."

He looked closely now at the face beneath him. It was a wide face on a squarish head. The nose was wide and short with half-open, opaque eyes placed unusually far apart. The woman carried some weight on her; she might be small-boned, but she was not a small woman.

"Recognize her?" asked Sloan. Everyone stopped their work and gathered around.

"No," said Osborne after a long, long pause. "I don't. Does anyone else?"

The group was silent. Sloan motioned to Roger to complete the exam. The deputy removed the sodden, frozen clothing with some difficulty. He looked up in surprise, "It's a man," he said.

"What?" Osborne leaned over. "Are you sure?"

"Give me a break, Doc. I know a dick when I see one."

He was right. Osborne stood up, mystified.

"What's going on?" Sloan leaned forward. His dark, thick eyebrows joined over his nose as he thrust his head close to the corpse.

"I don't know," said Osborne. "The bone structure is female, at least what I was taught was female, but obviously I'm wrong." He decided to examine the jaw again.

But before Osborne could move, Ray had moved in close over the body, his camera in hand. "Hold on, guys," he said, "I know someone who will want some good shots of this." The motor drive whirred and whirred as he shot from north, south, east, and west, jumping over and straddling the still form.

As he moved, one of his feet tugged at the tarp beneath the body, causing the fishing hat to slip back off the head. Along with the hat went the hair.

"Weird!" exclaimed the younger deputy. "Guy's totally bald." With a reflex action, he jumped to catch the soft swatch as it was lifted into the air by a sudden gust, then dropped it onto the tarp as if it was a wolf spider.

"Calm down. Haven't you ever seen a hairpiece before?" said Sloan sharply. "Now, don't lose that thing."

Sheepishly, the deputy reached back down for the hair-piece.

"Doc," said Ray, glancing over at Osborne, "you tell me if this doesn't look like those mink I was telling you about."

"Mink? For Christ's sake!" Sloan shook his head.

Osborne set down his instruments slowly. He was puzzled. Something connected him in a visceral way to this body, yet it just didn't figure. . . .

The clothing had been pulled away to expose the genitals. "Who-o-a, hold on Charlie. . . ." said Ray to no one in particular but with an unmistakable note of satisfaction building in his voice. "Do you see what I see? Or—should I say—don't see?"

Osborne's professional mind-set kicked in instantly and he moved the penis aside with his gloved hand to get a better look. Yep. Undescended testicles. No wonder Ray was happy. He just made himself an extra hundred bucks. At least. Maybe a lot more.

"It's all yours, Ray," said Osborne pulling his hand back. "But I sure hope you're wrong."

"What the hell are you two talking about?" said Sloan.

"You know the research that environmental studies group has been doing up at Dead Creek?" Osborne asked, looking up. Sloan and the deputies shook their heads no. "You better tell 'em, Ray."

"I've been guiding a Dr. Rick Shanley for the last year and a half," said Ray, "to a couple of sites where they've found adult mink, infertile mink, with malformed reproductive organs."

"Oh, for Chrissakes. What the hell would that have to do with this?" Sloan snorted. Roger rolled his eyes.

"Hey," Ray shrugged, "men, mink, whatever. When it comes to reproductive organs, the basics are the same. I've seen the deformed mink, and now I've seen this. One reminds me of the other. I'm conjecturing, Chief, strictly conjecturing."

"Like what exactly are we talking about here?" demanded Sloan.

Ray paused as if thinking over what he could and could not say. Finally, he spoke. "Shanley works for the Ford Institute of Environmental Health. His team is studying a range of problems affecting the reproductive systems in the fish-eating population up here. Eagles, hawks, otters, walleyes, bottom-feeders, salamanders—different problems at different levels of the food chain. FIEH has a half-million dollar grant from the National Science Foundation to investigate the extent of the problem in this region.

"I'm involved because I harvest specimens for them."

Osborne knew they paid him by the specimen. This would be a big one, probably bigger than they were expecting.

"Up here, you say?" Sloan looked shocked.

"You betcha," said Ray, his eyes very serious. "They have a significant situation over in Green Bay. No one knows yet how far it extends throughout the Great Lakes region."

Sloan shook his head. Green Bay was only 150 miles east of Loon Lake, Lake Superior less than two hours north.

"The scientists are finding all sorts of hormonal discrepancies," said Ray. "For example, a walleye or a trout might appear to you and me to be male, but the hormone count is off-the-charts female. Starting last September, Shanley asked me to watch for any mammals that appear to be one sex but have characteristics of the other—so that's all I'm saying about this body," said Ray, still straddling the corpse. "A human is a mammal. This one is unusual and, I repeat, John, I'm conjecturing, strictly conjecturing."

Ray stepped away carefully, capped his lens, and continued, "They suspect that chemicals used in paper and pulp production, which we all know have been dumped for years into the rivers and streams around here, are causing this. Over time, the chemicals break down, causing the hormones in these different life forms to go crazy."

"Ridiculous," said Sloan, his lips puckering as if everything Ray said left a bad taste in his mouth. Osborne didn't like what he saw: the rude dismissal of his good friend's remarks.

"The scientists call them endocrine disruptors," said Osborne, bolstering Ray's authority with medical jargon he knew would intimidate Sloan. He hoped Ray was happy now that he had taken Osborne into his confidence, even though Shanley had insisted Ray keep the project confidential. Ray's excitement over the project had led him to confide in his neighbor.

"As I understand it, John," continued Osborne, "over a period of years, some industrial chemicals dumped into the water up here have broken down into alkyl phenols, which are now known to have a direct effect on reproductive hormones and reproductive function. Dr. Shanley and his colleagues are particularly concerned with the chemicals leaching from our watershed. They have kept the study pretty quiet so as not to alarm anyone until they know the scope of the problem."

"I do hope I'm wrong," said Ray. "Can you imagine what will happen to my guiding if walleye guys think eating fish will stunt their sex lives?"

"Well, y'know . . . all this reminds me of the DDT scare at Dead Creek back in the fifties," said Sloan, "but I thought they cleaned that up years ago."

"Dead Creek is on my list," said Ray. "I haven't been in yet this spring. Shanley sampled up there last summer and found evidence of the stuff in the water, diluted but present. Remember the paper mill north of Dead Creek that closed down years ago? Well, they made food wrappings and used a process that generates exactly these alcohols—"

"Alkyl phenols," corrected Osborne. "You need to put

John in touch with Rick Shanley, Ray. He can explain it much better than we can."

Sloan's expression relaxed. Osborne's suggestion put him back in charge.

"Fine with me," said Ray. "I'm really not supposed to be talking about this, anyway."

"So they got other people up here with hormones like this guy?" Sloan, not quite ready to drop the subject, pointed to the fourth body.

"Not that I know of, John. And I don't even know if this guy has a problem. It just looks kinda different to me, and my job is to flag anything unusual. All I know for sure is Shanley's team has found very high estrogen levels in hawks and eagles and mink that appear to be male. The reverse, too. Females to the naked eye that register a high testosterone level. They all have one thing in common: they eat fish."

"Jeez, Ray, I'm a fish-eater," said Roger in a snide tone, rolling a toothpick in his teeth as he spoke, "does this mean I have to worry about menopause?"

"Well, Rog, I don't know," said Ray. "You tell me. If you eat as much fish as an eagle does—maybe."

The expression on the deputy's face changed. Osborne could see him mentally calculating his Friday night fish fries and Wednesday perch lunches. He didn't look happy.

Ray turned to Sloan. "All kidding aside, this is serious. I should phone Shanley about this tonight."

"You hold your horses," said Sloan. "I want to know exactly what I got here. Right now what I'm thinking is that this victim could be someone who lives around Dead Creek. If so, that's my district, and I need to contact the family first. Then we worry about the other."

"No one lives around Dead Creek," said Ray. "You know that. No one."

"They used to," said Osborne softly. "I remember folks were living up there back around the time I opened my practice. This could be someone who lived in that area years back . . . grew up there." As he reached to gather up his soiled instruments, Osborne noticed his hands were shaking.

"Hell—let the state boys figure it out," said Sloan. "Let Lew handle this. She's due back tomorrow late. Let's just wrap up and get out of here." The former police chief was a man who liked things in straight lines, and he was more than ready to hand this convoluted mess over to someone else.

"You look a little stunned, Doc," said Ray as the two deputies moved away to follow Sloan's orders. Osborne, still on his knees, had leaned back against a boat seat, his arms limp, his gloved hands still holding his instruments.

"I'm just . . . I'm racking my brain. That body is male all right, but every characteristic of the skull is female. Now, if your theory holds, Ray, and this individual has a high female hormone level . . . and if there's a good chance this is a person from around here, which is likely because I *know* I did the gold work, then you better get the news to Shanley as soon as possible. A health hazard like this puts all of us at risk."

"Doc, how can you be so sure you did the dental work on this corpse?" asked Sloan. "I mean, how do you tell one inlay from another for God's sake?"

"Gold is a very soft metal," said Osborne. "You rarely see it anymore because insurance companies refuse to pay for it. But it takes the natural contours of teeth so easily, it responds so well to your sculpting of it that in old days you measured the worth of a dentist by his skill in working with gold. You leave your mark in gold as distinctively as a fingerprint. My gold work is—well, I know my work."

What he chose not to tell Sloan was how he had prided himself on inlays whose edges could slip so smoothly into the soft slopes of healthy enamel that not even the most sensitive tongue could tell where the tooth ended and the gold began. He always regretted the escalating cost that eventually rendered gold inlays obsolete because the human mouth that carried gold looked better and the inlays lasted a lifetime. When they were given a chance, that is.

five

The last point of all the inward gifts that doth belong to an angler is memory. . . .

The Art of Angling (1577)

"**If** they had to cut the ice to drop that crate in . . . let's see if we can figure out just when. . . ." Ray's voice was low as if not to crowd the long, narrow room.

Sloan and Osborne moved forward to examine the photo he had pulled out of the developer. Sure enough, the picture showed the crate sitting in a pocket, an outline so crisply delineated in the thinning layer of subsurface ice that it had to have been man-made. Light and shadow captured on paper what the floodlights had flattened and disguised in the water.

"When the boys were winching it up, I noticed it sat deeper than the ice pack by a good six inches . . . so I'd bet they dropped it in there after the spring thaws had started, like within the last four weeks or so," said Ray.

"They didn't have to cut through more than two feet of ice before they could slip that baby right in, then figure it would stay anchored forever. Unless you really know your way around here, you'd never expect anybody to go fishing back in there, y'know? Looks too shallow. Takes somebody like me or the Doc who've walked it to risk it."

Sloan nodded. Sounded right to him. "I wonder where they got the tools."

"C'mon. Anybody who ice fishes can do that!" snorted Ray. "All you need is a chain saw or one of those old-fashioned ice saws. 'Course then we're probably talking locals."

"Something else here," said Osborne, who had been studying the photos Ray had pulled out earlier, the head shots of the bodies. "Notice how three of the men have light beard growth, but one doesn't. . . ."

"Which one is that?" Sloan crowded up behind Osborne.

"Guess."

"Ah," said Sloan, "I should've known, huh?"

"John, if I were you, I'd have the lab X-ray the pelvis of that body, too," said Osborne. "A female pelvis is distinctly different from a male's."

"Quiz time," chimed in Ray. "What else distinguishes our fair male?"

Sloan and Osborne looked over all the photos hanging from the racks over their head. Osborne couldn't see anything unusual.

"Doc, you disappoint me," said Ray. "Think coarse and curly."

Osborne saw it immediately, surprised he had missed it earlier: the photos of all the victims showed varying amounts of coarse body hair, visible on the arms in two cases, at the neck on another, on all with the exception of one.

"Ah," he said, "John, the Wausau boys can do a much better job once the bodies are properly laid out, so be sure to ask them to check for axillary hair on the chest, back, abdomen, and thighs. Right, Ray? Hair growth is definitely hormone-related."

"I think the lack of a five o'clock shadow is pretty darn significant," said Ray. "Oops! There's my timer."

Ray handed a wet photo over to Sloan and rushed from the small bathroom with its converted shower and tub stall back to the kitchen. A large black iron frying pan held two cut-up chickens slowly braising in a full cup of butter over a low gas flame. He lifted the lid and gently turned the pieces, nestling each one gently down between the others, taking great care not to dislodge any of the crispy batter—the same care he had taken when moving his strips of film from tank to tank.

"My grandfather's recipe. You won't believe how exceptional this is," he volunteered to Roger, who stood over in a corner of the living room, a cold beer in his hand, as he examined Ray's antique jukebox packed with old forty-fives. Ray poked at a drumstick with a fork. "I'll give it about ten more minutes." Then he checked the onion-fried potatoes warming in the oven and nodded approvingly at the tossed salad sitting in a large bowl on the kitchen table.

"Like that salad okay?" asked Roger, pride obvious in his voice. He had chopped and tossed while Ray, Sloan, and Osborne were crowded into the bathroom. The younger deputy had been drafted to drive the corpses to the morgue, but he was due back for his beer and fried chicken any moment.

Back in the bathroom, Sloan was taking a good look around while Ray was out of the room. "I'm amazed at how he got these tanks into a shower stall," he said to Osborne, who was still examining the photos Ray had strung on the lines crisscrossing over the cabinets and floor. "How the heck did he do that?" Sloan knelt to peer behind the shallow tubs that Ray had cantilevered up the walls of the shower. "Boy, did he jerry-rig this plumbing. I wonder if it's to code?"

"Ray's got that knack for how things work," said Osborne. He couldn't help adding dryly, "He's a real whiz at storm sewers." Then he shut up, realizing he could get his buddy in trouble. No doubt Sloan had not forgotten the confrontation between Mary Lee and Ray over the location of the trailer.

Immediately following that episode, Mary Lee had been apoplectic after she stumbled over a length of flexible pipe early one morning and discovered Ray was emptying his sewage not into a septic tank, but near their property line, right alongside her rose garden. Osborne, aware of a few violations of his own, had refused to let her report it. To this day, he wasn't sure what Ray was doing—nor did he care. Fact was, the roses flourished.

No siree, Osborne thought to himself, the last thing Ray needs is a five-thousand-dollar fine for violation of shore-line water treatment regulations.

"What d'ya mean?" said Sloan suspiciously. He stood up, unwinding his tall body carefully and brushing grit off the knees of his dark blue pants.

"Oh, you know—roto-rooting miles of pipe, that kind of thing—and leaky faucets, Ray's great on leaky faucets." Osborne talked fast to cover himself.

"He can be a real pain in the butt sometimes," said Sloan. "I don't want to tell you how many rainbows he's poached off Dick Svenson's private pond over the last fifteen years. And that's the tip of the iceberg. Ray Pradt has gotten away with a hell of a lot over the years. Don't need to see that razzbonya turn into a hero."

"He's a good neighbor," said Osborne, wondering why Sloan was so down on Ray. Was he jealous? Jealous of a man who lived a life money couldn't buy? Osborne let a stern note creep into his voice so he could end the conversation with his opinion overriding Sloan's: "I like the guy."

He was getting more than a little irritated with the pompous cop. After all, Ray was covering a lot of ground that would make Sloan look very good. Plus his hospitality for dinner was a not-to-be-underestimated bonus.

Once they'd moved the corpses from the boat to the police van, Ray had volunteered to process the film immediately since they were only a mile down the road from the neighboring lake where his and Osborne's homes were located. No, indeed, Osborne just didn't think it was necessary for Sloan to float any more negative remarks.

With the heavenly smell of buttery chicken wafting into the small room, Sloan seemed to get the message.

"Y'know, he's done a nice job on this trailer, hasn't he," Sloan said as if to make amends. He laid down the last photo and walked with Osborne back toward the kitchen. Ray's mobile home might look tacky from the outside, but inside it was spacious and quite clean. The living room held a plump, oversized dark blue corduroy sofa and matching recliner against cream walls with curtains to match. One corner held the jukebox, Ray's pride and joy; the other an antique wooden phone booth with a working rotary phone. A round oak table in the kitchen had been set for five with simple white china, cloth napkins, and stainless steel flatware. His two yellow Labs were calm, well-behaved, friendly dogs and currently sound asleep by the big-screen TV.

"Good-lookin' animals," said Sloan. "Ducks or grouse?"

"Both. Ruff and Ready got the softest mouths in the county," said Ray. "They can scoop a mallard without moving a feather."

"What happened?" said Sloan, looking over the dog with the bandaged leg.

"Coon," said Ray. "Nasty sucker, too. Poor Ready, hard to keep that bandage on 'im."

Osborne clapped his friend on the shoulder as he walked past him toward the table. "Ray, whaddya think?"

"I've been standing here mulling over some of those shots I got of that one body. . . . Thanks for giving me the go-ahead, John—I just put the call in to Rick Shanley.

I'm sure he'll ask if he can have copies," Ray said as he started to heap the chicken pieces high on a platter.

"Tell him to call me at the station," said Sloan as he and Roger pulled out their chairs to sit down. "I'll see after I talk to him." Sloan pulled the platter toward himself and lifted off a golden, crisp breast. Just then the door opened and the younger deputy walked in.

"Hey, smells great!" he said to the group as he followed Ray's finger, which pointed to an empty chair. "Bridget said the switchboard's swamped with calls. You boys are lucky to be hiding out here. Better enjoy it while you can. Oh, and Lew called. She's gonna call back later."

"Get those bodies checked in okay?" asked Sloan.

"Yes, sir. Our friends are resting in peace at Saint Mary's." The local hospital morgue served the purpose for the police as well.

"Do we need anything else?" Ray ran a critical eye over the table, then sat down and dove in with both hands like everyone else. The room was cozy and bright and filled with the sound of men happily chewing away. No one spoke, they were famished.

"Whoa! Wait . . . a . . . minute. I know where I saw a crate like that before," Ray's voice rose in excitement, and he set his chicken down on his plate. He rested his elbows on the edge of the table and held his greasy fingers carefully in front of him.

"I was at my sister's for Christmas two years ago. She and her husband live in Lake Forest outside Chicago, and they got a delivery of some art they'd bought in Japan. Two wooden boxes with matting all around and stuffed into a black wire crate very similar to this one. I remember now." He nodded his head. "Because I almost asked her for it. It was beautiful. Real tight weave, hand-soldered, copper wire at the corners. A little tighter weave and it would've made a great crayfish trap, a *huge* crayfish trap."

He looked from face to face as if expecting someone

to pick up that piece of information and run with it, but all he got was the sound of more chewing.

"Well, I don't think they flew these boys in from Japan," said Roger finally, reaching for his beer can with greasy fingers, "and I wouldn't hang those buggers on no wall of mine." No one reacted to this comment either. Sloan and Osborne just kept working on their respective pieces of chicken.

"Did you keep any records from your practice?" Sloan asked Osborne after a couple minutes had passed.

"I've been thinking about that," said Osborne, picking over his last set of bones and tidily wiping off his fingers. "I'm not sure. Mary Lee was such a nut on throwing things away. I know I moved my files out to the lake house when I closed the office, but I don't remember seeing them anywhere in the last few years."

Osborne remembered well his wife's frustration when he'd arrived home in a truck with two tall oak file cabinets packed with expandable charts, bitewings, and full-mouth X rays. The young dentist buying his practice took over all the charts of active patients, of course, but Osborne just couldn't throw out forty years of life's work. Once he had overcome his youthful urge to devote his life to the piano and sculpture, he'd come round to taking pride in his profession. When he retired, he genuinely missed the dentistry that had been his compromise in order to make a living. Mary Lee just saw it all as a big mess, however. And who knows what she'd done to it when he wasn't looking. His youngest daughter still hadn't forgiven her mother for throwing out her baseball cards when she went off to college.

"Jeez, Ray, I didn't know you were a Susie Homemaker." Sloan reached for a piece of the apple pie that Ray had just pulled from the refrigerator and set with plates and forks in the center of the table.

"One of Joanne's," said Ray quietly, referring to the premier pie maker of the Northwoods. "Taught her

•

sixteen-year-old son how to fish for muskie in exchange
for a pie a week for a year."

"You lucky son of a bitch." Roger reached for his piece.

"I remember when *you* were sixteen . . ." Sloan started,
pointing his fork at Ray. Suddenly he stopped, cautioned
by a serious glare from Osborne. "Doc," Sloan changed
the subject between bites of pie, "if you have those records, would they show what you think you saw tonight?"

"I'll have a diagram of the work done, I'll know the
lab that did it, the dates, everything," said Osborne, laying
his fork down and addressing the group, "*if* I can find the
files. That's a big if.

"I can tell you right now, though, that I'll not find that
record in my permanent patient files. I am convinced I
would have recognized the face if that victim was one of
my regular patients. Loon Lake only has 2,762 people, for
heaven's sake—and I know just about everyone. If I
didn't recognize him, someone else here would—right?"
Everyone nodded in agreement.

"If I find it, it'll be in my one-shots—the files I kept
on summer people. Tourists, camp kids. But I'll search
high and low tomorrow and give you a call right away if
I find anything."

"I'd appreciate that." Sloan wiped his mouth and set
both his arms on the table. He cleared his throat and
coughed, turning away. "Sorry, I think I'm coming down
with something."

Though he was in his late sixties, he'd inherited Italian
genes that gave him an olive complexion with so few lines
in his big, oblong face that he looked twenty years
younger. Even so, his smooth forehead was heavily fur-
rowed in thought as he pushed back from the table and
walked over to the sink to wash his hands. "This is a
humdinger, y'know? When I talk to Lew tonight, I'm
gonna see if she can grab an earlier flight tomorrow. We
need to get her into the loop on this as soon as possible."

•   •   •

An hour later, Osborne had barely shut the door to his house and flicked on the kitchen light when his phone rang. It was Ray.

"Did you find those files yet?"

"Ray . . ." Osborne let his irritation show in his voice. "I just walked in, and I'm exhausted. I'll look for them in the morning."

"If it was me, I couldn't wait. . . ."

"Well, you're not me. I'll talk to you tomorrow."

"That's why I called. I'm going up to see old Herman the German first thing, and I thought you might like to go along."

"I can't do two things at once." Osborne closed his eyes against the fatigue as he filled Mike's bowl with dog food. He sighed heavily. "Now, why are you going see the old man?" Much as he hated to get into a conversation of any length, Osborne was puzzled. Herman lived far on the other side of the county, deep in the McNaughton wilderness forest. If anyone could be less connected to everyday life in Loon Lake, it was that old hermit.

Ray dropped his voice conspiratorially. "He told me a Dead Creek story a long time ago when I was a kid. . . . I'm gonna check it out for Shanley. I don't know why I didn't think of it before."

"I see," said Osborne. It suddenly occurred to him that Ray would like nothing better than to beat former police chief John Sloan at his own game. Sloan, who'd locked him up in the Loon Lake jail for smoking marijuana in the high school locker room, causing him to miss the league basketball championship game the first year that he was star forward.

A few minutes later, as he pulled the covers up around his ears, Osborne made a mental note to mention to Ray that he should be careful what he said on the phone from now on. Osborne had heard at least two soft clicks on the party line after Ray'd hung up. It drove him crazy that he couldn't get a private phone line until the three old biddies, who were holding out on the pretense their phone bills would go up, agreed to the change. And there was nothing he could do. The damn phone company had a stupid rule that every subscriber on the line had to agree, or they wouldn't make the change. Saved them the cost of all the new cable that had to be laid.

Jeez, thought Osborne, as he drifted off to sleep, *by the time I get a decent phone line, the rest of the world'll have fiber optics to Mars.*

six

Some men fish all their lives without knowing it is not really the fish they are after.

Henry David Thoreau

The last place Osborne had expected to find himself at four o'clock the next afternoon was sitting at the bar of a stripper joint. And not just any stripper joint, but the infamous Thunder Bay Bar. Beside him, chattering away quite easily with no evidence of any embarrassment whatsoever, was Loon Lake's police chief, Lew Ferris. It was she whom he'd had to convince that Ray Pradt was missing. Not an easy thing to do.

The morning had begun innocently enough. Osborne got up later than usual for a Saturday, but all the excitement of the night before had been a little overwhelming.

He was just setting Mr. Coffee to brew when Ray's truck had rattled up and stopped sideways to Osborne's driveway, just long enough for Ray to lean out of the cab and give two perfect loon calls. Almost perfect. Even if he hadn't been able to see him, Osborne would have known it was Ray by the crazy cackle at the end of each. Osborne grinned. The annual loon call contest was happening Sunday in Boulder Junction, and if Ray could call like that, Osborne knew he'd knock the competition right out of the water.

Then Osborne had waved from where he sat at his kitchen table, knowing his friend could see him through the window, and Ray had trucked off, Osborne had figured, to do what he'd said he was going to do: see the hermit.

He did not have the dogs in the back of the truck, a signal to Osborne that he'd be back by noon. Ray always fed his dogs at noon. He was quite scientific about his dogs and their feeding habits, making sure they were never likely to be hungry during the hours they were used to hunt. These dogs got their food at nine P.M. and at noon without fail.

When Osborne had his first cup of coffee in hand, he set out to walk the property to see what that damn Mary Lee might have done with his files. Going to sleep before his search may have been the smartest thing he did, because as he was waking up, he had a vague recollection of seeing those old files behind a door he hadn't opened in at least five years: the storage room behind the fish shed. He stepped out into a crisp, sunny morning, temperature about forty degrees. Even though it wasn't yet eight A.M., the sun was climbing, and the air was full of spring smells.

He walked from the kitchen door across his yard to the back of the large garage where to the right and facing the house was a small room that held his lures, his tackle boxes, minnow buckets, old rods that he no longer wished to hang in the living room, and a beat-up wooden table where he cleaned his fish. At the back of the room was the door to a narrow storage room that ran along the side of the garage. Mary Lee had refused to use it much, saying the weather changes would damage anything good she might want to store there.

He pushed and tugged on the darn thing. The wood had

swollen in the warm spring air. Finally, it creaked open. There they were: his two oak files, dusty and cobwebbed but stalwart and full of secrets. Osborne stared at them with great satisfaction. He was happy he'd stood up to Mary Lee, miserable though the experience had been. He'd always known they'd come in handy someday.

Osborne set his coffee cup down on the windowsill and pulled the door wide open to maximize the sunlight so he could work. As he opened the middle drawer of the file closest to him, a breeze through the open door chilled the back of his neck.

Yes—his eyes scanned the contents swiftly—everything was there. By the time he'd finished his first cup of coffee, he knew the records he wanted weren't in the middle drawer. He went back to the kitchen to refill the coffee cup and call Sloan, but before he got there, he decided against calling Sloan until he knew exactly what he had, so he just refilled his cup and headed back to the shed. He hoped, too, that by the time he called, Sloan would know if Lew had caught an earlier flight.

He started through the records in the top drawer, the ones from the fifties. At first, he took his time. The familiar names on the manila files conjured the sights and sounds of old friends, now dead or moved away long ago, buddies with whom he'd fished and laughed and enjoyed the prime years of his manhood. Here was a file that brought back every instant of landing his first really big muskie: his good friend and patient Harry Everson had been so excited that day, he tipped himself right out of the boat. They used pistols on the big fish in those days, and with that monster moving every which way, Harry had done his best to keep from shooting the boat out from under the two of them. Harry got wet, but Osborne got his fish. Then Harry was gone. Prostate cancer. Osborne set the file aside gently. That was one he'd like to examine more closely later.

Another file reminded him of a very unpleasant feud

Mary Lee had had with a woman in her bridge club whose husband had been a partner in his hunting shack and, for a few years, one of his close friends. The women's disagreements had put an end to that friendship, however. His finger lingering on the tab, Osborne paused and sighed, feeling a sense of regret that time hadn't dulled. As the years went by, he'd come to see that Mary Lee was, more often than not, the troublemaker. Why on earth had she been such an unhappy woman? Osborne moved quickly on to the next drawer.

Because there had been only two dentists in town for many years, his life and his patients' lives were so deeply intertwined that when he treated a patient for a gum problem, he usually knew without asking what kind of stress was as much a cause of the problem as any physical factors. As he read the names on his records, ghosts of whole human beings rose before him. He heard their voices and remembered why they couldn't pay their bill for another month or needed to barter with venison chops or a summer's harvest of tomatoes instead of cash.

As he moved through the files, Osborne felt more sure than ever that the fourth body could not have been a permanent resident of Loon Lake. In a town so small, faces do not go unregistered, and this was one he certainly hadn't seen in the last ten to fifteen years.

When it came to one-shots, he had plenty in the fifties: thirty or more two-page folders tucked into hanging files, one for each year. Those years were the heydey of tourism in the Northwoods. First, the expensive private camps that flourished as the rich sent their offspring direct from private school to summer camp with scarcely a break between. Then the middle- and upper-middle-class families from Milwaukee, Chicago, Saint Louis, and Kansas City flooded in to stay in rustic little cabins at the lake resorts, resorts now closed as America's leisure habits had changed. Osborne shrugged. That fact of Northwoods life was a constant topic of the McDonald's coffee klatch:

Dad wants Montana fly-fishing, Mom wants the New Mexico spa, and the kids want Disney World. "Goofy," they said in unison as coffee cups were emptied.

The early fifties yielded nothing. By the time he hit 1957, his back was starting to ache from leaning over the open drawers, so he gathered up the next four years' worth of files and headed back to the house. He poured another cup of coffee and walked out onto the screened porch that overlooked the lake. The day was gorgeous. Osborne paused for a moment to enjoy the soft shimmer of the diamonds dusting the gentle waves. He settled into the beat-up easy chair and noticed it was already 11:15. Ray should be back any time.

He looked through 1957. Nothing. He opened 1958. In the middle of the folder, he found it.

Osborne sat straight up in the chair to examine and reexamine the file. He couldn't believe how perfectly his marks on the printed diagram in the upper left-hand corner of the page mirrored the work in the mouth he'd felt the night before. This was it. A small manila envelope paper-clipped to the file held X rays. Obviously, he'd been pleased with the work at the time because he'd shot X rays of the finished inlays. Those may have been the days when X rays were used a little too carelessly, he thought, but here was one instance when some people would be glad he had shot plenty.

He checked the name and address on the file. The patient was a boy from Kansas City, age 10. That would put him in his mid-forties, which seemed reasonable. Name, parents, address—the information was all there. The patient had been a camper at Camp Deerhorn, a camp just outside Rhinelander, which was about ten miles from Loon Lake.

Osborne hurried to call Sloan. Not in yet. That surprised Osborne. He left a message for Sloan to call the minute he arrived—it was urgent.

After he hung up, he decided to walk over to Ray's and

wait. As he walked. he remembered that Ray's sister. the lawyer who lived in Chicago. had married a man who'd been a counselor at Camp Deerhorn. They met one summer at a local bar where all the college kids hung out. Osborne remembered it well because Ray's mother had been so pleased her daughter had snagged a wealthy boyfriend that Mary Lee had been disgruntled for months. The wedding had been quite splendid with the reception held. not in Loon Lake. but at the Rhinelander Country Club. of course.

If we're lucky. thought Osborne as he leaned against a fence post outside Ray's trailer. *Ray's brother-in-law may remember the kid. Now, that would be interesting.* Osborne checked his watch. It was a quarter past noon. Ray should be there any minute. Ruff knew it. too. The dog was running in nervous patterns in his pen. anxious for lunch.

"Hey. boy. where's Ready?" Osborne was puzzled. *Where was the other dog? That's strange.* He tried the door to Ray's trailer. The wind was kicking up pretty strong off the lake. and he knew Ray wouldn't mind if he waited inside. He stepped into the trailer home. All the dishes from the chicken dinner had been washed and put away. The place looked pristine. as usual. But he heard scrabbling toward the back of the trailer where there was a little room in which Ray kept his washer and dryer, wading boots. and other outdoor gear. The door was pulled shut.

Osborne walked down the hall toward the door and listened. He heard movement. It sounded like the dog, skittering and yelping. He cracked the door open, then pulled it shut quickly. He had glimpsed small smears of blood on the tile floor. Now he remembered that one of the dogs had gotten into it with a racoon and hurt his paw. Ray must be keeping Ready inside with his sore paw. The dog yelped again as if in pain. Ray knew better than anyone the dog would be needing a new bandage. Where was he?

"Sorry, boy," said Osborne from outside the door. "This old man can't help you. Ray'll be here any minute." But he wasn't. Five, ten more minutes went by. Osborne got anxious. He walked back up the drive to his place and waited. Sloan didn't call either.

By one-thirty, with a constant chorus from the famished Ruff in the background, Osborne was really getting worried. He had just walked up to feed the dogs himself when Gordy O'Hearne from the Catholic cemetery drove in looking for Ray because he hadn't shown up to dig a couple of graves scheduled to be finished by four. Gordy wasn't worried, he was just plain mad. Now *he* had to dig the damn graves.

Lew Ferris picked up the nonemergency line in the Loon Lake Police Station when Osborne called in around two.

"Hey, Doc, I *just* walked in." Lew sighed, more than a hint of fatigue in her voice. "The place is crazy. The switchboard is all lit up, and I got stacks of messages on my desk. Can I call you back?"

"Didn't John tell you the news?" The last thing Osborne was going to do was hang up.

A brief pause, then Lew spoke. "Doc, what is going on? All I got so far is a message left at my hotel last night ordering me back here—as if Stoneface thinks he still runs the joint." She *was* tired. And crabby.

"So you haven't talked to him."

"No, I have not," Lew barked into the phone. She was beyond irritation, she was angry. "But I drove three hours in the dead of night to the Albany airport to catch a 5 A.M. flight. Now I'm here and no Sloan. No Lucy either, might I add. Bridget replaced her on the switchboard at midnight. All she left me is this cryptic message: 'Emergency! Talk to Chief Sloan ASAP.' Nice of her to forget who's chief around here. And ASAP? Well, hell—the man's nowhere in sight. I tell ya, Doc, is this some kind of punishment for taking three of the goddam fourteen vacation days I'm owed? I mean, jeez Louise. So if you know anything about anything, I would sure appreciate hearing about it."

Osborne couldn't have asked for a better opening. Without taking a breath, he rushed into the details.

"Whoa, hold up, slow down—let me grab a pen. . . ." Irritation subsiding, her voice took on a blunt, staccato edge. Lew was back all right, back and focused. Osborne started over. He tried to speak slowly. He could hear tremors in his voice, which surprised him. Quickly, he laid out the sequence of the previous night's events, anxious to get to the point.

"I'm sorry," Lew interrupted, "hold on a second, Doc. Bridget just handed me an envelope with a confidential memo from Sloan. I guess she finally moved her purse and there it was. Let me check . . . okay . . . and photos. . . . Holy cow! Doc, you found *this?* Wow! Am I glad John called."

"I thought you would be," said Osborne. "He and Roger and that new guy worked with me and Ray to get those bodies out of the water. I hope you don't mind; he deputized me again—"

"Heck, no, I don't mind. Good."

"I can't imagine why John isn't there, Lew, but I've tried to reach him three times this morning myself."

"I don't know either. After I got the message last night, I tried him at his house around eleven but got no answer."

"We were still at Ray's developing those photos—"

"I tried again from the airport early this morning and still no answer. I've asked Bridget to call Lucy at home, maybe she knows where . . . wait. . . ."

Muffled noises followed as Lew held her hand over the receiver.

"All right, all right, one mystery solved. Lucy said John felt like hell last night and was driving over to Rhinelander first thing this morning to see a doctor, get a prescription for antibiotics. You know him and his diabetes, he freaks out over the smallest infection. So let me finish reading his memo, catch up with a few things, and call you back, Doc."

"No. We can't wait, Lew. Something is wrong. *Ray is missing.*"

Osborne invested the last three words with all the authority he could muster, all the authority of his years of being listened to as if his was the ultimate word on all matters dental, medical, and even, on occasion, ethical. Being a professional in one field often, in a tiny backwoods community, translated to being a professional in all fields. Right now he hoped against hope that Lew would be intimidated by his tone and do what he was desperate for her to do: put Ray's disappearance first on her agenda.

"Ray missing? That's an oxymoron, Doc." Intimidated she was not. Osborne scrambled for a new and better approach as if fishing hazardous terrain: when one bait doesn't work, switch fast.

Meanwhile, Lew's silence on the other end of the line implied many things, not least that she could be reconsidering their relationship. Whenever it came to Ray Pradt, she was dubious, and rightly so. Ray—to put it mildly—had a checkered past. No felonies but a long, long list of misdemeanors. Years of misdemeanors. Only strategically timed deliveries of of fresh-caught bluegills had served to keep the stuffed trout hat out of jail on more than one occasion.

Nevertheless, Osborne plunged ahead. He owed Ray.

"I'm not kidding, Chief. I'm *very* worried." When intimidation doesn't work, try deference. Mentally, he crossed his fingers.

"Doc, you know Ray. You and I both know it is not unusual for that man to take off without saying a word to

anyone, to be gone for *days*. He's in Canada fishing walleyes, for God's sake!"

"Now listen to me, Lew," Osborne struggled to make
his case. "He didn't come home at noon when he should
have. The dogs weren't fed and Ray *always* feeds those
dogs on time, especially now that he's got 'em in field
trials. Also, he's got one that's injured and bleeding. Ray
would never deliberately leave a sick dog alone so
long. . . ."

"I'm still listening. . . ." He heard her shuffling papers.
Her tone was cool.

"Then Gordy from the cemetery just came by madder
'n heck 'cause Ray was supposed to have dug two graves
this morning."

"Ah. Doc, I'm sorry, but I need to return calls to the
mayor and the Loon Lake board before I do anything else.
I have to let them know this situation is under control—
which, of course, it is *not*."

Knowing that could take hours, Osborne dropped his
voice as if he was sharing confidential information in a
crowded room. "Lew, I hate to tell you this on my party
line phone, but you're forcing me: Ray said he had a lead
on one of those bodies, a lead he was checking out with
someone who lives way back past McNaughton. You
know that crazy truck of his—he could be stuck on one
of those back roads. . . ."

"Doc, if he's stuck, he can stay stuck. Ray Pradt is a
big boy who can pull himself out."

That was it. Osborne launched his last lure. If this
didn't hook her nothing would: "I think you should talk
to him before the Wausau boys screw it up."

"What does Wausau have to do with this?" A deadly
calm crept into her voice.

A nibble, thank the Lord. Could he get her to bite? If
Osborne knew anything about Lew, he knew she was ambitious. Ambitious, dedicated to detail, and determined to
keep the condescending know-it-alls from the regional lab

sixty miles south from messing around in her law enforcement operations.

"John told me he was sending the bodies down to the lab first thing this morning."

"Oh, brother! Now why. . . . okay, Doc, start over. Why on earth do I need to talk to Ray Pradt about all this?"

"Two reasons." Osborne went back over the dental IDs, his confusion over the sex of the fourth victim, and the information he found in his files. "I am sure his brother-in-law can ID that individual, and Ray is the only way we can reach him in Chicago." A long silence, and Osborne sensed he was more than halfway to victory.

"You mean Ray's brother-in-law knows something about one of those bodies?"

"Without doubt—but more important, you need to talk to Ray about Dr. Shanley's work before Wausau does anything. It's my opinion, though I could be wrong, that Shanley should run his tests before they do theirs."

"You mean before they screw it up so he *can't* run his tests? Geez, Doc, you're obviously nervous about this. I'll go with you; you don't have to talk me into it. I'll tell you what. Ray hangs out at Thunder Bay about this time every Saturday, looking for new clients. Meet me there in twenty minutes. I got problems with the new ownership anyway. They need some spot-checking."

"Lew, he's not at Thunder Bay. Something's wrong. The dogs . . ."

"Look, Doc, I know the man's habits, good and bad. If you want me to do this, we do it my way."

"Fine." Osborne hung up, marginally happier than when he had called in.

Much as he hated walking from the brilliant sunshine into the dark, smoky interior of Thunder Bay, Lew had a point. Ray did stop in here every Saturday. The bar was notorious for topless dancing, rumors of prostitution, and excellent barbecue ribs—all of which made it a natural hangout for "da boys" out of Milwaukee or Chicago when they headed north for hunting, snowmobiling, or fishing. Fresh meat for a Northwoods guide.

Ray wasn't always complimentary about the clients he picked up at Thunder Bay, describing some as "bearded wood ticks" and others as "Kenny Rogers throwbacks." But the reality was that after five or six rounds of draft Michelobs and a dose of Ray's ribald humor, Osborne's neighbor could name his price and fill his boat. Once, he bragged to Osborne, he pulled down a thousand-dollar tip. When it came to throwing money at women or fish, Ray knew he could bank on the clientele of Thunder Bay.

A major attraction of the bar was that it operated on both sides of the law, which produced a steady shift in proprietors. A recent drug bust had booted the former owner out of his liquor license and into the hoosegow, putting the bar under new management.

But that appeared to be all that was new, noted Osborne as he entered. As the bar door swung shut behind him, he took a moment to survey the two-room joint, left to right, for any familiar faces. This was only the second time he'd set foot in the place, and he would rue the day anyone he knew saw him there. He scanned the few full tables and the nearly empty bar. Any former patients? None. At least so far.

In the room to his immediate left, the action was just getting under way. A jukebox had started up toward the back of the room where there was a small stage. Osborne saw one cluster of three men sitting around a table in the far corner with a larger group at a table closer to the stage. A few were paying attention to a young woman who had strolled out and was moving lazily to the dance music. As best Osborne could tell in the dim light, she was wearing a one-piece swimsuit.

Off to his right he spotted Lew, perched on a stool at the far end of the bar, staring intently at something on the counter. The forest green of her winter uniform with its slim-legged pants and a close-cropped gabardine jacket over a tailored shirt and darker green tie suited her compact frame. She was a sturdily built woman with strong legs, a solid butt, and wide shoulders. Seen from behind, you might mistake her for a man of modest height but never would you make that mistake from the front.

She looked up as he approached. "Hi, Doc. Just reading over John's memo one more time. No sign of Ray yet, but I think we should sit tight right here. I'll betcha he walks in that door in any minute now. And I talked to Wausau. They'll hold on the autopsy on the fourth body until I can talk with Shanley."

Lew tapped the lid of the can of soda pop in front of her and lowered her voice. "Remember what I told you last time we were here: Don't drink from the glasses. If you want something, get it in a bottle or a can. Trench mouth." She leveled an informed, no-nonsense look at him along with the instructions. Lew had been a patient of his up until his retirement and took pride in letting him know she had memorized well his tips on oral hygiene.

Quite a bit younger than Osborne, Lew had had her children early and was the mother of three who had gone through school with his own. When she joined the police force ten years ago, she was the first woman on the Loon Lake force. He had wondered if she wouldn't be better off in a proper job as a secretary at the paper mill instead. He caught himself thinking that again when they first fished together, but then he'd remembered: Lew had divorced her husband many, many, many years ago, long before it was socially acceptable. She always was a little different.

Osborne nodded at the tip on trench mouth and asked the bartender for ginger ale—in a can. He turned to Lew. The soft glow of the bar lights heightened a healthy ruddiness in her cheeks. She might have sounded tired, but she looked great. Osborne loved the lines around her eyes.

"Well, Lew," he said as he eased onto the stool beside

her. "Have you been marinated in fly-fishing?"

Any guilt he felt for dragging her out to search for Ray vanished as her face lit up at the mention of her trip. "Doc, I hope I never have to sit through a trial like that again. Bor-ring. But three days at Wulff School of Fly Fishing made it all worthwhile. I swear," she slapped a palm on the bar, "it changed my life."

Then she cut her eyes to give him a look of pure mischief: "I have a new fly rod."

Osborne feigned shock. "Another one? Lew, rods aren't like trout flies—you don't need a hundred."

"And I won't tell you what I paid for it."

"Yes you will."

Lew chuckled and ran her right hand through the mass of dark brown curls that gleamed above her brow. She had a friendly way about her that always surprised Osborne. She was as easy to talk to as one of his fishing buddies. No fancy footwork, no pretense.

"I'll tell ya, they make it impossible for you not to buy the rod of your dreams. First you have six or seven hours of intensive casting practice, see. One on one. I still have problems with my backcast, but I am much improved. Anyway, then they set out thirty, maybe forty different rods around one of the ponds. Different makes, weights, lengths, and grips. You move around the pond, casting with each one until you find . . . magic."

"Magic?"

"Magic. This rod feels like an extension of my arm, of my hand even. It is like a part of *me*." It crossed Osborne's mind that she sounded like she was describing a lover, but he was too shy to even kid her about that.

"I had to have it—the Joan Wulff Favorite by Winston—the only one with the thumb groove. You won't believe how easy this rod is to cast. You'll have to try mine, Doc. They say it's a woman's rod, but two of the men in my class bought it, too. Picked up some new lead-ers and tippets and a very, very light fly line that I want to show you—"

He was enjoying the sparkle in her eyes when suddenly the bar door swung open. Osborne turned, hoping to see Ray Pradt's lanky form unfold itself through the doorway. Instead, a gaggle of five women crowded in. Five well-dressed, carefully coiffed women he pegged to be in their late thirties or early forties. Giggling and shoving at each other. Clucking as if they were embarrassed to be there, several, nevertheless, made sure their table gave them a sight line to the stage. From the corner of his eye, Osborne was relieved to see the dancer was still in her one-piece swimsuit. If he was lucky, he and Lew would be out of there before things got serious.

"Now what the heck brings them here?" Osborne whispered to Lew.

"I doubt they're up for crappies," said Lew after a cursory glance and a shrug. "A little too smart-casual for the boat, doncha know." She lifted her can of soda, clearly unconcerned. At times Lew had an edge and a vocabulary that surprised the hell out of Osborne. He was still hoping to be invited into her house someday. He wondered if he would find books on the shelves. Books on something other than fishing, that is. He wouldn't be surprised.

Smart-casual, huh? "Smart-casual and *expensive*," Osborne whispered back. Breezes wafting in from the door behind the women carried a wave of mixed perfumes, nudging enough of a hint of Mary Lee into his memory to remind him that these were exactly the type of women he wanted to avoid.

"And overaccessorized for Thunder Bay," said Lew with a lifted eyebrow, ready to have a little fun. "If gambling were legal in this joint, I'd put a nickel on Milwaukee—Shorewood."

"A nickel it is. I put my money on Chicago—Winnetka. Seriously, Lew, aren't you a little surprised to see them in here?"

"It's a tourist thing: cocktails at Thunder Bay, dinner at the Whitetail."

She was probably right. The Whitetail, one of the region's most elegant restaurants, had the bad luck of being situated just across the road from the Thunder Bay Bar. The owners had gone to great expense to put up a stockade fence in order to block their lowlife neighbor's lurid neon sign. Unlike today, patrons of the two establishments didn't usually overlap.

When it became obvious Thunder Bay didn't offer table service, at least for drinks, one of the women stepped up to the bar, standing just behind Lew and Osborne. Short and rounded with straight, chin-length black hair framing an open, pleasant face, the woman's bright, curious eyes seemed less involved in the drink order than in sizing up Lew.

Osborne watched her gaze take in the uniform, then the revolver on Lew's right hip. His eyes followed hers and, for the first time, he noticed that Lew had substituted a .40-caliber SIG Sauer for her usual airweight .38. Was she expecting trouble? Ignoring the woman behind them, Lew caught his glance, "Lends presence," she said.

As usual, she was educating him to the reality of the universe where he had been practicing dentistry for nearly forty years. Where once he couldn't imagine crime in the Northwoods beyond the off-trail snowmobiler or drunken deer hunter, since getting to know Lew, he had come to learn that the sins of the cities were as invasive to these forests as acid rain. And, of course, there were the random bodies in the lakes.

"Something is out of synch around here," said Lew. "I feel it in my bones. Judith Benjamin just paid over three hundred dollars per lake shore foot for this building and a thousand acres—"

"Geez," said Osborne, "that's half a million bucks."

"More," said Lew. "You didn't let me finish."

"Where'd she get that kind of money?"

"That's exactly what I'm wondering," said Lew as she flagged the bartender and motioned to the woman to step forward.

"Still waitin' on Ray?" the bartender said as he walked up. "You might be outta luck. If he comes, it's usually by now—round four o'clock or so. He wants to talk to guys before they get all drunked up. If he doesn't roll in here in the next half hour, I'd say he ain't comin.'"

Frustrated with the lack of attention from the bartender, the dark-haired woman moved off to the other side of Lew where she could crowd closer to the bar. Now he paid attention and took her order for the table. Another member of the group, a tall, slender, haughty-looking woman decked out in a buttercup-yellow cashmere sweater set with matching curls tucked crisply behind heavy gold earrings, got up to help carry the drinks. Waiting side by side, the two looked like Mutt and Jeff.

As they waited, they watched the dancer in the other room. A friendly banter was under way with the men at one of the tables, and the dancer was casually pulling down the top of her swimsuit to reveal a set of pasties on her abundant breasts.

"I guess we're the only women in the room not working," said the blond to her friend, her snide voice as piercing as a needle.

"I beg your pardon," said Lew. Her tone was jovial, but Osborne was aware of a tightness in her tone.

"Oh, she doesn't mean you, of course," said the dark-haired woman. She thrust a hand forward, "Hi, I'm Rosemary Barron from Evanston. This is a friend of mine," she gestured toward the blond, "Deirdre Thomson, and you—are you a forest ranger?"

"Lewelleyn Ferris, Loon Lake chief of police," said Lew, shaking the proffered hand, reserved but friendly. "This is Dr. Paul Osborne, one of my deputies." Osborne was happy to hear that. Did it mean Sloan's appointment of the night before was official?

"What brings you ladies out here?" asked Lew.

Rosemary's eyes had widened at the words *chief of police*. With her bright black irises set into pale skin under a smooth cap of black hair and wearing a black-and-white striped jacket that ballooned over the legs of her dark brown designer jeans, she reminded Osborne of a black-capped chickadee, a perky little bird, the kind that flew out of nowhere to perch on his shoulder as he walked from his house to his car on snowy winter days.

"Fun," said Rosemary in answer to Lew's question. The woman had a breathy, birdy voice, too. "We all belong to the same book club down in the city, and one of us, Miriam Wilson, has a cabin up here, so we escaped for a girls-only weekend. No husbands, no children," she trilled, then lowered her voice conspiratorally. "We came in here on a dare."

"My mistake," complained Deirdre, rolling her eyes, "I didn't think they'd do it. Now I have to buy dinner."

"Ouch! At the Whitetail?" said Osborne, though from the look of her, he figured the woman could afford it easily.

"Say," Rosemary jerked her head toward the dancer, "isn't that stuff against the law?"

Lew looked past her to study the woman who was now down to a G-string and bare-breasted, bobbing and weaving in front of the table of men. "So long as they don't violate Code 2116B, they're fine," she said matter-of-factly. "We haven't had any problems up here in, oh, six months or so. Tourist season is just around the corner, and they don't want to risk getting shut down before then. Now, if this was late August and some of the city boys were laying down some big bucks, it might get pretty raunchy. That's when we step in."

As the women watched, the dancer opened her legs to semistraddle one of the customers, her breasts deliberately sweeping his face. "That's not raunchy?" asked Deirdre.

Lew studied the action. "A little raunchy, but that's table-dancing. She's wearing her G-string." Lew turned away. The two women remained glued to the scene.

"How do you learn to *do* that?" mused Rosemary. "Can you take classes in table-dancing?"

Deirdre gave her a withering look. "It's a God-given lowlife talent. C'mon, Rosemary, that doesn't take training. The woman's a hooker. Pure and simple."

Osborne braced himself. She wasn't the first person to make such a remark in the company of Lew. He still cringed at the memory of his own loose-lipped faux pas. This was going to be interesting.

"O-o-h, I don't know about that," said Lew genially.

"Well, I do," snapped Deirdre.

"She's not a prostitute," said Lew. "The girls here are well aware of the legal limits."

"You think she cares?" Deirdre dismissed Lew with a toss of her blond head. "You don't do what she's doing and not go all the way." And with that, Deirdre swept up three drinks in two hands and walked off to join the others at the table. She was obviously a woman accustomed to winning all arguments.

"This establishment is pretty careful on that score," countered Lew as she walked by.

Deirdre paused and swung around to confront her, "And how would you ever know for sure?" Her strident voice electrified the air. Rosemary winced.

"Because one of my daughters danced here."

Lew's voice had remained calm, her eyes never leaving Deirdre's face.

Osborne watched a slow flush move up the blond's neck, past the collar of her buttercup cashmere sweater to her ears and across her cheeks. Her mouth opened and closed soundlessly, not unlike a smallmouth bass sucking in a minnow. And like a flailing fish, she spun away to-

ward the safe haven of the table where her friends awaited
their drinks.

Osborne leaned toward Lew, his voice low. "You didn't
warn her about trench mouth."

"No, I did not."

seven

Most anglers spend their lives in making rules for trout, and trout spend theirs in breaking them.

George Aston

Rosemary reached across the counter to touch Lew's arm.

"Don't mind Deirdre," she said, a sympathetic glow in her eyes, "she's got the personality of a fork." Then, as if to further distance herself from her companion's remarks, she added in a low voice, "She's a travel agent . . . a doctor's wife."

Rosemary unzipped a fanny pack she was wearing under the balloon jacket and pulled out a business card. She handed it to Lew. "Unlike Dierdre, I live in the real world," she said, her eyes intent as she talked fast. "I'm an editor for the *Chicago Tribune* metro section—investigative stories. What you just said fascinates me." Now she moved around Lew to stand between her and Osborne, her back to her friends.

"I mean—what a juxtaposition," she kept her voice determinedly low and thrust her hands deep into her pockets as if to keep herself from hopping and flapping about too excitedly. "Mother a police officer, daughter an exotic dancer. If we were in Chicago, you'd be a cover story. Do you mind if I ask you a few questions?"

"Only if it's off the record," said Lew, a little taken aback at the force of Rosemary's reaction. Then she relaxed. "Sure, I don't care, I'm proud of my daughter." She slipped a small napkin under her soda can as she leaned her left elbow on the bar. Rosemary, glass of wine in hand, moved in even closer.

"What made her choose bar dancing in the first place?"

"We're talking about my eldest, Suzanne," said Lew. "She had a rough streak starting out. She had to get married right after graduating from high school, to a no-good creep, had twins four months later, a divorce six months after that, and the bum she married never paid a cent of child support."

"When was this?"

"Oh, seven, eight years ago. So at nineteen she has no money, two kids, no future, right? The mill offered her a secretarial job, but she couldn't make enough to cover day care. Then she heard what the girls here were making and ended up getting an offer she couldn't refuse. She worked the six-to-eleven shift, I watched the kids, and the money she made she saved. And she made good money. But she was a dancer, she was *only* a dancer," Lew said pointedly.

"What about the other dancers?"

"The same. Thunder Bay was under different management at that time, with owners who knew the minute you let that other stuff happen, you've got problems with the mob, with law enforcement, with hysterical wives. You get an element you can't control, and those folks did not want trouble."

"You have the mob up here?"

"Since Prohibition," said Lew. "This is a good area for cooling off. It's easy to disappear in the Northwoods." Then she lowered her voice, "I know people think the women who dance here are all hookers, but if they are, it's strictly on their own, off the premises. I'm here today to be sure the new ownership understands the law. Believe me, I've been doing this job for eight years now. *I* know what goes on."

"Does Suzanne still dance?"

"No." Pride crept into Lew's voice, "She worked here about a year, and the money made it possible for her get out of town and back to school. She met a nice guy down in Milwaukee, and she's married and doing just great now. She's a CPA—makes fifty-two thousand a year." Lew beamed.

While Lew and Rosemary chatted on about Suzanne's successful second career, Osborne's mind slipped off to thoughts of his own daughter Erin, his youngest, wife, mother of three, and president of the Loon Lake School Board.

They had breakfast together once a week, and he thoroughly enjoyed hearing about the frustrations of daily life in a small town, the kids in school, her husband's law practice. He'd developed a strong friendship with his daughter since Mary Lee's death. Through her he'd learned it wasn't the money but the listening that counted. She was happy in her life. He knew that.

Osborne tuned back into the women's conversation just as Lew took a slow sip from her can and chuckled. "Yep, when it come to kids, you never know, y'know. Suzanne was my little one who played the Madonna in the Christmas play in third grade and—"

"I remember," said Osborne, interrupting. "She got the part instead of my daughter Mallory. We certainly had the weeping and gnashing of teeth in our house over that. But Suzanne did a very nice job." Truth was, he knew Mallory never did understand how she'd lost out to Suzanne. Nor did her mother.

Mallory went on to get everything else: the expensive degree from Radcliffe, the big wedding to the investment banker, and the estate in Lake Forest. Mallory. The one

with the bad year, last year, whose words slurred on the
rare occasion that she called, and Osborne knew it wasn't
a problem with the phone line. But that was changing
now. At least he hoped it was.

Lew caught his eye. As if she knew what he was thinking, she looked over at Rosemary, "We do all we can as
parents and then just hope for the best, you know?"

Her eyes shifted suddenly toward the back of the room
to check the door, which had just opened. Osborne
looked, too, only to be disappointed. Just two men he
didn't recognize, no sign of Ray.

Rosemary lifted her wineglass, ready to return to her
friends. "Can we stay in touch?"

"Certainly," said Lew. "I have a case right now that
may involve some people in Chicago. Don't be surprised
if you get a call from me."

"Please," said Rosemary. "My reporters have very good
sources on the street. And I'm so glad you weren't upset
by Deirdre."

"Takes more than that to upset me," laughed Lew.

"What do you say to a person like that?" Rosemary
shook her head.

"Tell her what I used to tell my kids," said Lew. "When
in doubt—be kind."

"Like she'll get it?" Rosemary rolled her eyes as she
left.

Suddenly Osborne didn't want to be sitting in the bra-
zenly seductive haze of women and booze another minute.
He checked his watch. "Lew, it's twenty after four. Ray's
not coming. I don't like this place. And I rea-a-ally don't
want to stay here much longer."

"I can see that, Doc," Lew said. "It's written all over
your face. But it was our best shot for finding him.
Brother, you'd never make it in law enforcement long-
term," she chuckled. "I'll tell you, some of the places I
have to go . . ."

"That's why I'm not in law enforcement," said Osborne, hoping he sounded curt enough to get her out the door.

"Oh-h, yes you are!" she answered in surprise. "John's memo said he made you a deputy so that ID you did will hold up legally. You're in the game again, my friend."

"Uh-oh, I guess you're right." His spirits lifted. Her words meant he had a job to tackle. And with that, the bar took on a slightly more comfortable feel: if it ever made it back to the McDonald's crowd that he'd been seen at Thunder Bay, Osborne could say he had the *authority* to be there. He liked the sound of that.

Still, Ray had not shown up. The bartender let Osborne use the phone next to the cash register. Nope, still no answer at Ray's home, either.

"Maybe we should check in with Donna?" offered Osborne. "Ray might have called her or she might know which direction he went."

From the corner of his eye, Osborne checked on the dancer's progress. The men at the large table were keenly interested as her body was writhing on the small dance floor, dollar bills tucked into strategic sections of her costume.

"Five to ten more minutes," said Lew, glancing at her watch. "This is high traffic time. If Ray doesn't walk in shortly, he ain't comin'."

The bar had been filling up as they waited. Groups of men in twos and threes. Rosemary and her friends gave up their table to one foursome that looked like out-of-towners. Most just glanced casually at the dancer and headed straight for the bar or a table nearby. No one entered that Osborne knew well enough to be concerned about, thank goodness. Now the sound of frying and clanking pots could be heard behind the kitchen doors that were just to the left of where he and Lew were seated near the end of the bar. The smell of fresh-popped corn mingled with the bourbon fumes.

"Okay," said Osborne, pacified. A quick glance confirmed his residual worry over the activity on the stage. The young dancer was rapidly approaching complete nudity. This was a far cry from a spring Saturday of two years ago when he and Mary Lee had attended Saint Mary's annual quilt show. In spite of his mounting anxiety, Osborne allowed himself a small, secret smile.

"By the way, Doc, how would you like to fish the Bois Brule with me? I want to try out my new rod, and I know a series of holes up between Stone's Bridge and the Winneboujou that are classic trout water."

If she was trying to divert his attention, she succeeded. Osborne's spirits soared. "A day trip?"

"Oh, no, this requires a weekend, Doc. Do you have a good tent? Or you can share mine, but the big browns only bite at night. We have to night-fish if we want to see some action."

"Night-fish? Really?" Osborne hesitated. "I heard there's quicksand."

"No, no, you're thinking of the White River. I don't fish the White, too risky. Whaddya say? Want to give it a try?"

"Well . . ." He tried his darndest not to say yes too fast. "What do I need for trout flies?"

"Deer-hair mice are my favorites. And a big, bluntnosed, red-and-white deer-hair bug called a Hank's Creation. I'll get you one, Doc. Most folks use Hank's Creations for smallmouth bass, but, brother, do they work on browns. I cast right along the edge of the weed beds and retrieve with sharp strips of line. Those big browns want commotion. They want it glugged and popped, and when they hit, man, it is *ka-whomp!* You won't believe those fish—thirteen, sixteen inches. It is wild."

Her eyes were sparkling again. The perfect moment to propose an exchange: a weekend on the Bois Brule in exhange for equal time in Osborne's muskie boat. Just as he opened his mouth to set up the trade, the expression on Lew's face changed.

"Well, well, that's interesting," she said, tipping her head back toward the door. Osborne's eyes followed hers. In had walked a curious couple.

Whether they were together or not was unclear. The tall, broad-shouldered, blunt-nosed blond who led the way was Judith Benjamin, new owner of Thunder Bay Bar. Her large, dark eyes were framed by tortiseshell glasses, which seemed to restrict the quick, darting glances that took in every detail as she headed toward the bar. Her mouth was set in a sullen straight line and her very yellow hair was lacquered into a tight French twist. If she had a body, not a curve could be seen under the boxy beige trench coat that was buttoned to the neck and tightly belted. If Judith Benjamin looked like anyone, she looked like a cross between an old-fashioned school marm and a linebacker for the Green Bay Packers.

The darting eyes seemed to linger for a fraction of a second on Osborne. He felt rather than saw her march down the full length of the bar, sensing a long, tall shadow fall over him as the advancing footsteps neared. She stopped just short of his bar stool. Her lips parted in a slit of a smile that exposed the edges of perfect white teeth, a pale, large-fingered hand with rather bulbous knuckles jutted out from her sleeve.

"Hello, Dr. Osborne." Her voice was very low, husky even, as she shook his hand. She did not seem surprised to see him there, even though it was his first visit to any establishment of hers in the seventeen years that she'd owned taverns in the region. Taverns that always had a reputation. Yes, thought Osborne as he shook her hand, Thunder Bay was the perfect addition to her portfolio and, yes, Lew's decision to put Benjamin on her watch list was wise.

"Nice of you to stop in." And then she was gone, vanished behind the kitchen doors. Osborne was a little stunned. All he could think at the moment was that she looked exactly like she looked when he saw her every

Sunday, rain or snow, at 6:30 Mass when she took her place in the last pew at Saint Mary's Church. She never took Communion, but she never missed Sunday Mass. And she wore that trench coat winter and summer, spring and fall.

It had been a long time since he'd seen her up so close, too. That nose. A Loon Lake landmark. A mark of shame and violence, proof that man's inhumanity to man starts very young. For reasons he couldn't explain, Osborne was in awe of Judith Benjamin. She frightened him.

Years ago she'd endured the humiliation of being different in a small town where being different made you a target of those stronger and meaner—and turned it around on those who tortured her. She walked the edge of the law to gain a crude but effective control over the fantasies and realities of their sex lives. Her lakeside brothel was not just her livelihood, it was her revenge: Osborne had lost count of the number of Loon Lake marriages that were irretrievably strained after a wife learned her man had been with one of Judith's girls.

Eventually, a local judge, one of her protectors, passed away, and Judith refocused her business: investing in taverns, scaling back on the higher-risk enterprise. But if the history of her business acumen was still grist for bar tales, the story behind Judith's remarkable face was a chapter long closed. Twenty-seven years had passed. Osborne wondered if anyone even remembered.

The man who had walked in behind her was also advancing on Osborne. But now the good dentist could not repress a groan as he turned away, hoping against hope he wouldn't be seen. He despised Brad Miller. He had despised him since he was a child and took a big chomp out of Osborne's right thumb during a school dental exam.

Osborne was new to Loon Lake at the time and had just opened his practice. He also had just met Miller's father, Joe, who would become one of his favorite hunting and fishing buddies. But Brad, who was adopted, had nothing in common with Joe. He had nothing in common with most people. Osborne always felt very guilty that he'd taken such a strong dislike to this child, small for his age with pinched features, a mouthful of teeth that rotted too easily, and so uncommonly bright that he scared grown-ups.

Peggy Miller, Joe's wife, had doted on the boy, and town lore was that she dressed him in all white, sometimes in frills even, until he went to nursery school. That was absurd, of course. Osborne doubted the story was true, but it did help explain Brad's fastidious ways. When she finally let Joe take him fishing, it was too late. The kid wouldn't get close to a worm much less hook a wriggling mud puppy or a leech. Actually, no one could take much of Brad. He had a supercilious way of appearing to sniff the air around you as you spoke as if something bad had entered the room. When Brad had won every scholarship there was to win and left Loon Lake, few regrets were whispered behind him.

Joe died in a boating accident during one of Brad's vacations from Princeton. Osborne had helped Brad and Peggy with the funeral arrangements but then he hadn't heard from him in years. Brad, Peggy had bragged to Mary Lee, had had a stellar career as a professor of art history at Yale University.

Then, nine months ago, he took early retirement and returned to Loon Lake. He moved into his mother's house on the best street in town, talked of someday donating an art collection he told someone was worth over a million dollars to the town and, after much arm twisting, condescended to the wishes of the local arts council to teach a few classes at the local university branch.

Why he had to arrive at Thunder Bay Bar just as the dancer challenged Code 2116B was beyond Osborne's ken. Sometimes life just wasn't fair.

"Huh?" asked Lew in response to the strange grunt from Osborne. Her eyes had narrowed to watch Judith's reflection in the mirror that ran the length of the bar, not unlike a cat cautiously considering a spider. Now she slowly swung her gaze from the kitchen door behind which Judith had just vanished to look at Osborne.

"Oh, jeez," said Osborne, tapping his empty can with irritation on the bar and raising his eyebrows in grim anticipation. "Getta load of this. . . ."

Miller had spotted him and stepped right up behind the two of them, a big grin on his squarish face. Even though it was a cool day and a little early in the season, he was wearing khaki bermuda shorts under a red plaid woolen jacket. Academic horn-rimmed glasses perched on his nose. Osborne thought he looked like a hunter out of a *Far Side* cartoon.

"Why, Oz-z-zie, what are *you* doing here?" Only Joe had ever called Osborne Ozzie, and the dentist cringed at the sound of his nickname nasally abused by Miller. He turned around to face Miller, noticing with some surprise that the creep had lost a lot of weight since Osborne had last seen him.

Once quite portly, now he was remarkably thin through his legs and shoulders, though he still carried a doughy tire of a midriff. Only the too tightly cinched belt of his khaki shorts kept it from expanding farther. As he planted himself behind Osborne and Lew, he leaned back like a pregnant woman, a pose that emphasized he was all angles and no muscle. He looked very out of place in Thunder Bay Bar, which didn't seem to bother him in the least.

"Oh, my goodness, I don't believe we've met. What lovely breasts you have, my dear." He extended a hand to Lew, who swung around on her chair and looked at him. She didn't take the proffered hand.

"Wha—?" Osborne looked at Miller in amazement.

"Oh, don't get nervous, Ozzie. I'm quite serious. The college is working with me on a marvelous exhibit." He raised his right hand, fingers touching, as if to emphasize how classy this would be.

"We're bringing in a very hot, very prestigious New York artist, Kiki Smith. If you haven't heard of her, you will!" This time both hands were raised in an effeminate wave. "She does an absolutely *phenomenal* series of female nudes urinating glass beads, glass moths, that type of thing. Quite phenomenal." And with that, he laughed the old Brad Miller "Ha, ha, ha, ha"—the signature dry cackle, totally humorless, that had always raised the hair on the back of Osborne's neck. "I stopped out here to do a little research—"

"Brad—" Osborne tried to interrrupt.

But Miller refused to let him in. "Oh—this is so new for this region and we *have* to explain it—so I plan to hang a photography exhibit of more traditional female nudes alongside. I would love to shoot you, Mrs.—?" He paused for only a second, not really expecting Osborne or Lew to volunteer her name.

"I can see your figure is just so—so—*Boucher.*" He pursed his lips as he uttered the French word. And then again, "Ha, ha, ha. Oh, Ozzie, you are always too much."

He winked at Osborne. It was quite clear he knew exactly how uncomfortable he was making his father's old friend. And how much he was enjoying watching Osborne squirm.

"Brad. Stop." Osborne was determined to shut him down. "Just stop—"

"Stop what?" Miller leaned back on his heels and raised his eyebrows. Osborne swore he was feigning surprise. But Miller still refused to let Osborne get a word in. "Don't misunderstand, madam. C'mon, I know she's not a hooker, Doc. That's obvious. We're wearing a uniform, aren't we? But big, beautiful breasts *are* big, beautiful breasts. Ha, ha, ha, ha. Really, I must shoot you. Next week, perhaps?"

And then, suddenly throwing both hands up in mock horror, Miller tipped his head in mock disappointment.

"My dear," he sniffed, "I'm doing my best to make you famous."

Lew just continued to stare directly at him, quite calm and unperturbed.

"No, thank you, I'm not interested."

That was it. She didn't appear to be insulted or upset by the remarks. Nor did she say another word. She simply swung around on her bar stool to face the bar, her back to Miller.

That stopped him. His face fell ever so slightly. But he recovered quickly to look over at Osborne. "Of course, if you two are so involved—"

"Bradford!" A sharp voice sounded a warning, and Judith Benjamin slammed a mug of beer down on the bar a good three to four stools away from them. Osborne hadn't even seen her approach, but now he noted with great relief that Miller seemed to take her word as an order. She said nothing else, but walked back into the kitchen. Miller moved in the direction of the beer and left his sentence hanging.

"We're out of here," said Lew softly, standing up. Osborne followed her lead. Neither of them spoke as they headed toward the door. And when they had stepped out into the dusk and the crisp, cool air and closed the door behind them, Osborne began to apologize, but Lew stopped him with a harsh, "Huh? That wasn't about me, Doc. The professor hates your guts. That was all about you, my friend."

eight

Fishing is a cruel sport...how would you like it if fish and angler were reversed?

Robert Hughes

The day had changed. They stepped into a brisk breeze that had lowered the temperature a good twenty degrees, and the sun had the late-afternoon fade to it that made it seem later than it was. That plus the smell of hamburgers.

Lew and Osborne hadn't moved ten feet toward Lew's cruiser when they heard a sharp barking noise from the rear of the wooden building, the side toward the lake. It sounded vaguely human to Osborne, who turned his face into the wind and squinted, trying to see through the shadows thrown by the huge Norway pines that protected the bar from the road.

"Wait! Mrs. Ferris, Mrs. Ferris!" the dancer from the bar came running and waving at them. She had thrown a short leather jacket over her shoulders. Her long legs teetering on spike heels looked painfully bare in the dimming light and the icy air. But she didn't look cold, she looked upset. She stopped at the corner of the building and beckoned to Lew to come toward her. She leaned forward anxiously. It was clear that for some reason, she couldn't go farther.

Lew started toward her, but Osborne stayed right where he was, midway in the parking lot, until Lew motioned to him to follow. Together they walked over to the woman.

"Step over here, okay? I don't want them to see me. If anyone comes out, talk about Suzanne, okay?" Up close, Osborne could see she was shaking.

"Laura, calm down. What's wrong?" Lew put a motherly arm around the young woman's shoulders. Her compact fireplug frame was a good two inches taller than the slender dancer's. She looked at Osborne over the woman's head, her eyes dark and concerned.

"I dunno—but I'm like really, really worried." Laura's words rushed out. "I can only talk for a minute—I said I needed a cigarette, y'know. But really I wanted to get to you—I heard about those bodies and how no one knows who they are and stuff and I—"

"Slow down, Laura, take it easy," said Lew.

"Well—I'm just real worried one is my roommate Annie."

"Annie?"

"Yeah, Annie Potter. From England. She came over to work as a baby-sitter—y'know, a nanny they call it—for a doctor over in Rhinelander. When they didn't need her anymore, she got a job working here, and about six weeks ago, she disappeared."

The girl dropped her head into her hands, clearly fighting back tears, then looked up again.

She took a deep breath, then she spoke. "I didn't tell anyone because I thought maybe she had somethin goin' with a guy or something. But I got all her mail, her car, all her clothes at my place. Something isn't right. She woulda told me what to do with her stuff, y'know?"

"When was the last time you saw her?" asked Lew.

Laura looked at her with frightened eyes. "I'm not supposed to tell anyone this, okay? She did a party gig. Judith lined up a bouncer for her, and he was s'posed to get her to the Burdeens for a party. The bouncer didn't stay very long though. He told me Annie said she didn't want him at the party."

"The Burdeens had a party?" Lew's tone was incredulous. And rightly so, in Osborne's opinion.

Everyone in Loon Lake knows that lowlifes don't come lower than the Burdeens. They're shanty trash. They might have a drunken brawl but not an organized party. But even a brawl isn't likely because that implies group interaction. The Burdeens are loners, rarely seen. And they are mean, silent men: three brothers you don't want to meet and they don't want to meet you. They don't even like each other.

Osborne shuddered at the thought of a young woman even getting near one of them. When his girls were growing up, he'd warned them about necking out in the woods with boys. "You never know what's back there," he'd said, very satisfied to see their eyes widen in surprise and fear. And when he'd said it, he'd been thinking quite specifically of creeps like the Burdeens.

Laura thrust a photograph at Lew, who took it and studied it briefly before tucking it into a pocket on her shirt. "I'll look into it right away." She patted Laura on the shoulder and tucked her jacket around her. "Now, you go back to work and don't worry. I'll get in touch with you when I know something. Why don't you stop by in town if you think of anything else I should know. Give me a call and let me know you're coming."

"But you won't tell anyone I said anything, okay?"

"Of course not. Laura—who's the bouncer?"

"Ted Bronk."

In the police cruiser, Osborne turned toward Lew. "Why didn't you tell her that her friend isn't one of the bodies we found? We didn't find a woman—"

"I don't want to say anything to anyone until we know

what we've got, and I don't think we'll have that ID out of Wausau for another couple days," said Lew. "Those boys don't like to work weekends."

She was quiet for a moment. "Doc, you never know who's doing what in this town. You can't really assume things are as they appear, you know? Now someday, if I get to know you better, I'll tell you a thing or two about Miss Judith Benjamin back there." She cut her eyes to look at Osborne. "But it isn't very pretty stuff. I'm not sure yet you want that kind of thing in your head."

Osborne nodded and looked away. He wasn't sure either. On the other hand, the more he knew, the more he was likely to have an opportunity to work with Lew. That seemed quite benign and a hell of a lot more interesting than anything else he'd been up to lately. This afternoon had just beat the dickens out of looking for antique muskie lures at garage sales—his usual Saturday occupation, if he wasn't fishing.

Ray's sometime girlfriend, Donna Larson, sold mobile homes. Her office was in a mobile home that sat in a lot crammed full of mobile homes. Cloth banners slung with Christmas lights and trumpeting sale prices were criss-crossed over the dirt driveway.

"Tornado alley," commented Lew as they pulled into the lot. "I see Donna in the window."

"I haven't seen Ray since Monday," said Donna, a tall, slender woman with a head that looked disembodied within a halo of long, overpermed bright red hair. She was stubbing out a cigarette in an overflowing large green ceramic ashtray that Osborne noted was identical to one he'd had in his office in the early sixties. "Pisses me off, too. He's s'posed to be here by now to take me to dinner. It's my birthday today."

"See?" Osborne whirled in excitement, but Lew ignored him.

"How many other birthdays has he missed?" asked Lew.

Donna grinned, "Every one. Every one of six, counting this one," she said, lighting up another cigarette. "I should know better. Coffee?" She walked over to a microwave, mixed herself a cup of instant, and shoved it in the oven as she hit the buttons. She had an easy way about her. Then she chuckled, looking at Lew. "Don't tell me—he poached Whitehead's trout pond again?"

Osborne had cleaned and filled eleven teeth in Donna's mouth when she was on ADC and struggling to raise two children she'd had by a man who went to prison for shooting a state trooper after robbing a liquor store. She'd been in the process of divorcing the creep and finishing her high school education by correspondence. That was over ten years ago.

In the years since, she had remained a patient of his, and he had seen her life improve slowly but steadily. If he found her short on class, she made up for it with common sense. Donna might be hard-bitten, but she was going somewhere. In two short years, she moved up from sales rep to sales manager for the region, and Osborne often wondered why Ray didn't just bite the bullet and marry her.

But, of course, he knew why: Elise Martin. The old high school flame. A beautiful girl who fled Loon Lake and became a New York model married to a wealthy stockbroker. Like a bad dream, in Osborne's opinion, she came back every summer to see her aging mother and just enough of Ray to keep him enthralled. Love with Elise was going nowhere, Osborne had tried to tell him one lazy summer afternoon while casting for muskie; love with Donna was home-cooked food on the table and a good friend when it counts. Ray had just listened, his eyes soft and confused.

"I know, Doc, you're right," he'd said, "but she always wears the wrong thing when I try to take her out." Osborne wasn't sure exactly what that meant. After all, Ray's entertainment scene was more likely to be local fish frys, not dinner parties with bank presidents. Osborne figured right then that the man would never grow up; he was a hopeless romantic with no concept of compromise.

"Have you any idea where he might be?" asked Lew. "Dr. Osborne thinks he's—"

"I think something's happened," Osborne jumped in. "He hasn't fed the dogs, and he missed a job at the cemetery."

"Yeah," said Donna, "they called here for him. I dunno. You could be right. He usually lets me know if he's gonna leave town for a while. I always feed the dogs for him. You want me to stop by later?"

"I did it," said Osborne. "But I'm real worried."

"Well . . ." Now Donna looked worried, "I guess I talked to him on the phone last night. He said he was going out to see his old friend Herman the German up in McNaughton. You know that old hermit up there?"

Osborne and Lew, with Donna in the backseat, bumped along a gravel road that took them deep into the wilderness off old Highway 47. Very few patches of woods like this remained in northern Wisconsin, isolated areas of wilderness that the lumber barons didn't lay bare in the late 1800s. So dense were the drooping branches of the ancient pines that the road seemed to snake into pitch-black infinity.

"Okay," said Donna, "slow down, the turn is just past this stand of birch, you'll barely see it . . . right, take it slow so you don't knock hell out of the bottom of your car." Osborne felt the minutes stretch one by one as they lumbered deeper into the woods, the headlights picking out trees, trees, and more trees. Suddenly, they came upon a small barn in a clearing that held the skeleton of an old pickup, a rotting rowboat turned upside down, and a large stack of firewood. A light shone in the one window set beside two double doors.

"Well, if this isn't the middle of nowhere," said Lew softly. "I've never been back in here."

"I used to hunt this area," said Osborne. "This is one region of the backwoods where you don't ever want to get lost. The genetic throwbacks that live out here aren't very nice people."

"You make it sound like they eat their young," said Lew.

"The old man is okay," said Donna as she opened the car door. "But you're right, Doc. You can stumble on some scary characters in these parts—and Ray knows 'em all. He picks blackberries with Herman every fall." She rapped sharply on one of the double doors.

A dark old man peered up at Donna, his figure in the doorway illuminated by a spill from the lights on the police car. Lew stayed in the cruiser, her window rolled down. Osborne followed Donna to the door and stood behind her. Old Herman Ebeling stood just under five feet tall. He was wearing a scruffy brown tweed jacket over overalls and everything seemed crusted under the same layer of brown something. His beard was scrubby and his eyes kind of rheumy-looking. Osborne didn't peg him for drinking, but he didn't see any signs of positive health habits either.

"Herman, how ya doin'?" Donna's bright, friendly voice sounded startlingly out of place. "We're looking for Ray. You seen 'im?"

"Mmrhumm." The old man rolled his jaws and opened his mouth slightly. Osborne could see there were no teeth inside. Herman, though one of his patients many years ago, had never been comfortable with the bridges Osborne had argued him into. Some of his best work, too. Osborne sighed.

"Oh yeah?" said Donna, who apparently understood what the old man was saying. "Where'd he go?" The old man responded again in what Osborne determined was a cross between gumming and a patois he could barely discern. Donna, however, appeared quite tuned in to the old man's language. They jabbered for a moment, and then Donna thanked him. The old man plucked her sleeve as she turned back to the car, and she reached into her purse for a package of cigarettes. "I'll have Ray bring you a carton next week," she said. "You take care of yourself now."

Back in the car, Lew and Osborne turned toward Donna.

"Herman said Ray was here early today. He wanted Herman to tell him about them little orphan babies that Herman found years and years ago. He said Ray was real interested in exactly where the babies had been born, so Herman told him how to get there."

"Get where?" asked Lew and Osborne simultaneously.

"Up behind Dead Creek," said Donna. "I know where that is. My ex-husband's family was from up around there. We're about thirty miles away. It's up behind Shepard Lake. I think we better get up there right now. I'll go if you don't have time. . . ."

Osborne could see Donna's attitude had changed about Ray's disappearance. No longer just worried, Osborne thought she seemed frightened. He exchanged glances with Lew and knew he was right.

As they passed a tavern, once they were back on the main road, Osborne volunteered that they might be wise to pick up another man to go along, but Lew just pressed her foot harder on the gas, and Osborne knew he'd said the wrong thing. Would he ever learn? They covered thirty miles in about twenty minutes, the police light swirling silently as they sped down the highway. Donna gave terse directions, then pointed, and Lew swung the car hard down a dirt road. Osborne rolled down the window on his side and inhaled the cold night air. "I think we're close to water," he said.

"Fork left," said Donna when they came to a split in the road about five minutes down the dark lane. Once again, the police car bumped along in the dark, this time the pines and birches and random maples were shorter, more densely packed. The high beams picked up something pale in the road ahead.

"Oh, boy," said Lew under her breath.

"That's him," said Donna. "I know that's Ray." Lew stopped the car, leaving the engine running and the lights focused on the figure sprawled across the dirt tracks. All three burst from the cruiser and ran toward the body.

nine

Third Fisherman: Master, I marvel how the fishes live in the sea.
First Fisherman: Why, as men do a-land; the great ones eat up the little ones.

Shakespeare, *Timon of Athens*

Lew got to the body first, jumping nimbly over ruts and loose brush in the barely visible ruts of the road, the beam from her flashlight bouncing off the trees. Osborne was surprised to see how gracefully she moved in spite of her stocky build.

"We got 'im!" she shouted. She bent over with her flashlight and ran the beam slowly, carefully, over Ray Pradt's entire six feet six inches. "He's alive and his color's not bad—but he's out cold." Stumbling, Osborne nearly squashed the stuffed trout hat. He stooped to pick it up. As he did, he looked up. The headlights beaming across the chest of the still figure lying in the road seemed to outline each detail with extreme clarity. It took only a few seconds for eyes long trained to avoid a patient's gag reflex to note the slight movement in the man's chest. "He's breathing!" Donna and Osborne ran up behind Lew and looked down. His eyes half-open, Ray appeared to be staring at his boots from where he lay flat on his back, arms to his sides and legs straight ahead almost as if someone had carefully laid him out.

"Ray? Ray? It's me, Donna." Donna dropped to her knees and leaned to grab for Ray's shoulders.

"Uh-oh, don't do that," said Lew, catching her arms gently but firmly. "We don't want to move him. I'll call for an ambulance."

Lew ran back to the cruiser and quickly radioed in the emergency. Then she turned off the headlights. "Don't panic. I've got a road lamp in the trunk," she shouted. "I'll set that up so we don't run down the battery on this tank of mine."

Tucking the bulky stand under her arm, she started back to the group, but as she hurried, she tripped. Recovering, she stopped and retraced her steps. Something caught her attention, and she pushed the beam of her flashlight slowly along the ground until she was back to the ruts around Ray.

"Hold on, folks," she said, her voice very firm and low. "Stay right where you are—both of you." Again, she moved the beam slowly around Ray's body. Now she knelt close to him and turned the light off for a moment, leaving all four of them in the dark. Osborne watched the outline of her form as she dropped her head down toward Ray's and gently patted her hand in the dirt around his head and shoulders. Finally she stood up and flicked the flashlight back on.

"Look." She spoke very softly as she moved the beam along the ruts in the road beside Ray's body. "See all these muddy clots? But it's been dry all week, hasn't it? Where's this mud come from? And here, right on the edge of this clump, you can see ridges from a tennis shoe or a running shoe." Osborne peered into the circle of light. She was right: fresh mud and a large shoe print. No doubt about it.

"But Ray is wearing hiking boots with much deeper

treads," said Lew. "Now look down the road just a little way—see how these ruts are broken down? I think his body was dragged along the road here where it's dry by one party and then," Lew swung the light beam, "from the brush over there, it looks like we get this other set of footprints."

"You've lost me," said Donna from where she sat on the ground beside Ray.

"Two things happened here," said Lew. "First, someone or some people dumped Ray. Second, someone else came walking by with very soggy shoes, walked around our injured friend here, and left in that direction. They haven't been gone long, either." She rubbed some of the wet mud between her fingers. "A couple hours maybe? Maybe minutes. Certainly long enough to get to a phone and call for help. Very curious."

The three of them stood over Ray Pradt. The dark silence of the heavy woods seemed to close in around them, and Osborne found himself trembling slightly in the dark.

"What's that?" asked Donna, twisting suddenly at a nearby rustling in the forest.

"A deer, maybe a bear," said Osborne.

"I don't need a bear," said Donna.

"Don't worry, they're more afraid of us than we are of them," reassured Lew, setting up the road lamp and turning it on. The warm glow made it seem safer.

But not for Osborne. Rational or not, night in the deep woods always made him uneasy. His friends ribbed him because he was always the first one into the deer shack from his stand during hunting season. One night as they sat around a fire pit roasting marshmallows, he'd scared the living daylights out of his children saying, "The forest is full of secrets, dark, black secrets, more secrets than the ocean." Mary Lee had been furious because both girls had to sleep with the lights on for weeks after that. Tonight he admitted that he believed those words of his. *Oh, come on, enough of that.* Osborne made himself shake off a vague feeling of dread.

To curb his unreasonable fear, he knelt and gently palpated Ray's extremities, then moved on to his neck and chest. The medical skills trained into him during the war many years ago came back as easily as if he'd just read the textbook. "He's got a big lump on the back of his head behind his left ear," said Osborne, trying to sound casual. As he looked Ray over under the shadowy light of the road lamp, Lew walked back to her car to check on the status of the ambulance.

Osborne continued, "Otherwise, he doesn't appear to have a mark on him. I think he's got a concussion due to someone clocking him from behind, that's what I think."

Donna leaned over, this time gently touching Ray's body as if to reassure herself it was alive and warm. She glanced around suddenly. "Where's his hat? Oh, here it is. He'd die if he lost his trout hat." Osborne saw her take a firm grip on the hat and clutch it to her breast.

"Hey," called Lew from where she was sprawled half in and half out of the cruiser. "It'll be about twenty minutes before the paramedics get here." She came running back. "Here, I found a blanket shoved back in a corner of the trunk." Donna spread it carefully over Ray, tucking it in around the edges. Lew walked back down the road a short way, trying to push flares into the semi-frozen ground. She succeeded with one and returned.

"No change," said Osborne, standing up. He picked up Lew's flashlight and stood over Ray's still form, leaning over to study the ground around him, working hard to take his mind off his worry over Ray and the bears while they waited. There was nothing more he could do.

"Jeez, Lew, where'd you get that eye for tracking? There's not *that* much mud here, much less enough to see those little ridges from shoes. Hell, I can barely make out these clumps, and I know they're here."

"Comes from tying on too many size twenty-six

Midges, Doc," said Lew, resting against a convenient tree.

"You know, Lew, if you hadn't stopped me, I'd be tromping all over this, this evidence here."

"Well," said Lew, "you didn't, so don't worry about it."

"I am worried. Not about the road here—but my eyesight. How the heck *do* you tie on those tiny trout flies? I'm going to have to invest in some kind of magnifying lens."

"Yep," said Lew, "maybe some clip-ons. You can wear 'em on your fishing hat."

Osborne thought that over. Then he inhaled deeply; the crisp night air felt good in his lungs. In all his years as as a dentist in good standing with his peers, as a man who tried to be a good father and a caring husband, as a somewhat lonely widower and grandfather, he'd never felt so alive as he did right now.

"Excuse me a minute, folks," said Osborne, looking down at his watch. A sudden call of nature overwhelmed his fear of bears. "Before that ambulance gets here, I need to see a man about a horse."

He shifted the beam of the extra-heavy-duty flashlight that Lew had handed him and started down the narrow road. Branches hit him from both sides as he followed the outlines of ruts along the seldom-traveled trail. Bear or no bear, he really had to pee.

About twenty yards from where Ray lay in the road, he figured he'd reached a polite distance where he couldn't be heard. He stepped into the brush about three feet, not too far, and unzipped. As he stood there, he mulled over the second set of footprints around Ray's body. They puzzled him. In Loon Lake, if a hunter or a fisherman comes across an injured person, he tries to get help. It's an unwritten code of honor in the Northwoods. You could find your worst enemy having shot himself in the foot, and you'd still help him out. So just exactly who would look at Ray lying unconscious and leave?

He was just zipping up when he heard a sound in the brush off to his right. Osborne froze. He knew instinctively it was the soft inhale of something breathing. Swiftly he finished hooking his belt, then slowly, slowly reached for the flashlight, which he had set on the ground behind him. Light would startle the beast long enough for him to escape. He whipped the beam toward the sound.

Not ten feet away but nearly hidden behind thick brush and looking down at him was a human face hanging like a bulb from black branches. The flashlight beam hit at a strange angle, flattening the eyes into slits of glittering light, flattening the nose against the face so it looked like a fleshy knob. Tiny black holes marked the nostrils and a larger black hole the slightly open, downturned mouth. The last thing he noticed in the split second that he had the thing in focus were the bald spots on top of the bulbous head: a mushroom with hair.

He was so stunned, he couldn't speak. He couldn't breathe, he couldn't move. He could tell time was passing from the heartbeats in his ears, but he only heard three before the ambulance siren wailed toward them. His eyes must have shifted to the right, and in that instant the thing vanished without even a rustle of a branch, not that Osborne could have heard anything over the pounding in his ears. Osborne didn't try to follow with the flashlight; he was stumbling backward as fast as he could.

Lew and Osborne and two other deputies who had responded to her call tramped through the area long after the paramedics had loaded Ray quickly into the ambulance and sped off to the Loon Lake Hospital. They found Ray's pickup about fifty yards down the road but no sign of Osborne's vision in the woods, although they did discover a good-sized stream and many muddy footprints about fifteen feet beyond where the figure had been standing.

Osborne figured the creature might have had a canoe tucked away or just waded out of the area.

"We can check this out better tomorrow in the daylight, can't we?" asked Osborne after an hour of fruitless searching. Lew didn't argue.

"And what did it look like again?" she asked him for the umpteenth time.

"Just . . . a round, globular face, a big head with a worried expression on it," he found himself saying finally.

"Oh, now, *that's* interesting," said Lew. "Not threatening but worried. What about frightened?"

"Both . . . maybe."

"I should've known better," she said during the drive back. "I felt like someone was watching from the moment we got there, but I thought I was just being too much of an alarmist. The guys at the station kid me because I follow my hunches so often. I'm not saying I have ESP, but I have feelings. I have feelings, and I ought to pay more attention to them, damn it."

Osborne said nothing. A residual feeling of dread, generated by the image of the fat head with its slitty eyes, made him feel exhausted.

"I'm too old for this," he said as Lew parked in the hospital lot. "It's—it's just so creepy how close that thing was to me. I might've touched it, for God's sake." He noticed as he got out of the car that the wind was blowing colder. The forecast was for zero to ten degrees that night, even though May was just around the corner. The wind chill would push it close to ten below zero.

"Thank God we found him," he said to Lew as they hurried toward the brightly lit entrance. "Another twelve hours in this cold, and he might not have made it."

"I'm sure that was the plan," said Lew. "I'm reporting it as attempted murder."

ten

The muskie is truly the king of the freshwater fish.

Tony Rizzo, *Secrets of a Muskie Guide*

"His vital signs are fine," said the emergency room physician, a tall, lean young man who looked to Osborne to be all of age twelve. "I checked him over, and that lump is the worst. A few minor abrasions. He needs to lie on that ice bag for another twenty minutes or so, then you folks can take him home."

It was late, but they all hoped for some answers. Lew leaned against the wall on one side of the bed, Osborne and Donna had taken chairs on the other. Everyone was staring at Ray, who had come out of his coma about two minutes after the ambulance crew managed to dump him onto the gurney.

The doctor leaned over the patient. "Ray, you're gonna feel like you've got the worst migraine in the world. . . ."

As he spoke, Ray pulled the sheet that covered him up over his head, "Ohhh," he groaned, "light hurts. *Sound* hurts."

"You never know with these concussions," the doctor said, looking at the three visitors. "Some folks are out for days. Ray's doin' great. He may have some short-term memory loss, and that headache'll be with him for a day or more."

"Is it okay if I ask him a few questions?" asked Lew. "I can wait, but the sooner I can get some direction here—"

"No problem," said the doctor, "just be aware the man doesn't feel so hot."

"Doc?" Ray muttered from under the sheet. "Can you make me a deal on a hundred thousand aspirin? I'll show you and your better half the best bluegill fishin' in the county."

"Sure thing, Ray, you take what you need and don't worry about it." The doctor patted him on the shoulder and left.

"Ray?" Lew was insistent, "I hate to do this but—"

"I know, I know," Ray groaned and threw the sheet back, "I really do not know *what* you're talking about."

"I'll get back to it. Can you tell me what happened out there—from the beginning?"

"I . . . don't know. . . ."

It was clear to Osborne Ray *was* trying to think back.

"Where were you going?"

"I . . . I can't remember. . . ."

He looked so frustrated, Osborne thought he might burst into tears.

"Ray, what's the last thing you do remember?" asked the exasperated Lew.

There was a long, long pause. "Ordering a waffle with maple syrup at the Sportsman's Bar down in the hollow . . . with a side of link sausage and some of that home-made toast they always got in the back . . . then . . . here, I remember coming here to the hospital and the sound of the siren as we were coming into town."

"Okay, Ray, we found you north of Shepard Lake. Does that jog your memory?"

"Nope. Lousy fishin' up there. That's Dead Creek. Why would I want to go up there?"

"Ray," Osborne decided to interrupt, "you told me you were going to see old Herman the German. He said you were by his place earlier today."

"I was? Yeah . . . okay, I vaguely remember. . . ." Ray pulled the sheet down from his face. Donna helped him adjust his pillow and ice bag so he could sit up against the back of the bed. He blinked, then rubbed his eyes with both hands and kept his hands held tightly over his eyes. "Please, the room spins if I don't do this, I'm sorry. . . ."

"You don't remember anything later? You don't remember driving or walking down that road?" asked Lew. "Ray, if I tell you there was someone watching us, watching you, not helping you but hiding back in those woods, do you have any idea who that might be?"

"Ohh . . . you mean that woman?" Ray's response was almost automatic.

Lew's eyes darted to Osborne's. He shook his head. The thing he saw in the beam from the flashlight—a woman? He couldn't believe it.

"A woman?" asked Lew, surprise in her voice.

"Well, yeah . . . I mean, I dunno." Ray was clearly struggling to remember something. "Y'know you asked me that question and I said that and now I don't know why really. I don't *really* remember anyone. I don't remember a face, y'know? But I remember *something* about a woman."

"Ray. Did you spend the day with another woman? This is not the time to be coy because Donna's here. It's way too late for that." Lew's voice was insistent.

"No," said Ray so emphatically he winced. "Donna's my main heifer." Donna slapped him lightly on the hip. "Ouch!"

"He's feeling better," warned Donna. "A lousy joke is a good sign. Ray, shut up and be serious."

Osborne noted for the umpteenth time that rough edges

aside, Donna had just the right spirit to go up against Ray and his kidding. He could see she looked relieved for the first time that night. She was right: for Ray to kid at inappropriate times was normal behavior for the guy.

"Okay," Lew pressed. "We still have a woman in the picture, however. You don't know what she looked like, but was she blond? Dark? Short? Tall? Fat? How did she smell?"

Ray kept his eyes closed and dropped the smart-aleck tone. "I don't know, Lew. I don't remember a thing except the sense of something female being around me . . . but I'm trying." He paused for a long time, the muscles in his face tensed. No one spoke, waiting. "It's like I remember being close to a woman. Not sexually. This sounds crazy, I know, but the most acute sense I have right now is that I've been with my mother very, very recently. That . . ." He paused and his voice lowered to barely audible. ". . . she held me."

"Your mother's dead, isn't she, Ray?" said Osborne softly.

"Fifteen years."

The room was quiet. A cool chill crept up Osborne's spine.

"Maybe he had one of those near-death things," said Donna.

"Okay," said Lew, "anything else?"

"It's so weird you ask how she smelled . . . because I can tell you exactly how she smelled."

"Okay," said Lew. "Shoot." She didn't look surprised as she scribbled notes.

"Like garden soil . . . she smelled like rich, black, garden dirt," said Ray. "You know what I mean?"

"I do," Lew reached over and patted his hand. "That's good, Ray. That's enough. You keep thinking about that. Anything else you remember, please write it down. I'll give you a call in the morning, and we'll go back over this."

She heaved a sigh and flipped her notebook closed. "Now it's time for everyone to get some sleep."

"What day is it?" Suddenly Ray dropped his hands from his eyes and sat up straight. "Did I miss Sunday?" he demanded. His eyes were bloodshot, and he still looked pretty pale.

"No, no." Osborne patted him back onto the pillow gently. Donna moved quickly behind him to adjust the ice pack. She stood at head of the cot and began to massage Ray's shoulders while Osborne spoke. "It's Saturday night a little after midnight. Take it easy. I fed your dogs this afternoon so they're fine—"

"And I'll take you to my place tonight, Ray, so you can sleep in tomorrow," said Donna. "Doctor Osborne'll take care of the dogs. You just relax."

"Boulder—ouch—Junction," said Ray wincing, closing his eyes to cut out the light.

"What about Boulder Junction?" Lew, who had been about to leave the room, stopped and turned. She flipped open the notebook she'd closed a moment earlier.

Once again she had that no-nonsense attitude, and Osborne found her compelling to watch. The alert dark eyes against her lightly tanned, roundish features made her look much younger than her fifty-plus years—that and a body that was well-toned and trim, even if it wasn't a petite size. The woman had a presence and an authority that continued to impress him.

"Tomorrow's the Spring Muskie Festival and the finals of the North American Loon-Calling Contest," said Ray, his voice quite serious. "I'm a finalist for the fifth year in a row. Last year I came in second. This is my year to win. I've been practicing for weeks. I *can not* miss it."

"Think again," chimed in Donna. "Nature has its way of telling you to take it easy, honey."

"Nothing natural about it, Donna." Ray's tone was grim for the first time since he'd come to. "Natural is not getting hammered from behind by someone you can't see.

Hey, maybe that's *it*, Chief Ferris." He raised his eyes to Lew's. "That Canadian goombah that beat me last year hired a hit man. See, he *knows* I'm going to clobber him tomorrow."

Ray threw back the sheet covering him and sat up on the gurney. "I'll feel better if I'm on my feet. I'm going to Boulder, folks."

Then he cupped his hands around his mouth and let loose with the strange, fluttering wail. "There . . . that wasn't so bad." But the rush of blood from his head took its toll, and Ray flopped back on the narrow bed, throwing the sheet back over his head. "Oh God, it hurts, it hurts, what did I do to deserve this?" he wailed.

A nurse poked her head in through the curtain and motioned to Lew, who followed her out of the room.

Donna threw her hands up in despair and looked at Osborne. "Doc, you tell him he's crazy. He's gonna break a blood vessel or something."

"Ray, you probably ought to take a day in bed, watch some TV—"

"Forget it, everyone. Forget it. I'm going. Doc, if you want to help me out, you're welcome to come. You, too, Donna."

"I can't," said Donna, "you know tomorrow I leave for Chicago to visit my daughter for a week."

"I forgot," said Ray. He looked beseechingly at Osborne. Osborne knew well Ray's maniacal drive to win this contest. He'd talked of little else for weeks now.

"All right, I will," said Osborne, "on the condition you let me drive."

"It's a deal," said Ray and heaved a sigh mixed with pain and relief.

Osborne didn't mind making the ninety-minute drive north at all. It had been years since he'd been to the Muskie Festival. Not since his kids had grown up. He vividly remembered the huge bed of red-hot coals always carefully tended by a team from the local Lions Club. Dozens of fresh muskies, caught during the first week of the season, then donated and flown in from around the state, would be wrapped in aluminum foil and steamed in butter and juices over the coals. By ten in the morning, each silver log would be unwrapped, and slabs of the flaky white fish dished up with little pots of butter. Not even a fresh Maine lobster could rival Osborne's adoration of that steamed muskie. If that was the price for driving Ray to his crazy contest, he'd pay it—easily.

"We need to be on the road by seven, though," he said to Ray, "so the sooner we get you into bed, the better."

Lew rushed back into the room.

"We got an ID on one of the bodies," she said. "That partial plate belongs to the owner of a small insurance company in Des Moines, Iowa. Family didn't report him missing because they thought he was on a fishing trip, even though he's been out of touch for three weeks—"

"Oh my golly, I completely forgot! Ray," interrupted Osborne, "my charts! I've got a record of doing that gold inlay on a ten-year-old who went to Camp Deerhorn one of the summers, I think, that your brother-in-law worked there. It's too late to call him tonight, but first thing tomorrow, we got to get in touch. He might remember this kid. He was from Kansas City."

"Hold on. Before you call anyone, guys," said Lew. "I've got a problem. Sloan caught the flu from Pecore, and he's flat on his back. That leaves me very short-handed.

"Also, the Wausau boys had some more interesting news. Seems the victims were frozen *before* they died. I mean, Wausau's pretty excited. These are the juiciest remains they've ever seen. Perfectly preserved. The medical examiner thinks he may have 'em talking by noon tomorrow. But only the one ID so far. Shanley contacted them, and he's running tests first thing in the morning."

Lew paused, and her eyes darkened as she stood with her hands jammed into her jacket pockets. "Given that I have other problems to deal with here in Loon Lake, I am hoping that both of you—Dr. Osborne and Ray—wouldn't mind continuing as deputies for another twenty-four hours, and perhaps you'll find some time to go back up to Dead Creek—"

"You asking the victim to check out the scene of the crime?" asked Ray.

"Kinda like that," said Lew with another wave of her hand and sheepish grimace. "Frankly, you're the best one to do it, which you know. But I have to be there, too. So what if you two do your Muskie Festival in the morning, win that trophy, and we'll celebrate over a late breakfast? Then let's try to set up a conference call with Shanley, and after that, if you're feeling okay, let's head for the woods together. But only if you're feeling up to it, Ray. . . ."

"We'll do it."

"Doc?"

"Fine with me," said Osborne, "though I may pass on the pancakes if that muskie is as good as it used to be. Why don't we meet you at Susan's Café in Saint Germain around twelveish? They serve late on Sundays."

"Good," said Lew. "I'm taking off."

She left the cubicle, and Osborne followed her out so Ray could sit up and get dressed to leave the hospital.

"Call us in the morning if you change your mind and want to watch the contest," said Osborne.

"If I change my mind, I'll come by," said Lew. "You boys have that damn party line out there, and I don't like letting your forty-seven best friends know what I'm doing. That's a hint, by the way."

"I know, I know. But we're stuck with that party line, Lew, until three lovely old ladies depart this Earth. They love it, and the phone company won't route new line without one hundred percent participation from all residents currently getting service. Believe me, I've called a thousand times to change the damn service."

Suddenly, the curtain was flung back and a half-dressed Ray, still pulling his jeans up over his shirt, confronted Osborne and Lew. He appeared to have forgotten his headache. "Hey, you guys, I just remembered something. Where's my boat? Did you leave my boat back there?"

Twenty minutes later, the boat was still the only detail Ray seemed to remember. As Osborne turned down the lake road, Ray raised his head from where he'd been resting it against the seat. He'd decided it would be better to sleep at his own place instead of Donna's in order to get a good start in the morning.

"Nothing like goin' home some nights. You know, we lucked out, you and me. First Lake is the best lake in the Loon Lake Chain, doncha think?" The painkillers were making him drowsy and not a little happy.

"How many times have I agreed with you, Ray?" said Osborne, checking his rearview mirror. Back in his own car at last, he found he was still edgy from the encounter in the woods. He kept checking all the familiar intersections, parking lots, and other landmarks to be sure no one was behind them, no one was watching. "Let's think twice before we talk to each other on the phone again. You told me last night you were headed to old Herman's, and I keep wondering if someone might've heard you."

"Nobody's up that late, Doc," protested Ray weakly. "I don't think." He was quiet as Osborne's car bumped down the lane to Ray's place. "Plus all we got are young families and old ladies on the line—no homicidal maniacs in that crowd. Seriously, we know everyone."

As the men stepped out of the car into the dark surrounding Ray's trailer, they were buffeted by a rough wind blowing off the lake. One dog barked joyfully from the pen, and they could hear the racoon victim howling from inside. Ray opened the gate for the first dog.

"It's a good twenty degrees colder out here than in

town," shouted Osborne as Ray fumbled for his keys. "I bet it's blowing forty miles an hour."

Ray flicked on the interior lights, and everything was as Osborne had left it earlier. Osborne exhaled in relief. He realized then he'd half expected Ray to have an obese woman with a bald head waiting for him. But the only occupant was the wounded dog, who leaped happily at the sight of his master.

"Jeez," Osborne said, backing out of the door as it was apparent Ray could manage for himself, "I'm getting old. I'm still a little rattled over all this."

"Me, too," said Ray, looking over at him. His eyes were clear and the expression deadly serious. "Maybe you'd like to sit down and hear what Herman had to tell me. But first, why don't I give that sister of mine a call?"

"Oh, I wouldn't do that," said Osborne, "not on the goddamn party line. Lew'll have our heads."

"You're right," said Ray. "I'll give her a call first thing in the morning. Sit down, sit down. You want a ginger ale?"

Osborne nodded. Then he walked over, closed the curtains on the windows, and was about to check the lock on the door when Ray looked over at him. "Relax, Doc. If anyone comes, the dogs'll bark."

"It's coming back, your memory?" Osborne sat down on the couch and leaned forward, his elbows on his knees.

"Oh no. No, no, no. I *never forgot* what Herman told me," said Ray as he let his long frame down into his favorite armchair, tipped his head back, and closed his eyes. The dogs immediately found their places beside the chair and curled up in tight donuts beside their master. Ray looked exhausted, but he kept talking. "You might say I don't remember if it's time to share it with the authorities. The chief thinks I'm kinda goofy, ya know? So I'd like to be sure I know what I'm talkin' about before I say anything."

"Ray," said Osborne, "is this going to be a long story?

I'm exhausted. You need to get some rest. Why don't we talk in the morning?"

"If you don't mind, Doc, I'd like to tell you now. Right now. Just sit here with me, okay?"

The cool shiver went up the back of Osborne's neck again. He couldn't help but think that Ray was making sure to share his information just in case something happened to him in the night.

eleven

Fish die belly-up and rise to the surface, it is their way of falling.

Andre Gide

"**I've** known Herman since I was eight years old," said Ray, leaning forward over the kitchen table, his fingers pulling gently at his beard in the absentminded way that Osborne knew signaled a verbal trip into Ray's world.

"He looks today just like he looked then! All bent over and gnarled. Y'know, I think that old man was *born* old. Yep. . . ." Ray paused for a long, long minute, fingers pulling, an obvious series of thoughts passing though his head if the changing expressions in his eyes were any clue. Osborne watched and waited. He knew there was no rushing Ray.

"I first saw him one day after he'd been in to pick up some cigs at old Ruthie's place. Remember Ruthie? That big fat old lady who lived right off Highway 8 behind the Labor Temple and ran a little grocery store out of her house?"

"Barely," said Osborne. "I think she died a couple years after I moved here."

"Bludgeoned," said Ray crisply, his eyes widening and his face relaxed. His headache appeared to be lifting.

"Brains all *over* the Rice Krispies boxes—now there's a sight you don't forget." Ray shook his finger at Osborne. "I snuck in around the side, but that's another story. Back to old Herman the German, right?"

"If you want to win the Loon-Calling Contèst, we'll both need some sleep."

"Yep, okay. I'll make this fast." Ray hitched up his chair and crossed his arms in front of him.

"I was about eight or nine years old and fascinated by that old guy and his rickety banged-up truck. One day when I was way the hell out in the woods, I spotted him checking some traps. I was hiding behind a stand of balsam thinking he couldn't see me, y'know, when he turns around, stares right at me, scares the living daylights outta me. Just the sight of him. Then he laughs and hollers at me to come give 'im a hand. Which I did. And me and old Herman've been buddies ever since."

This part of the story was one Osborne had heard many times in the muskie boat, but he said nothing. If he'd learned anything over his many years as a fisherman, it was that when men of the Northwoods talk, the secrets often lurk between the words, not exposed in the sentences. Half the time they don't even know they're telling secrets. If Osborne's hunch was right, Ray was about to work his way somewhere with some intriguing turns that even Ray might not be aware of yet.

"Summers I'd ride my bike out to his place," Ray continued in a soft voice, "the whole goddamn ten miles, every Saturday morning, just to hang around, pick a few blackberries, and listen to the old man talk. Winters he'd pick me up in that old truck and drop me off later. One winter we nursed a young bald eagle together. The bird flew away in the spring, but he always came back to sit in the trees and watch while we picked those berries. Herman taught me everything I know about these woods and their lakes. When I guide, people always think I must be part Indian, but I'm really just part Herman."

Ray dropped his forearms onto the kitchen table and leaned forward. His voice lifted in intensity, and he talked faster.

"One night, I was about fifteen, I'd just gotten into acid in a big way, and I was having one really bad trip. I mean I was in deep shit that night. I decided I had to kill myself and that old Herman and the eagle had to watch. Don't ask me why—this was all in my head. So it's the middle of the night, I swipe my dad's car and drive way the hell out there. Herman was good. He let me rave on for a while, and then he talked me down. He talked me down by telling me about his evil angels."

"His evil angels?" Osborne mulled that over. This was indeed a new story.

"Yep. I've never told anyone about this because Herman asked me not to. See, Herman moved here in 1925 from Canada. He was only nineteen, but he'd made a little money already in lumber up north, and he was ready to buy a little land. About ten years later, another friend of his and that fella's wife also moved here. The couple was French Canadian. Well, Herman buys his land from the state and gets a pretty good deal, but his friend gets a real deal, buying from the Cantrells just this side of Starks. Cantrell owned a trucking company out of Kansas City that did big business up here hauling lumber and branched out into paper and pulp mills."

"Down below Dead Creek?" asked Osborne.

"Yep—on the Crane River. They basically bought Dead Creek," said Ray. "Old man Cantrell never told the couple he was running effluent from that paper mill he owned right down through the water there. For years. Remember, the paper industry ran this region in those days. Cantrell's mill made the type of paper used for wrapping food. He made millions pumping out twelve-foot rolls of the stuff, and at the same time he was dumping liquid by-products into the river up there, which he could do legally 'cause there were no regulations then.

"So the couple builds a log cabin right on the riverbank about a mile down from where the creek enters the river, they start farming some potatoes and corn and stuff. They do okay, and they want to have kids, but the wife keeps miscarrying. Finally, she's well over thirty now—which is real old for those days—the wife gets pregnant. She has one kid. Then she gets pregnant again. But they had started having problems out there. A lot of dead fish drifting down that creek, and then they all got so sick off and on, but they figured that might be caused by their well water. Little did they know the scope of the problem, but they had enough difficulties to make it pretty hard on 'em. And a shame, said Herman, because they'd built a fine little cabin."

Osborne found himself curiously soothed by the rhythm of Ray's voice. He felt himself getting drowsy and hoped the story ended before he fell asleep sitting up.

"Herman doesn't see 'em for a while. And then he gets a visit from the husband who says he's really worried about his wife. She had these triplets, see, and she's real upset. The babies came early, they were real small and had to be hospitalized for awhile. Money was tight, and the last thing they needed were three more mouths to feed. They were surviving on fish and venison. He told Herman that she was in hysterics half the time and had taken it into her head that the infants were possessed—sent to punish her for something."

"I don't like the sound of this," said Osborne.

Ray nodded. "Herman tried to reassure the poor guy that she was just very tired. I mean they didn't have help or any of the conveniences you have today. So he just assumed that was the problem. The husband didn't say too much else, but he invited Herman to their place for Thanksgiving. He said the company would pick up her spirits and give her something else to focus on.

"So Herman goes out there on Thanksgiving Day and the place is real quiet. No smoke from the chimney. He just knows something's wrong. First thing he sees going in is the wife hanging from an overhead beam. Chair kicked away—he's always been convinced she did it herself. She looked like she'd been there a day or so, too. Then there's his friend hunched over the kitchen table with his brains blown out. Put a shotgun in his mouth . . ."

"And the babies?"

"Sound asleep in a orange crate with blankets and clothing and a note from the father asking Herman to do something with them. The older child, maybe two years old, was sitting by the babies, not crying, Herman said, but just sitting and waiting and very calm. She held her arms up to Herman, too. She wasn't afraid or anything. He said it was just like she'd been expecting him.

" 'Cute as bugs, each one of 'em,' said Herman. Four beautiful children. The triplets were maybe five or six months old and real alert. So Herman takes the crate and drives into town. He goes first to Saint Mary's and leaves the little ones with the nuns. While he's there, they lift them out of the crate to check them over and change some diapers. That's when they see a problem with two of the little ones. . . ."

Ray looked intently at Osborne as he leaned forward in the kitchen chair.

"See, this is what I *thought* he told me years back, and I asked him this morning if I remembered this right. Those babies were fraternal triplets—one girl and two boys. Healthy except both boys had undescended testicles. Not just one, but both boys. The doctor told Herman that he might expect one child to have such a problem but not both. Also, triplets were highly unusual in those days.

"Then, after I started working with Shanley, I trapped some mink a little to the south and west of Dead Creek that had malformed reproductive organs. Like that family, those animals could have been eating fish from the Crane River, south of Dead Creek."

"The only thing is, Ray," said Osborne, "undescended testicles are not uncommon. Kids are born that way all the time."

"Yes, but don't they descend within the first few months?"

"I'm not sure."

"Maybe I'm working it too hard, Doc, but Shanley asked me to flag any anomalies, and I think this is one, especially since this is an adult male. Now you find he went to a camp up here?"

"A camp that is too expensive for local kids, which shoots your theory that the victim is from the area," said Osborne. "Go back to your story. What happened to the babies?"

"The note the husband left behind asked Herman to find help for the 'evil angels.' He couldn't take it anymore."

"I'm surprised he didn't kill the babies," said Osborne. "Sounds like he was as bad off as his wife."

"Herman said he couldn't kill anyone except himself," said Ray. "Herman figured they were both despondent, not just because of the situation with the kids but the water affected their heads. I agree. You know they sealed that whole area off for years in the fifties and sixties because of the wildlife kill?"

"It was off limits when I moved up here."

"Well . . ." A sly look crossed Ray's face. "I'll bet you didn't know that for a while the state thought that some chemicals found in the water table around Dead Creek had worked their way into the aquifer used by the town?"

Osborne shook his head.

"Yep, they've kept it quiet until they could be sure there was no problem. That's how come Shanley arrived on the scene in the first place."

"Ray—the babies—after the convent?"

"Unfortunately, that's where Herman's story comes to

a grinding halt. He's a good ninety-four, ninety-five years old, and his memory isn't too terrific. He knows they were all adopted, but he was having a hard time recalling anything more."

"But it was years ago that he asked you not to say anything?"

"Right."

"Why did he do that, I wonder?"

"I don't know."

"Ray, if he could remember all the details of finding those children, why wouldn't he remember the rest?"

"You're right, Doc. I'll tell ya something else. He started in to the story real strong, then right in the middle, he slowed down. As if he decided he had said too much."

"Did you tell him what we found?"

"Yes."

"I thought Sloan said—"

"Doc, that old man is one of my closest friends."

"Maybe, but it sure sounds to me like he doesn't trust you."

"Trust me? Or the people around me?"

Osborne pondered that for a moment. "He's a hermit for a reason."

"Yep."

In the middle of the night, Osborne woke to the sound of his own moans. The woods woman was leaning over him: white and swollen, her massive head fringed with wisps of hair. A towering fringed toadstool. She reached for him. She wanted him. She knew him. He sat straight up in bed, the nightmare woman still moving like a video in front of his sleep-dazed eyes. That's when he knew he'd seen her before. But where? When?

He turned on the small lamp to his right. He was wet with sweat. He got up, pulled on his robe, and padded out to the kitchen for a drink of water. The house was warm, not hot. Mike slept peacefully. Everything was fine. But where the hell had he seen that woman before?

twelve

I fish because I love to; because I love the environs where
trout are found, which are invariably beautiful . . . and,
finally not because I regard fishing as being so terribly
important but because I suspect that so many of the
other concerns of men are equally important—and not
nearly so fun.

Robert Traver

At six-twenty-five A.M., Osborne walked into Saint
Mary's Church for early Sunday Mass. He took his seat,
as he always did, on the right side of the church ten
benches behind the choir. After receiving Communion, he
circled back to his seat, as he always did, by walking
down the center aisle toward the back of the church and
past Judith Benjamin, kneeling in the last pew, her eyes
downcast.

Out of habit, he looked straight ahead at the reflection
in the glass doors as he turned to pass in front of them
and return to his seat. To his surprise, he saw Judith turn
her head first to the left to watch him pass and then to
the right to follow him as he walked behind the last row
of pews. He turned to go down the side aisle back to his

seat with the uncomfortable sensation that she was watching him every step of the way.

He glanced back as he knelt in his own pew, his eyes traveling between bent heads to connect with Judith's staring eyes. She looked away quickly. Osborne knelt very slowly. Knowing he was the target of such intense interest bothered him, and he wasn't sure why. He found it difficult to concentrate on the Host and for the first time in years, he did not take five minutes to thank God for the property on the lake and the health of his children. Instead, as his tongue worked on the sticky little wafer, he wondered what it was that Lew knew about Judith.

Ray was waiting in his old pickup outside the church at seven-fifteen. He motioned to Osborne and moved over to let him drive. Fortunately for Osborne, the driver's side door was the one that opened. The other door was permanently stuck so you had to crawl through the window to enter.

"Go-o-od morning, Doc," Ray boomed, pulling happily at his beard as he slid over and angled his lanky frame into the passenger's seat. "So why do the blind hate to sky-dive?"

"I haven't a clue," said Osborne as he pressed the clutch, turned the key, and pulled the steering wheel to his left to back out of the parking space, "Why?"

"Scares hell outta the dogs," said Ray and laughed his old laugh: a silent bouncing of his body accented with twinkling eyes.

"Feeling better, I presume," said Osborne dryly, pulling into the temporary traffic gridlock generated by everyone leaving Mass.

"Much better. Much, much better. You are driving with the champ, my friend."

"Any luck reaching your sister and brother-in-law?"

"Not yet. I got their answering machine, and I left a message. I'll try again around noon."

The two drove in silence. It was a phenomenally beautiful spring day with sunshine glistening on the dewy firs. Osborne didn't even mind that the driver's side window wouldn't close all the way. It made for a comforting flow of yeasty smells: leaf buds and fresh-melted snow. The loamy Wisconsin soil, ploughed last fall and almost soft enough for planting, gave off a warm, fertile odor with just a tinge of cow manure. The pickup sped up Highway 51 toward Boulder Junction, and Osborne listened patiently as Ray told one of his long, long stories about old Doc Shanahan and his mistress.

It seemed that about thirty years earlier, Ray and two young friends, one of them Shanahan's grandson, witnessed a pleasurable though illegal act being performed on old Dr. Shanahan in the privacy of his very own home. The little scamps were watching from outside the living room window. Years later, the lovely lady engaged in the activity had walked into Loon Lake. Walked until she drowned. A suicide. Ray had his own theories on that, however, and Osborne heard them all in detail as they drove north. He listened with half an ear, keeping an eye out for the first buds on the tamarack and nodding whenever Ray paused for breath. They pulled into Boulder Junction twenty minutes before the festivities were to begin. Ray wound down his story with the punch line: "So y'see, the interesting thing is, Marsha was Judith Benjamin's first girl."

"What?" Osborne finally tuned in, but it was too late.

The one-street town was bustling as if it were a midsummer sidewalk-sale day. Banners hung from the gift shops, fly-fishing centers, and bait stores that lined the quarter-mile strip. Osborne felt good in the bright sun and crisp air. He swung the truck into a space near Coon-Sports, a sporting goods shop.

A good crowd for the season, given it was too early to see many out-of-towners, had gathered for the loon-calling event. Most of the attendees were familiar to Osborne, and every one seemed to be a best friend of Ray's: predominantly male, including members of the sponsoring Lions Club, local fishing guides scouting business, seriously addicted muskie fishermen, and lots of mothers with small children. *Ray sure does know the world,* observed Osborne as he witnessed a parade of encouraging handshakes and backslaps. *He should run for office.* The contestants took their places on the small stage set up in the CoonSports parking lot.

Osborne sat down to wait patiently in a folding chair set toward the rear of the gathering. He was more than a little disappointed to discover the muskies hadn't even been wrapped in their foil bakers and the charcoal was still cold. The fish wouldn't be ready until late that afternoon. Darn! he thought. The news cast a pall over what had promised to be a fine day.

"Excuse me, Dr. Osborne?" Someone tugged at his sleeve.

He turned to see Winnie Grumbach, a former patient, and her husband, Walter, standing behind him. "I heard you asking about the muskie, Doctor," said Winnie. "We're going to be bringing some back to Loon Lake this evening for our son and his wife. Would you like us to drop some by for you?" She was a short, good-humored lady with a broad hook nose that made her look like a parrot. A parrot with dyed-black feathers and motherly eyes.

"Really?" said Osborne, reaching for his wallet. "I sure would. That's very nice of you. Here—"

"No, no, Doc." Walter put his hand out to push the two ten-dollar bills away. "Our treat." Walter was all beige with a moon face and a very genial manner, which had served him well in the men's clothing business. Osborne had known them since he arrived in Loon Lake. Nice people. Now that he could get some muskie, the day was good again. The obvious pleasure on his face must have served as an invitation.

"Doctor . . ." Winnie, who had put on about forty

pounds since Osborne last saw her, parked her khaki-clad butt in the seat beside him and motioned to Walter to sit beside her, "I want to talk to you about those bodies you found."

"Shush—after the contest, dear," her husband said, patting her knee. "We need to include Ray, you know." He pointed ahead.

They all focused their attention on the stage then as the MC for the festival introduced the contenders. About twenty-five people had shown up. However, hand votes from the crowd winnowed the competition down to two in less than half an hour.

Now the pros stood to challenge each other. The Canadian, a tall, handsome Metis, was good, very good. In fact, he was so good that Osborne had to applaud and felt sorry for Ray. He was sure the head injury was bound to take a toll on Ray's wind if not his general well-being.

Ray ambled his long torso up to the microphone. He was wearing a warm red plaid Pendleton shirt with clean Levi's and a good-looking deerskin vest that Donna had given him for his birthday. His eyes were serious over the carefully brushed and trimmed beard that reached to his chest. The stuffed trout was cocked jauntily over his ears. Though he had rolled his way up to the mike, shoulders slightly hunched, now he seemed to remember Osborne's advice to stand up straight and pull in his gut. He threw his shoulders back and looked out over the audience.

Osborne closed his eyes and held his breath.

The haunting call of the loon started low and distant as if far across lake waters at dusk. Then the bird swept closer, its dark tones echoing over the reeds and gentle waves. He heard the mate answer and the two call back and forth, each distinct in tone, one overlapping the other. No sooner had the crescendo risen than the birds fell still, and the male turned his noble head to a rising moon. Now a low flutter of sound, then mounting urgency, then a hush . . . and a final aching hymn to the wild winds that kill

and maim. With exquisite control, Ray gave voice to the
ultimate challenge: the call of the wounded loon. Osborne
exhaled slowly. He opened his eyes.

Walter and Winnie rose with him, the Lions Club members, the fishermen, the guides, and all the mothers and
children to give Ray a standing ovation. He won hands
down. He got the silver muskie to hang on the living room
wall in his trailer for the next year. He also got coupons
for free dinners at several restaurants, a gift certificate
good at the men's clothing store where Walter worked,
and a case of Leinenkugel's Original beer.

And he got Winnie glued to his side the minute he
broke free of his admirers.

"Ray, about those bodies," she said, looking up and
tugging hard at his sleeve. "We need to talk."

"She needs to talk to you," echoed Walter from behind
her. "Maybe in private?"

"Well, I dunno . . ." Ray's eyes searched over their
heads for Osborne, who nodded a silent okay.

"We're headed for Susan's up in Saint Germain," said
Ray, "I need pancakes."

"We'll follow you," said Winnie.

During the twenty-minute drive, Ray and Osborne decided how much to tell, and Osborne was assigned to
alerting Lew to the nature of their sources.

"I remember Mary Lee always looked down on Winnie
for being a hairdresser part-time and for being an invet-
erate gossip," said Osborne. "Not that Mary Lee wasn't a
vicious gossip herself when she had the chance."

"Yeah? Well, gossip works both ways," said Ray. "You
give and you get. I'd like to know exactly what Winnie
has picked up. That old gal is wired better than AT&T."
Osborne nodded.

With business covered, they drove in satisfied silence,
Ray tickled with his success and Osborne pleased with
the sunshine and the promise of a buttery muskie dinner.

Susan's was bustling. Every table and even the twelve

chairs at the counter were full. Something about the sunny Sunday had everybody in for late A.M. pancakes.

"Not to worry, Doc." Susan, the proprietress, pushed her six-foot broad-shouldered frame through the crowded chairs and tables toward the doorway where Osborne, Ray, and the Grumbachs were standing. "I got a four-table opening up right now."

Even as she spoke, four fishermen whom Osborne didn't recognize rose to wave them over and introduce themselves. They'd been in the crowd for the loon call contest. Handshakes and back pats were exchanged as they congratulated Ray. "Now, be sure you have that homemade bread toast," said one to Osborne as they finally turned to leave. Then everyone took a chair except Ray, who continued walking about the restaurant, happily accepting congratulations or announcing his victory to the ignorant. Osborne figured he'd be working the room for a good ten minutes or so.

"I never miss the homemade bread toast or Susan's ham off the bone," said Osborne as he pulled back a chair for Winnie. She plunked her chunky rear end down so fast, Osborne wondered if she thought someone was going to steal her chair. He was close. She certainly wanted to be sure no one stole his attention. Before their table was cleared, she had her purse open and had thrust a list of names in front of his face. It was clear Winnie had something to say.

She moved dirty plates and glasses back so the list sat squarely on the table in front of Osborne. "See this?" she started, leaning forward and keeping her voice low. "Do you know what this is?" Walter had also leaned forward. "I think these are the men you found in the water."

"Winnie," said Osborne, "I really can't. . . ."

"No, no." She waved her hands at Osborne's protest. "The word is out, Doc, and I know about the bodies. Now, you listen to me for five minutes." Osborne knew when he'd been given directions, so he shut up, wrapped both hands around his coffee mug, and watched, his eyes intent on Winnie as she spoke.

"I've been working twenty hours a week as a receptionist at the Dairyman's Association this year, and these are the names of four guests who disappeared six weeks ago. Everyone's been frantic about it, but no one's said anything to the police. In fact, we've only called one family so far. What's weird is no one has called *us*. But these men are missing. I am ninety-nine percent sure they must be your bodies. So I want you to tell me what to do next, Dr. Osborne. Someone needs to know."

Osborne looked at her blankly. He was stunned. "Jesus. Let me get Ray over here. Then we'll talk." He stood up and motioned over the heads of nearby diners to Ray. The look on his face must have been enough, because Ray stopped in happy midsentence and excused himself to hurry over and sit down.

"Winnie thinks she knows who the victims are," whispered Osborne into Ray's ear as they both sat down. He pushed the list in front of Ray and waited. Ray looked down. Osborne pointed to one name with a Des Moines, Iowa, address. Ray nodded.

Everyone around the table knew the Dairyman's Association, known locally as the Dairy. It was the odd name for a very exclusive hunting and fishing preserve whose membership had once been exclusively bluebloods from Chicago. In existence since the late 1800s, the Dairy was a favorite haunt of the wealthy scions of the meat-packing fortunes. Few locals, including Osborne, had ever set foot behind the huge wrought-iron gates.

"Who the hell are these people?" asked Ray. "These names mean nothing to me."

"We checked 'em in as a group," said Winnie, ready to launch into her case. "But see how they come from all over the country? They're members of something called the Young President's Organization. My boss calls it the YPO."

"I know of the YPO," said Osborne. "Wausau's got a chapter. There was a gal in Mary Lee's bridge club whose first husband had been a member of the YPO out of Milwaukee. Mary Lee was quite impressed, but I thought it all sounded pretentious as hell."

"I'll bet you didn't tell Mary Lee that," interjected Ray.

"No, I did not," said Osborne, shooting Ray a dirty look. He was not real happy to be caught capitulating to a woman he was beginning to dislike more and more. Now that Mary Lee was gone and he had the opportunity to spend more time with folks like Winnie and Walter and Ray, he was realizing what a small world he had let Mary Lee restrict them to, small in several senses of the word.

"Hell, he wanted that meat loaf on the table," humored Walter. He winked at Osborne.

"Thank you, Walter," said Osborne, clipping his words, "confirmed bachelors have no idea how treacherous are the reefs of marriage. But seriously, Winnie, I *do* know what the YPO is. It's a prestigious social club for men who become presidents of companies before age forty. Most of them inherit the position from their fathers, but there's a few self-made types. It's an upscale Rotary Club."

"Why were they staying at the Dairy?" Ray asked Winnie.

"A two-week fly-fishing clinic," said Winnie. "We do a lot of those with classes and guides, and we mix in business-type speakers so the guests can write off the hunting and fishing. Sort of silly, if you ask me. These people have so much money the last thing they need is a write-off."

Walter interrupted, anxious to keep the conversation on track. "But, Dr. Osborne, no one arrives, then disappears for six weeks, almost seven now, like this group did. That's what Winnie and I think is so strange. Why did they all leave together one night and never come back?"

"Right," said Winnie. "We have all their stuff, we have

their clothes, their fly rods, we even have their rental cars.
. . . I finally called one of the wives to see what she knew
about it."

"And?" asked Osborne.

"She wouldn't tell me," said Winnie. "She said that her
husband often went on YPO business and it was confidential. She was concerned about the length of this trip,
but she said he had been gone as long as eight weeks
before without telling her where he was. She said they
were into 'study groups' and would 'go to the source'—
whatever that means."

"That means they don't have enough to do, they're trying to justify being alive, they've got too goddamn much
moola—that's what that means," said Ray.

Winnie had paused to pour almost a half cup of cream
into her coffee, stir it in gently, add a packet of sugar,
take a sip, and now she looked around at the men. "I
thought that wife actually sounded relieved that her hub-
bie wasn't back yet. She wasn't making a big deal of it,
know what I mean? I'll tell ya, I thought it was pretty
weird she wasn't even worried!"

Osborne and Ray looked at each other. Walter leaned
forward, his chin cupped in his hand. More hot coffee
arrived along with menus, which everyone glanced at
quickly. They all ordered the same thing: buttermilk pancakes, ham off the bone, side orders of homemade bread
toast, orange juice, and more coffee.

"Did you meet these men?" asked Ray.

"I saw them," said Winnie. "I took their reservation
cards and I told them which way their rooms were."

"What were they like?"

"Just . . . the usual. Businessmen. Fly-fishing shirts,
ironed Levi's. Very pleasant." Winnie stirred her coffee
again. "Frankly, I barely looked at them. But when I heard
you found those bodies, I couldn't help but think it might
be these guys. We've just never had guests go off and not
return. It's a big problem, you know. Those rooms were

booked for new arrivals, and no one knows what to do. When people pay five hundred dollars a night, you don't just boot them out."

"Five hundred bucks a night!" Ray was incredulous.

"Yeah, see?" said Winnie. "The wife I called said it was just fine to keep on billing it, too."

"Who's running the Dairy these days?" asked Osborne.

"They brought in a guy from Minneapolis who used to run one of the big hotels and wanted to semiretire," said Winnie. "He's in a panic over this. I guess—now, I don't know this for a fact—but I think the Dairy has not been doing that well financially for the last few years. So he wants no publicity on this. I'll be fired if he finds out I'm talking to you. But I was going to call you today anyway." Walter reached over and patted his wife's hand. It was clear they'd discussed the risk before approaching Osborne.

"Don't worry about that," said Osborne. "Did they drive themselves off when they left?"

"Oh, no," said Winnie. "The college hired Ted Bronk to drive them. That's the next weird part. A number of us from the Dairy have been calling Ted's house, but there's no answer. He seems to be gone, too."

Ray looked around the table and scratched at his beard. "Now, why the heck would the college have ol' scumbag Ted driving some head honchos around? That sure as hell doesn't figure."

"Yeah, Ray, they coulda hired you," laughed Walter.

"For their money, yes, they could," said Ray. Suddenly his eyes shifted to the doorway. "Doc, Lew just walked in."

Osborne set down his coffee cup and looked around to wave Lew over.

"I want you to tell Chief Ferris everything you just told us," said Osborne to Winnie and Walter. He moved over to make space at the table and motioned to Susan they needed one more place setting.

● ● ●

"Ted Bronk is a popular guy," said Lew after Winnie and Walter had cleaned their plates and left Susan's. Her dark eyes caught and held Osborne's. "Remember the dancer out at Thunder Bay yesterday? She said our Mr. Bronk took her friend somewhere, too." Lew looked at Ray and Osborne both as she spread honey on her toast. "Time to talk to Ted.

"But, first, I have some other news for you two. Sloan was admitted to the hospital this morning with acute pneumonia and a collapsed lung. So I continue to need help. Doc, do you mind staying on as a deputy to work with me on this case? I'm sure it won't be for much longer."

"Me, too," said Ray, wiping up the last yellow of his yolk with a small piece of crust. "Count me in."

"Ray . . ." Lew looked hard at him, "I'm having a hard time with that. Professionally, I can't risk it. Sloan reminded me it's only eighteen months since the warden booked you for smoking dope out on the Flambeau Flowage."

Ray chuckled and looked down at his plate, "I blew that one, didn't I."

Osborne looked surprised. He hadn't heard. Seeing the look on his face, Ray volunteered, "Yeah, I had some weed on me and there I was out in my boat minding my own business when ol' Joe Schmidt rolls up and we haven't liked each other since first grade and he wants to know what I'm doin' sittin' in my boat minding my own business so I said I was fishing for golf balls and wham he hits me with a misdemeanor and wrecks my budget. You know what they say about that asshole: 'Joe happens.'"

Lew was unimpressed with the excuse. "How do I know you don't have grass growing on your back porch these days? Ray, I'm not kidding. You cannot work in law enforcement with felonies on your record."

Ray shrugged, "Misdemeanors, Lew. I got off, remember?"

"Only because Schmidt went easy with you after he received a package of frozen venison chops," said Lew.

Ray folded his arms and leaned forward on the table. He looked straight into Lew's eyes and lowered his voice. "Lew, I do certain types of work for people not unlike yourself, relationships that must remain confidential. Dr. Shanley is one I can mention. I'm not breaking any laws unless it suits my purposes, and when it does, I'm protected. I hope that explains something. Please don't ask me to tell you things I'm not supposed to tell you."

"I see," said Lew. "I'm not surprised."

"I didn't think you would be," said Ray.

Osborne listened in quiet amazement. He had no idea what they were talking about, and he didn't think it would be wise to ask any questions at the moment.

"Fine, then," said Lew. "I'll count on both of you, and please stop by the station to do a little paperwork for me later today. The town will pay you, of course."

"Do we have the report in from Wausau?" asked Osborne.

"I'm expecting it any time," said Lew. "This delay is getting ridiculous."

"Excuse me a moment," said Ray, standing up and wiping his chin with his paper napkin. "Let me use Susan's phone to try my sister again."

He got up and went to the phone back in the kitchen while Osborne watched Lew scarf up two eggs over easy, three pork sausage links, homemade bread toast, and a side of ham off the bone. *No wonder she looked so healthy,* he thought as he downed another cup of black coffee. He waved to Susan for a refill.

"Hey, Doc," warned Lew, "you drink way too much coffee. How many cups have you had just since I've been sitting here? That stuff's gonna rot your stomach."

"Lew, it's my only vice," said Osborne with a sheepish grin.

She looked at him and smiled. "We oughta do something about that. . . ."

Suddenly Ray was back, wearing a big grin on his face, "Sis said Bill remembers the kid well. His name was Robert Bowers, and he was from Kansas City. Parents were very, very wealthy, Bill said, and he thinks the family may still live there. He said that young Rob was a good kid, quiet type. He was a junior counselor Bill's last year there, and his family paid for him to have his own cabin, which was considered outrageous by the other counselors. But that fits for what we're looking for, don't you think? Bowers is the family name. Bill figures the guy'd be about 42 to 43 years old, which is right—"

"Bowers? That's one of the names on Winnie's list," said Lew, interrupting and pushing back her chair. "Time to call Kansas City. Which one of you has some time? I have a couple calls to make before I can get back to work on this."

"I'll do it," said Osborne. "An old college friend runs the newspaper in that town. Let me check in with him and see—"

"Great," said Lew, "just be sure he knows we have no firm ID yet, and we can't release anything to the press until that report is in."

"I'll tell you what, Lew," said Osborne. "Let's go over a few things right now so I don't make any mistakes on this."

Fifteen minutes later, after Lew's detailed instructions, Osborne was headed back to Ray's to get his own car.

"So how's the new management at Thunder Bay?" asked Ray as they got in the truck, a twinkle in his eye.

"What was all that about 'working for certain people'?" countered Osborne.

"Oh, that. That was pure bullshit," said Ray, pulling on his beard and glancing at Osborne with eyes that seemed to be smiling. Osborne thought they also looked sly, and he looked away, uncomfortable. "Now she thinks I do surveillance for the DNR or somebody."

"Do you?"

"Nah," said Ray, "that would add stress to this good ol' boy's life. But it got me what I wanted, didn't it?" Ray winked at him.

Osborne decided not to believe him, but he kept his mouth shut. "Thunder Bay is quite the place," Osborne said to change the subject. He offered up the details of their visit. Ray got real interested when Professor Bradford Miller showed up in Osborne's story.

"You're serious? The professor walked into Thunder Bay Bar and strip joint with Miss Judy?"

"We-ell, it was close; you couldn't swear they were together, but it sure looked to me like she was giving him free beers," said Osborne.

"How so?"

"Of four or five of us around the bar, he was the only one she served and I never saw him go for his wallet."

Ray took it all in thoughtfully. "Now, isn't that an odd pair: Brad Miller and Judith Benjamin? Maybe he swings both ways. . . ."

"Brad Miller is one of the few people that I really, really dislike," said Osborne. "He was a creepy little kid, even if he was my best friend's son, and age has just made him worse. The man is smarmy, if you know what I mean."

"Gee, Doc," Ray looked at his friend, "give the guy a break. At least he's smart. What does he have—a Ph.D. from Harvard or something like that?"

"Yeah, well, there's smart and there's smart. What I *really* don't like about him is just what's happening now: I feel guilty for thinking the creep's a creep. Now, why is that? It makes me mad because then you bend over backward to be nice to the guy because you feel guilty, and before you know it, you've just about invited him to dinner. I give up."

Ray laughed, "I think a lot of us feel that way. When we were kids, you knew that he was the guy to pick on, and everyone did. He was such a runt. So I think a lot of people in Loon Lake put up with his BS because they haven't forgotten they were pretty mean to him way back when."

The two men drove along in silence for a while. "But you know," Osborne finally spoke, "he asked for it."

thirteen

*Men lived like fishes; the greater ones devoured the
small.*

Algernon Sydney, *Discourses on Government*, 1698

An hour later, Osborne parked his station wagon in front
of Erin's big white Victorian house. His heart lifted at the
sight of the open porch with the bright yellow and green
trim. His youngest daughter had a way of making everything around her seem sunny.

"Hey, Mike," he directed his voice at his dog's crate in
the back of the the station wagon, "I'll be back in about
thirty minutes. You be a good dog."

And he set off up the sidewalk, humming.

"Gee, Dad, I think that's pretty neat," said Erin. Her long
blond hair hung down her back in a braid as she bounced
18-month-old Cody, Osborne's first grandson, on her knee
as they shared the dregs of the coffeepot at the big oak
table in Erin's kitchen. The house was the oldest Victorian
in Loon Lake, and Osborne could never get over how
much hard work had gone into restoring it, and how much
of it Erin and her husband, Mark, had done themselves.

"Lew said we'll be paid by the town," continued Osborne. "I just hope I don't grow dependent on this new income." He grinned broadly. He was finding that being paid for his services did make him feel good, even if he also felt a little sheepish: His job description sounded more dramatic that it was.

"You're kidding, of course," said Erin. "You don't really want to become a police officer, do you, Dad? I mean, not permanently, not after this case. Right?"

"And ruin my muskie fishing? You know your old man."

"Say, I'm going to be calling an old college friend of your mother's and mine. Remember Dick Halstead? He was an editor for the *Milwaukee Journal* and now he runs the *Kansas City Star*. Didn't he have a daughter your age?"

"Marci. We went to Girl Scout camp together, remember? Hey, Dad." Erin jumped up. "I've got to change this kid's diaper. Why don't you call Mr. Halstead from here? Find out what Marci's up to and get her phone number for me. I'd like to give her a call."

"Oh, hon, this is going to be a long call. I don't want to tie up your phone."

"Dad, it's Sunday afternoon, for heaven's sake. Take your time. If you don't call from here, I *know* you'll forget to ask about Marci. Here." Erin pushed the cordless phone across the kitchen table toward him. "I'll do diapers, you do phone." With a grin and a flash of braid, she was off to conquer poopy pants.

Osborne smiled. Then he reached into his left shirt pocket and pulled out the small, dog-eared address book that held what was left of his life. His blunt fingers turned the pages carefully. He picked up the receiver.

Dick was home. He was nursing a bad cold and glad to hear from his old buddy. Osborne took a good five minutes to catch up on personal news: Dick's wife was recovering from a hysterectomy, the paper was down to a miserable 20 percent profit margin due to newsprint cost increases, Dick thought their new publisher was a little young for the job, and Marci had a thriving law practice. She also had a phone number. Osborne scrambled around the kitchen for a pen, which he finally laid hands on. He took down Marci's number before he could forget.

"Dick, I've got a couple of questions for you." Osborne finally got to the point. "I'm helping out as a medical investigator up here on a murder case, and there may be a Kansas City connection. Are you familiar with the name Bowers?"

Silence greeted the question. A lengthy silence.

"I am very familiar with that name," said Dick. His voice was suddenly subdued, measured. He spoke in a staccato, as if rehearsing facts he had reviewed many times: "An old blueblood family here in town, major donors to the Nelson Museum, money goes way back to the early days when Kansas City was a hub for the rail industry. They made their money in transportation, then diversified. The late Mrs. Bowers was a Cantrell, another old Kansas City name. Her husband worked for her family, then made his own fortune as a very successful commodities trader on the Kansas City Board of Trade. He died a good twenty years ago. His widow passed away about three years ago, leaving the whole kit and kaboodle to their only child, an adopted son. I know all this because I'm a trustee for the museum, along with Robert Bowers."

"So you know Bowers pretty well?"

"In a manner of speaking, Doc. A slight matter of class difference perhaps. Irish Catholic still doesn't cut in some circles in this town," said Dick with the touch of irony that had led to the friendship between him and Osborne years earlier.

"When was the last time you saw him?"

"Oh, gosh . . . six or eight weeks ago? It's funny you ask, because we've been trying to schedule a board meeting, and that guy has been out of town for over a month now. We can't get an answer from his office on when he'll be back, either."

"He may not be coming back if we're both talking the right Bowers," Osborne said. "We've had a multiple slaying up here, and his may be one of the bodies."

Dick was very quiet for a long moment. Then his voice tightened, and Osborne got a very real sense of how his old pal behaved in the office. To say Dick Halstead could focus was to put it mildly, thought Osborne later. The sudden appearance of breaking news catapulted Dick from the easygoing banter of his Sunday afternoon foot-on-the-ottoman style to the terse style of the newspaperman driven by the urgent, ongoing need to get it first and get it right and get it before TV, damn.

"Listen, buddy," said Dick, "I have a Pulitzer-winning investigative guy on staff that I want you to talk to. He can give you some background, and I'm gonna tell him to give you some off-the-record stuff, too. Now is this . . . Are you official on this?"

"I'm deputized to help with the investigation, but we haven't made any official announcements. We don't have positive IDs yet," said Osborne.

"Great. I need you to do something for me in return. Don't talk to any other news media about this before you confirm with us, all right? Call me immediately when you have that confirmation," said Dick. "If one of those victims is Bowers, this will be big news down here. And, Doc, here's something that my reporter knows but that we haven't released to the public: there's a sting investigation under way down here, and we have to keep it under wraps until the KBI gives us the go-head."

"The KBI?"

"The Kansas Bureau of Investigation. But let me put you through to the reporter, because he's got the details. His name is Grant Moore—"

"What's his phone number?"

"Don't worry about it, I'm going to patch you through

to him. I think he's downtown, just hold on."

Less than a minute passed before Osborne heard a new voice on the phone. "Dr. Osborne? This is Grant Moore. The boss said you've got some interesting news. . . ."

Quickly Osborne told the reporter exactly what he had just said to Dick Halstead. He went over the details of where the bodies were found, what he'd seen for physical evidence, but he said nothing about the peculiar genitals of the corpse that appeared to be from Kansas City. He didn't think he should share that information until they had a solid ID. He did tell the reporter about Ray's disappearance, the assault, and the strange woman in the woods.

"None of this makes a lot of sense," he apologized, "but my dental records do seem to point in the direction of Kansas City."

"I see," said Moore. "I'm going to air freight a packet of clips for you—photos and background on the family. That will help with your investigation, but you need to talk to Bowers's lawyer right away. She's been bugging me for weeks to look into where he is because she's sure there is something wrong. We didn't have a clue where to start because he didn't leave any word with his house-keeper or anyone else that we could find."

"What kind of a man is he?" asked Osborne.

"Very private person," said Moore. "Midforties, single, very unassuming. I guess he's worth about two hundred million bucks, but I'd never heard anything about him until the robbery. Dick set up the interview—that was about two months ago—but we haven't run the story yet."

"A robbery?" asked Osborne.

"That's what Dick asked me to tell you about," said Moore. "The Bowers family home, which he inherited from his mother, was robbed of a very famous collection of European sterling silver, which is what precipitated the paper's involvement. The police down here weren't as responsive as Bowers thought they should be—the silver collection is worth millions—and he mentioned it to Dick during a board meeting. He refused to let us publicize the robbery, but he is cooperating with the KBI, which has set up a fence operation they think may lead them to the perpetrators—which, in my opinion, it won't."

"You sound pretty sure of that," said Osborne.

"I know that," said Moore. His voice was genial but serious. "I have a source in the Kansas City, Kansas, police department that told me they know exactly who took the silver: when, how, what happened to it, and why it will never be found."

"But no one believes them?"

"Oh, they'd believe them just fine," said Moore. "But this information is off the record. I can't publish this. I can't even tell Bowers—but Dick Halstead told me I better tell you. So I have to ask you to agree to keep this confidential before I tell you anything more. Agreed?"

"Of course."

"There's a known silver thief who operates out of Canada," said the reporter. "He gets his information from antique dealers. We think he masquerades as an antique dealer himself. Then he flies into a city in the morning, pulls the heist, and is out on a plane that night. He's pulled maybe six or seven jobs in Kansas City over the last ten years because this is a center for some fine collections. A lot of money in this town."

"Why don't the police get him?" Osborne asked.

"Two reasons, no, three," said Moore. "First, they don't usually know he's been here until he's gone; second, police departments don't share information. Kansas cops may know one thing, but they aren't talking to the Missouri cops. None of the cops, Kansas or Missoui, talk to the KBI. The KBI wouldn't listen if they did. Bowers lives in Missouri, and my informer is in Kansas. The third reason is that on the Kansas City, Kansas, side they really don't care. That's the poor side of town. They could care less if a major heist occurs on the other side of the state line."

"I'm sorry," said Osborne, "but you lost me. Why the is the KBI involved if Bowers is a Missouri resident?"

"The University of Kansas's art museum was robbed of a similar silver collection that had been donated by Mrs. Bowers several years ago. The same thief, of course.

"But I have a theory on this, Dr. Osborne, and I couldn't get Robert Bowers to listen to me. He has been working with two art experts, private dealers, over the last year, and I think they're involved. I am *certain* of it. And the reason I'm certain is because those two have vanished.

"First the silver disappeared, then Bowers took this unexplained business trip, then his lawyer found hundreds of thousands of dollars paid out of his personal account to one of the dealers—who is missing. Well, we think he's missing, although we can't really document that he lived here. He was around a lot, but we can't find a local address for him."

"We have more than one body," said Osborne.

"You can't miss the woman," said Moore, "she's built—like thirty-eight Ds. Very chesty."

"Nope, that we don't have," said Osborne. "What about the male? What does he look like?"

"Middle-aged, kind of stout."

"That's it?"

"I only saw the guy once and from a distance at a gallery opening."

"What about other businessmen in the area—anyone else missing?"

"No," said Moore. "Dr. Osborne, I know Bowers's lawyer will be anxious to hear everything you've told me. Why don't you give her a call, then let's talk again. Here's her number. I've got some reporting on fire here right now, but I'd like to see if Dick won't send me up there in a day or or two, but let me get back to you on that. . . ."

Osborne placed the second call, and within ten minutes,

he was making arrangements to pick up the lawyer at the Rhinelander airport the next morning.

"Dad? I overhead you talking about Ray Pradt getting beat up out there by Shepard Lake." Erin was waiting for him in the long, airy living room. She was sitting on the sofa, little Cody sound asleep on her shoulder. She spoke softly so she wouldn't wake up her son.

Osborne loved the picture he saw: his lively-eyed, slender-bodied daughter, jean-clad knees akimbo on an old overstuffed sofa in a room full of interesting and colorful things. Not expensive, traditional stuff like Mary Lee had always wanted, but what Erin called "funky." Old furniture and antiques, comfortable sofa and chairs, nothing their three children couldn't clamber on. The room was full of life, and her face was full of thought. Serious thought.

Osborne smiled and sat down carefully on the plump sofa beside Erin. The expression on her face seemed to grow darker, more concerned. This was beginning to look like something requiring lengthy discussion. Was she going to tell him he was making a mistake taking the assignment from Lew? Maybe she had reservations about Ray. Ray was always controversial, and his daughters often chided him for being seen too often with the stuffed trout hat. They had inherited their mother's conventional attitudes, though in less toxic doses.

Osborne glanced at his watch. If he didn't leave in five minutes, he'd be late for his meeting with Ray and Lew.

"What about Ray, hon? I told you we found him on one of those old logging roads farther north," said Osborne. "Why?"

"But didn't I hear you say it was up behind Shepard Lake?"

"Well, it was," said Osborne, "closer to Dead Creek but back beyond that old B-and-B."

"Dad, I had a terrible thing happen to me up there."

Erin laid the sleeping form of her son carefully on a blanket she'd spread beside her on the sofa. "I didn't want to tell anyone this because I felt so stupid later." She stood up and motioned him back toward the kitchen.

Osborne followed her, a nasty feeling tightening his shoulders. The look on Erin's face frightened him. "What is it, Erin? You've got me worried."

Erin leaned back against the kitchen sink and crossed her arms. She looked hard at her father. "You know Jeannie Phelan is running for county clerk, right? And I'm her campaign manager. So we got all these flyers printed up last Wednesday, and I got everyone to take some and start dropping them off in mailboxes.

"I took a bunch myself, and I decided I'd go out toward Crandon a ways and then north to Pine Lake. I had about three hours to kill, so I put Cody in the van and I just started to drive down the different roads, dropping off flyers at every house. Some houses have mailboxes by the road, and some have them right on the door or the porch. If they were on the door, I'd get out of the van and go shove one in the box or wherever.

"So I'm heading toward Pine Lake, and I'm driving past the sign for Marjorie's Bed and Breakfast when I see this road I've never been on before. Looks like new houses going in or something because it's getting traveled. I go up about a mile, and I see this old building with a truck in front of it. I was turning around when I noticed the road swung back behind the building. So I keep going, I go over a hill, and on the other side there's a brand-new house—a big, fancy, log house. I pull in the drive, get out of the van, and walk up to the house. It has a porch that runs around it on both sides.

"So, Dad, I'm standing at the front door and I'm looking for a mailbox. I can't find one. Then I sort of peer into this front window by the door because I'm intrigued by this incredible house when all of a sudden—I heard him before I saw him—I heard someone pounding across the porch. Then this guy comes around the corner of the house right at me like he's going to hit me or something."

"Are you serious?" Osborne was stunned.

"I can't even remember exactly what he looked like except he was big, he was wearing these huge black boots, and he had this intense look of hate or fury or something in his eyes. I mean—he came at me! I screamed and ran," said Erin. "It makes me shake to talk about it."

She was right; Osborne could see her arms trembling even through her heavy sweater.

"Did he follow you to the van?"

"No, thank God. He never left the porch. He never said anything, either. I don't even know where he came from. He just loomed up with these eyes and this hate, and I thought I was going to die. Taught me a lesson. You won't catch me back in *those* woods again. I swung that van in a circle and beat it out of there, but I looked back in my rearview mirror, and I could see him waving his arms at me. It was so freaky, Dad. Don't go near that place, whatever you do."

"But you don't remember what he looked like?"

"Just . . . like big and bearded, these sharp, blazing eyes, and those boots. A real big guy." Erin paused and thought hard. "He was in farmer overalls and a dirty old sweatshirt, but I don't remember too much more than that. He had this look in his eyes, Dad. Like he hated me and *like he'd been waiting for me.*"

Erin had begun to tremble again. Osborne reached to pull her close and put his arms around her. This was strange, thought Osborne. He couldn't help but wonder if Ray had run into the same situation.

"Well," he stroked Erin's hair, "take it easy. You're fine, and that's what counts. I'll tell Lew and Ray. We're going out that way to retrace what happened to Ray yesterday, and I'm going to check out this house you've mentioned. You know, I don't recall anyone building back in there. You know me, I'm pretty tuned in around here."

"It's a prefab, Dad," said Erin. "We know the manufacturer, and you can put those up in less than a month if you get your foundation poured. The other weird thing is the little lake it's on. It looks man-made."

"A man-made lake in this part of the country?" Osborne shook his head. "We've already got three hundred and twenty lakes in a ten-mile radius of Loon Lake. Why would anyone want to make another one?"

fourteen

There is more to fishing than catching fish.

Dame Juliana Berners, fifteenth century

Leaving Mike in Erin's backyard, Osborne hurried across the street and over the sun-dappled courthouse lawn. Lew's office in the new wing attached to the jail was just a block and a half away. A brisk east wind gave the air a cold edge, even though the sun was still high. Osborne broke into a jog. He did not want to be late for the conference call with Rick Shanley.

The door to Lew's office stood open. Lew sat at her desk, rocking back in her chair as she chatted with Ray, sprawled in one of two leather-seated wooden armchairs pulled up in front of the big old oak desk. The room was airy and light-filled, thanks to three wide, tall windows whose sills spilled over with green plants. The southern exposure agreed with them. To Osborne's right as he entered was a small table, which held a coffeepot, its red light glowing. As he stopped to fill a mug, Lew straightened up in her chair, pushed a multibuttoned telephone console toward the center of her desk, and waved at him.

"Close that door behind you, will you, Doc?" she said.

"I've got the speakerphone all set up. Are we ready?" Osborne nodded as he sat down, steaming mug in hand, and crossed his legs.

"Okay, Lucy." Lew leaned toward the console. "You can put us through." A brief pause, a distant ring, and Dr. Richard Shanley identified himself.

"Hey, Rick." Ray clasped his hands as he leaned forward, elbows on the arms of his chair. "Ray Pradt here. I've got Police Chief Lewellyn Ferris with me and Dr. Paul Osborne. You and Doc Osborne met at my place, remember?"

"Sure do, how are you, Dr. Osborne? Caught any trophy muskies lately?" Shanley's voice boomed into the room, causing Lew to turn the volume down a notch. Osborne got the impression she didn't want Shanley's remarks heard outside the room.

"Season's just opening, Rick," said Osborne. "I like to fish shallow water right after the ice leaves the lake. That's why I was scouting upstream when I found the bodies you've been looking at. Now, I don't know if you know or not, but muskies are very territorial, always feeding in the same spots if the temperature is right. There is a heck of a trophy muskie I've been stalking for years now. So when I get a spring sun and a west wind, I know right where to go. Otherwise, Rick, I would never have been up that creek, and no one else fishes that spot. Chances are real good no one would have come across those fellas ever."

"He's right," said Lew. "We're lucky Doc Osborne found them when he did—before the water warmed up. I want to thank you, by the way, for changing your schedule to run your tests. I know Wausau appreciates it, too."

"You have no idea how much *I* appreciate it," said Shanley.

He sounded downright buoyant, quite different from the tight-lipped academic Osborne been introduced to one October afternoon seven months earlier. Ray had swung into his drive that day with Shanley in tow, right after the two men had agreed on Ray's participation in Shanley's research. At that time, the environmental expert, identified only as "a new client," was obviously anxious to keep a low profile, was probably running late for another appointment, and had been rather curt to Ray, cutting him off just as he had launched into a discussion of Shanley's search for chemical pollutants affecting wildlife in the region. No such abruptness was apparent in the voice coming through the speakerphone today. Expansive was more like it.

"I have to thank you for this, Ray. A bonanza. I've spent all morning here in the lab, and I will probably be here . . . well, I'm planning to stay overnight. I apologize if I sound gleeful over someone's bad fortune, but I've been on the lookout for something like this for a good, oh, three, four years."

Ray's eyes sparkled at Shanley's response.

Lew caught his expression and shook her head. She leaned off to the side of the phone to whisper to Osborne, "Can you imagine two guys so thrilled with a corpse? Only a grave digger . . ." She rolled her eyes.

"Rick, Chief Ferris needs to hear from you directly on some of the background behind your research," said Ray.

"Of course," Shanley responded swiftly. "And I'll be brief, Chief, because I have a paper I just published that I'm sending up by messenger Monday morning. It will fill in a lot of details. As Ray may have told you, I head up a team working for FIEH, the Ford Institute of Environmental Health.

"We are a privately funded national consortium of chemists, zoologists, and endocrinologists. My team has been looking for evidence of alkyl phenols, a family of chemicals that can best be described as superestrogens, which are very powerful synthetic hormones affecting many life forms, both plant and animal. We have found traces of the alkyl phenols in lower life forms in your area. But before I detail what I found this morning, let me say that three of your victims do not fit the pathology I am researching."

Shanley paused for several beats, and Osborne could hear papers shuffling, "The fourth body is remarkable. Absolutely remarkable. As Ray would say, 'This is one trophy specimen.'

"But before I get into this, Chief Ferris, I must be perfectly clear: I do not have all the answers. No one has the answers. The research on *naturally occurring* hormones, such as estrogen and testosterone, is so new that every answer generates ten new questions. My research is on how *synthetic* hormones affect our natural hormones—raising even more questions. By that I mean that everything I'm about to tell you is open to interpretation. I may have a Ph.D. in my field, but there are scientists who disagree vehemently with my findings. On the other hand, while I cannot prove my case definitively, they cannot disprove it, either.

"Chief, it's critical that you know this because the results of my tests and what will stand up in a court of law are two entirely different matters."

"Does anything you found concern the cause of death?" asked Lew.

"Oh no, no, no. But if you are looking to assign blame for the source of pollution . . ."

"Not an issue for me," said Lew. "I am interested only in how these people died, why and, frankly, at this point, we are still trying to figure out who's who."

"Good," said Shanley. "Then what I have to say may help you do that. Let me back up for a moment to explain why. Almost everyone is familiar with the DES scare in the late seventies. DES—diethylstilbestrol—is an estrogen-like drug that was administered to pregnant women for over twenty years. While the intent was to prevent spontaneous abortions, the result was a disturbance of the balance of hormones in the womb, which caused genital defects in the children. Among those defects were undescended testes, which is what we have with the victim in question.

"However, since DES was banned, it has been documented that at least forty-five *other* synthetic chemicals, particularly industrial chemicals in common use, have been found to affect the endocrine systems of various animal populations, including humans. That is, they disturb the delicate balance of naturally occurring hormones and have a profound effect on health. These chemicals happen to be chemicals used in paper and pulp production, including food wrappings—chemicals that have been released into the water around Loon Lake.

"We call them endocrine disruptors because that is, essentially, what they do. Once ingested by an animal or a human, they elbow their way into the cells of the reproductive tracts in fetuses, where they attach themselves to molecular receptors, which are like docking sites—for lack of a better description—cells that are normally reserved for natural estrogen. But these endocrine disruptors make themselves at home and proceed to become more and more active than normal estrogens, hence we call them superestrogens.

"And what these superestrogens do is biochemically feminize the embryo so that females end up with over-developed reproductive systems and males the opposite. Where females may experience an early, precocious puberty, males are feminized. Their puberty is delayed, almost canceled. In both sexes, the developmental growth that is supposed to happen during early adolescence is disrupted—but how severely depends on the level of exposure and over what period of time. And it gets more complicated.

"For example," Shanley's voice rose with excitement, "research done by another group, not mine, has shown that some of these superestrogens are capable of mutating into testosterone, the male hormone responsible for masculine development, wholly on their own. This changes the picture significantly. It explains why some of the feminized life forms have displayed unexpected male characteristics.

"But let me simplify what we know to date. We know the majority of the changes caused by a mother's exposure to any of the superestrogens during her pregnancy won't show up in a female child until the child is supposed to enter puberty. If she gives birth to a boy, then an early clue is undescended testes. In fact, the testes may never descend and the intra-abdominal tissue may degenerate over time, which is what I found in this victim.

"But back to puberty, when the most serious symptoms occur. Because the superestrogen blocks a natural release of testosterone, a boy will not experience a normal growth spurt, leaving him not only small in stature but with a feminized skeletal framework as well. He may experience little or no axillary hair growth, whether pubic, facial, or other body hair. In fact, your report from the pathologist here in Wausau will show that in addition to wearing a hairpiece, the victim had traces of adhesive on the lower jaw and above the upper lip, indicating the victim tried to disguise the lack of a beard. The superestrogens will also promote the development of a high level of body fat rather than muscle mass. *Again, I found evidence of each of these characteristics in the victim.*

"Other signs, which I cannot document, are a delay in the deepening of the voice, and the emotions may be affected, causing him to experience severe depression and anxiety.

"So, short of the emotional markers, which, of course, I cannot judge, it is remarkable how many signs of endocrine disruption I found in the victim. But not textbook. My guess is he had testosterone administered medically in his late teens, which accounts for his medium height. Otherwise, the hormone count is off the charts for female levels and, as I said, I found no evidence of testicular tissue in the abdomen, which confirms a severe hormonal imbalance during fetal development that restricted reproductive development.

"Not only is the skeleton feminized, but the victim also has a feminized corpus callosum, the bridge joining the two halves of the brain, which is always larger in females. I mentioned the marked lack of body hair, and I found some swelling of breast tissue, but that appears to have been arrested, probably with testosterone injections. And, finally, this body has the cleanest arteries I have ever seen in a male this age—the one good thing excess estrogen can do for you."

"Rick, what are the signs of endocrine disruption in a female child?" asked Osborne, getting up to refill his coffee mug.

"Female development is affected in several different ways. Not only do some of the girls experience puberty much too soon as a result of excess estrogen, but if some of these estrogens mutate into testosterone, thereby boosting testosterone levels at the same time, an imbalance between the two can have a disproportionate effect on the growth of the spine. In addition to height, in some girls you will see the shoulders broaden, muscle mass develop, the voice may deepen and, often, the girl is hirsute."

"Hirsute?" asked Ray. "What does that mean?"

"Hirsute means hairy, Ray. Affected females will have the misfortune of developing excess body hair. They may show evidence of pubic hair much earlier than expected in a young girl and, generally, a pattern of coarse hair growth down the midline of the abdomen and across the medial surface of the thighs. Some will have excess facial hair—they'll need to shave."

"Baldness?" asked Lew.

"I don't know. That could be a secondary defect, but genetics play a role, too. Please remember what I said when I started: Our research raises ten questions for every answer. May I add one more factor to all this?"

"Go right ahead, Doctor."

"This discussion is so focused on the physical defects caused by the superestrogens, I don't want you to miss the psychological impact. The emotional and psychological damage can be devastating. Puberty may be a time to grow and develop physically, but it is also a time when you are learning what is good and evil in the world.

"Take a child whose puberty is totally askew and you throw in an entire new set of problems: sexually precocious children are at risk for sexual abuse, kids whose physical development is delayed may not be able to participate in sports. Teenagers seek the company of kids like themselves. These kids get left out.

"Left out and singled out because they look different. Normal in every other way—bright, enthusiastic, full of imagination. Think about it—at a time of life when peer pressure is all-powerful, they can easily become targets, objects of ridicule.

"This is what drives my reseach, people. The need to save children from disaster."

Lew's office was silent. Osborne sat perfectly still. Lew and Ray both shifted in their chairs. Lew cleared her throat.

"Rick, do we know exactly when and how the mother is exposed to these industrial chemicals during the pregnancy?" she asked.

"Yes and no. Our studies have found that plants affected by the industrial chemicals that produce endocrine disruptors make compounds called phytoestrogens, which are passed along to plant-eaters. We are finding phytoestrogens in the plant life in a number of lakes, rivers, and streams around Loon Lake. Minuscule amounts so far."

"Plant-eaters like fish? I didn't think fish ate plants," said Osborne, uncrossing his legs to sit forward in his chair.

"Not fish, but frogs, salamanders, otters, mink, eagles—you name it," said Shanley. "So far we have only seen it in nonhuman life forms in your immediate area. The contaminants enter the food chain in organisms lower than fish but are transmitted up through a food chain that includes fish. This is the first human male exhibiting so many female characteristics that I've ever seen—and, I want to emphasize, my observations are quite theroretical.

"More frequently observed, in your region, has been the feminization of male fish and some birds and mammals, along with decreased fertility and, in some cases, impaired metabolism. I would be hard-pressed to tell you just how a pregnant woman might have ingested the chemicals. For problems as severe as those I see in the victim, the mother had to be living in a veritable hothouse of superestrogens. Also, it could have been for a brief period of time but during a vulnerable stage of her pregnancy."

"Doc, going back to the problem I have identifying this individual," said Lew, "I have information that points to this victim being from the Kansas City area and having spent just a short period of time up here. I think that shoots Ray's theory that the victim is from this area."

"But you don't know the individual's life history. Where was he born? Where did he grow up? As Ray may have mentioned to you, the question my team has been dealing with is just how widely distributed are the source chemicals in the Great Lakes region. More specifically, throughout the watershed that includes Loon Lake."

"Why choose Loon Lake?" asked Lew. "Why not an area farther north? Like around Lake Superior?"

"Because we know the industrial chemicals in question have been released in your region. For years, they were spewed by pulp and paper mills into your streams and rivers. More to the point, your area had mills that manufactured food wrappings, a primary source of alkyl phenols, which break down to produce the superestrogens. The big question is: How seriously has your groundwater been affected?

"But again, I must hedge and say nothing is certain. We are having a heck of a time because different species metabolize these chemicals in different ways. Also, the mix of endocrine disruptors in the environment is constantly changing. All we know for certain is there have been times in your area when the concentration of the chemicals in question has exceeded acceptable thresholds.

"That's why I am going to go out on a limb and theorize that this victim was exposed to a unique environmental situation. This could lead us to a more potent source in your region than any we have found to date. Back to your question: The individual could be from somewhere else, but the coincidence is rather striking from my point of view. To find a body in this region, a known source region, exhibiting so many signs of endocrine disruption . . . well, you get my point."

"We have the name of the victim, Dr. Shanley," said Lew. "When our investigation is complete, you may want to check over the medical records, but I'm afraid I have to cut this short. We have a site we need to investigate before dark and a list of possible victims to check out."

Osborne could see Lew was anxious to get off the phone and out to Dead Creek before dusk.

"I have a favor to ask, Chief Ferris," said Shanley. "When it is appropriate, would you allow me to talk to the family? It would be of enormous value to our study if they would donate the remains."

"That's a tough one," said Lew, "I'll certainly do my best."

"Do you have any more questions for us, Rick?" said Ray.

"No, just a heartfelt thank-you, everyone. This just pushed my research forward a good couple of years."

"Does this mean I get a bonus?" asked Ray, winking at his friends.

"A bonus? Let me put it this way. When I publish the paper that will be written as a result of what I have observed this morning, I can guarantee FIEH will get funding for future projects up the wazoo. You won't be able to get me enough specimens. You'll get calls from scientists around the world looking for someone to harvest for them. A bonus? Man, you got a *business*."

"Dr. Shanley, thank you for your time and for your immediate attention to this." Lew stood up, directing her voice toward the speaker on the telephone. "I'll get back to you as soon as I have a confirmed ID. Please keep these results confidential."

"Of course. Chief Ferris?"

"Yes?"

"Tragic though it may be, this is very exciting stuff."

Lew managed a weak smile. "Not to someone who loves pan-fried bluegills."

fifteen

God never did make a more calm, quiet, innocent recreation than fishing.

Isaak Walton

They decided to use Osborne's car so he wouldn't be worried about the dog. Ray took the backseat with Mike sniffing over his shoulder. At Ray's urging, the three had attached a trailer carrying one of the police boats to the car. Osborne noted Lew's 9mm semiautomatic was strapped securely to her hip because she patted it about six times as if to be sure she hadn't forgotten it.

By now, it was four in the afternoon. The light was flattening out, and the air had a cold, damp edge, though it still smelled of spring.

"Perfect day for muskies." Osborne looked back at Ray. Ray nodded in agreement. But neither of them seemed to mind being where they were. As the car sped toward Shepard Lake and Dead Creek, Osborne told Lew and Ray about the Kansas City conversations. He also told them what had happened to Erin. Just as he finished Erin's description of the threatening figure on the porch, they drove past the very road she had taken: the road with the sign for Marjorie's Bed and Breakfast. Osborne slowed. The road they wanted was the next one, just around the bend in the highway.

"Well, that's interesting." Osborne turned to look back at Ray. "We found you in the same area where Erin saw that guy."

"I always feel like it's *Deliverance* territory back in there," said Lew. "I don't think Erin was too smart driving in there all alone."

Osborne turned onto the dirt road where they'd found Ray. The car bumped along on rough sand and gravel, heaving from side to side. It ran alongside a desolate-looking swamp where water appeared to have drowned thousands of trees. The spiky, leafless, needleless skeletons spread in gray formations for miles.

"Beaver," said Ray as they drove along. His comment said it all: A beaver dam could trap acres and acres of healthy forest and turn it into a swampy wasteland almost overnight.

"Who on earth would want to live back here?" shivered Lew.

"Somebody who doesn't need company," said Ray. It seemed like ten miles before Osborne and Lew recognized a police flag Lew had left behind to mark the spot where they'd found Ray. Osborne pulled his station wagon into a small clearing. They parked, leaving the dog in the car, and continued on foot along a fairly well-worn track.

"My hunch is I probably put my boat in back here," said Ray, loping ahead of the other two along a nearly invisible deer trail. "Boy, I sure hope it's still there." He pulled at his beard and talked as he walked. His strong legs, used to striding through brush and climbing beaver dams, cleared low branches off the path for Osborne and Lew.

"That boat's a collector's item. It's one of the last ones old man Terney built, y'know. Two years to select each strip of that wood, twenty-seven coats to laminate it just so, without ever changing the color of that cedar, just gorgeous. You can't buy a boat like that today."

Ray paused and looked back at his friends. His tanned face had its color back, and his eyes seemed happy in spite of his concern. "I traded ten bucks, each one six points or bigger, for that boat—ten bucks over five years of deer hunting. I paid through the nose, but it was worth it."

"Ten bucks in five years isn't legal, Ray," said Lew.

"Whatever," said Ray with a wide grin.

"Now, what would anybody besides you be doing back here?" asked Lew, her attention back to the dense brush around them. "You got no houses, not even trailers back here. I don't have a thing on my fire maps. I checked after we found you, Ray."

"Place is desolate," said Osborne a little crossly as a branch whipped across his face and nearly poked him in the eye.

Ray stopped suddenly and thrust his arms out to his sides so that Osborne and Lew bumped into him from behind. "Wait a min-ute. . . . I know where we are! I know this place. It's coming back to me. Lew, you won't find anything on your maps. C'mon, I'll show you why."

"Wait, wait, wait, slow down," said Osborne. "Are we on private land? I don't want to get into any trouble back here." Lew looked relieved he'd asked the question.

"Trust me," said Ray, "we're safe."

Osborne and Lew glanced at each other. Neither with confidence. "So far, I think we're on state land," said Lew to Osborne. "We're okay."

"We are not on state land," said Ray to his partners. "This is the old Cantrell place."

"Cantrell?" said Osborne. "Where the mill used to be?"

A look of deep satisfaction crossed Ray's face. "Yep. I drove over here after I saw old Herman that morning to check out exactly where he said he found those little babies years ago. That's what I was after, all right. Just foolin' around really. I haven't been back this close to Dead Creek since I was a kid."

"Oh my God, duck!" Lew shouted, crouching suddenly. From over his left shoulder, Osborne felt rather than saw a huge shadow sweep up from the brush alongside the trail. A sickish, sweet odor had just drifted into the air around them as the magnificent bald eagle spread its wings, hovering momentarily as if to shelter the three of them, then rose in a simple elegant spiral to disappear over the tips of the Norway pines guarding the narrow trail.

"Now what the heck road kill would you get way out here?" said Ray, marching toward the spot where the bird had obviously been feeding on something. He stepped off the trail and moved forward slowly, brushing the tall, dried grasses away with his hands. Lew and Osborne remained rooted where they were, waiting.

"So that's what they didn't want me to find," said Ray. He stopped and looked down. "Don't move too fast, folks. We've got a ripe one here."

"What is it?" asked Osborne, happy to stay back.

"You mean what *was* it." Ray's voice was calm as his eyes studied whatever it was at his feet. Dead grasses hid it from Osborne's view.

Then, as Lew strode toward him, Ray looked up at her. "Walk carefully, my friend. You'll be looking for evidence in them thar briars."

Then his tone turned serious. "Ted Bronk," he said. "I recognize the boots. He got those up in Alaska last year when he did some heavy construction work for his brother-in-law. Nobody else in town's got boots like that. Boots and bones, Lew. That's all the Wausau boys'll have to go on with this one. The fox and the eagle have done their job on old Ted. Too bad, too. There's a lotta folks would've liked to have had a piece of Ted before he checked out, ya know?"

Osborne watched Lew nod her head solemnly. He knew

she knew what an evil guy Ted had been, doing way too much damage over his thirty-four, maybe thirty-five years. He'd been a bully, a wife beater, and a man who was suspected of raping an eleven-year-old girl on her way home from the ice rink. The parents of two classes of junior high boys had been appalled ten years ago when they found out Ted had been running an after-school porno film club for the kids, charging two bucks an afternoon. No, thought Osborne, few would mind Ted's departure from Loon Lake, and many would be pleased if he'd suffered on the way out.

As if she was reading his thoughts, Lew looked over at Osborne. "I just wish I'd been able to ask him about those parties he was driving the dancers to," she said. "I am sure he knew what happened to that English girl. Well, let's keep going. I'll call this in on our way back."

Ray had moved past the carcass to the woods behind. He seemed to know where he was going, though Osborne could see no evidence of a trail. The front line of brush and shrubs gave way to a darkly lit and vast, silent space. The forest floor was wall-to-wall pine needles, the ceiling broad branches of Norway pine, spruce, and tamarack. The skeletons of fallen, dead trees lent an eerie cavelike quality. But it wasn't absolutely quiet. They could hear a soft burble of water, even if they couldn't see it.

Osborne leaned forward to peer over a massive fallen log and spotted a stream running just behind it. Five feet wide, maybe three feet deep at its deepest. And hidden from view behind the same log, neatly tucked under dead limbs so no winds could shift it, tipped over to protect the interior, was Ray's canoe. Ray leaped over the fallen log and ran to his boat. He smoothed his hands over the cedar-strip surface and gently turned it over, his eyes rapidly scanning the interior. Two paddles lay on the ground beneath it.

"Not a scratch," he breathed with relief.

Lew put her hand on his shoulder, "Ray, is this where you left it?"

"No, I didn't. I know I didn't because I always store my paddles up inside the gunwale on these racks, see? Someone else put this boat away. I am absolutely sure I didn't leave it here."

"Then you have a guardian angel," said Osborne.

Lew and Ray looked at him a little oddly. But Osborne barely noticed. *It was the mushroom woman*, he thought. Now the expression on her face made perfect sense, she had been watching over Ray, waiting to make sure he was okay.

"Does Ted Bronk have a sister?" asked Osborne.

Ray looked over at him as he carried the canoe toward the stream. "Nope. He had a brother who was killed in a knife fight a few years back, but no sister that I know of. Why?"

"Just a thought."

The canoe slipped downstream with Lew in the front, Osborne in the center, and Ray at the back. It was a beautifully proportioned, steady canoe that moved across the water like a mother duck, serene and perfectly silent. The creek grew wider and deeper, which Osborne could judge from the dark shadows of rocks below the surface. As Lew and Ray dipped their paddles, the boat glided forward. Twice they ducked below ancient railroad ties carrying rusted rail.

"Some of this forest was clear cut in the late 1800s, and no one's been through here since," said Ray, "not even the beavers. But the water looks okay. It used to have a gray-green tinge to it. Now it's clear."

Suddenly, he pulled his paddle back, halting the canoe and forcing its nose into the brush to hold it in place. He handed his paddle to Osborne as he raised a finger to his lips, signaling quiet. He scanned the water running under the canoe, then leaned forward and thrust his arm down.

He brought it up immediately, a muddy-colored creature, about twelve inches long and looking like a cross between a dog and fish, twisting in his hand. He held the thing down on the floor of the canoe with his knee, turning it onto its back and pulling the legs away so he could see the torso.

"That's a mud puppy, for you," said Osborne, backing away. He hated the slimy bottom-eaters. They looked like something God detested.

"Let's take a look," Ray said, "if we're on Dead Creek right here—and I'm pretty sure we are—then this little mother'll show us just what shape the water's in." He examined the underbelly of the creature closely, then held it out toward Osborne and Lew. "Looks okay to me."

"Be interesting to know what the hormone count is," said Osborne. "Shanley's got me spooked. My fish intake is going to be minimal until we know what's going on around here."

"Dead Creek is a special situation," said Ray. "They say it's another twenty years before anybody should be eating fish or even living around here."

"Too bad," said Osborne, "I've always heard that once upon a time Dead Creek had some of the biggest browns and rainbows—"

"You betcha," said Ray, "I had an old, old geezer—I'll tell ya this guy fished here around 1920 or so—he told me he took a twenty-two-inch brown trout out of here. Called it Crescent Creek in those days."

"Wow," said Lew, "what was he using? Did he say?"

"Worms," said Ray, "plain old nightcrawlers."

"Hey, guys," said Lew with an edge of concern in her voice, "it's going to be dark pretty soon. Shouldn't we go back?"

"Hell, no," said Ray, "I want to see where it takes us. We got an hour until it's dark, and I promise we'll be back at the car by then."

"But—" Lew protested.

"Five minutes," said Ray, "I know we're close—"

"Now how the hell do you know that?" Lew thrust her paddle into the water with obvious exasperation. "I see no sign of this creek ending anytime in the next century." She was right. Below the canopy of branches, they could easily see the creek winding ahead through the woods several hundred feet at least.

Slowly, Ray pulled back on his paddle. "O-o-kay," he said, "I'll show you." He pointed with the paddle to a flat-topped rock along the bank. A branch of Norway pine hung over the boulder. Strewn across the top of the rock were small, hairy pellets, smaller than a fingernail. "See those? Owl poop. Northern hawk owl. Where do they like to sit? On power lines and metal fence posts. I spotted the first of these pellets about three minutes ago, and now they're everywhere. Look." Ray pointed the paddle four times.

"We are very close to where the owls are roosting, and that means we're close to people. They only retreat in here during storms. This is a good sign that we're coming out somewhere very soon, and we'll find some sign of life when we get there. Trust me, Lew."

The canoe continued swiftly downstream.

"Say, Lew," said Ray as they passed over a deep hole, "When does trout season open? If I were you, I'd try a weighted nymph in here just to see if the trout are back. But . . ." He looked up into the dense canopy of Norway pine. " . . . with so little sunlight, I'll bet it's at least another three to four weeks before this water gets close to sixty degrees. What do you think? Maybe a little black stone fly? Just to see what happens . . ."

Lew looked back at Ray in surprise. She set her paddle down. "Ray, I had no idea you fly-fished."

"Years ago. Many years ago—with the old man. Didn't go often enough to really feel comfortable with it. Dad was always on call, so his time was limited. Bein' I was a kid who loved to fish, I was damned if I'd wait for him.

That's how come I talked my way into fishing with a couple of the old guides. You remember Quigley and Kirsch, Doc? I learned everything I know from those guys. They fished everything—muskie, walleyes, bass, panfish—everything except trout. Of course I paid dearly. I had to clean the catch.

"I fly-fished just a couple a times with my dad in my teens, and I never did go again after I started guiding."

"Well . . . that's very interesting," said Lew. "I'm glad to hear this, Ray. Restores my faith in humanity now I know you have one redeeming quality."

"Oh yeah. What's that?"

"Some familiarity with a trout fly or two. Means there's hope, y'know?"

"Just don't go telling anyone. You'll destroy my image." Ray lowered his voice and hunched his shoulders to ape a wrestler: "Me tough guy. B-i-i-g fish man. Muskie hunter."

"So how 'bout you, Lew? How is it you fly-fish?" asked Ray.

"Ah . . ." said Lew slowly, as if debating whether she wanted to give up a secret. Sweeping her paddle with a sure, steady stroke, she kept her eyes straight ahead as she spoke. "I fly-fish because it's just me and the water. No boat, no motor running, no gas fumes. Just me, the riffles, and a canny old trout.

"Maybe . . ." She paused, resting her paddle on the edge of the canoe. "Maybe I like trout fishing for all the same reasons I like my job: takes a predator to know a predator. Right, fellas? As true for muskies as it is for trout: a good fisherman thinks like a fish. Law enforcement isn't catch-and-release, of course, it's catch-and-arrest."

With that, Lew chuckled, dipped her paddle deep into Dead Creek, and the canoe sped forward.

Ray was right. In less than two minutes, the canoe poked its nose out from a cove on the edge of a small lake. Lew stopped paddling as they emerged, and Ray pulled back on his paddle immediately so the canoe would remain hidden in the shoreside brush.

"Looks like the beavers made a lake out of Dead Creek," he said. "This is very interesting. I know this little lake wasn't here fifteen years ago."

At first glance, there was no sign of human life along the lakefront to their right or to their left. Insects buzzed, the water was glassy and still, even under a light breeze. To the right they could see the entire perimeter of the lake and no sign of people. Ray let the boat glide forward so they could see farther to the left.

"Smoke," whispered Osborne softly. A dark plume lifted above a dense patch of tamarack, still golden with their winter needles, that guarded the lake across from them and to the left. It was black smoke with a touch of gray brown color along the edge, visible even in the darkening sky. "Someone's smelting," said Osborne very, very softly, keenly aware his voice could travel across the lake.

"How do you know?" asked Ray. Lew shifted in her seat and looked over at Osborne.

"I know because I used to sell the silver scraps from fillings I made, along with old silver and gold fillings that I replaced, to a fella in Crandon who melted them down. He had his own smelting oven. He smelted on Saturdays, which is when I would drive over to drop off my silver scraps. I was always struck by the strange color of the smoke it produced. Somebody's smelting silver, I'm sure. You get a different color when you smelt gold."

Lew and Ray nodded and studied the smoke.

"I see where it's coming from," said Ray, and he pointed even farther to the left as he let the boat drift out onto the lake.

Sure enough. As the boat swung out and made a sharp left turn, they got an angle on a house set far enough back from the shore that it was nearly, if not purposely, hidden from view by towering pines. The smoke came from a

distance still—somewhere behind the house. They could
see just a corner of the house but enough to make out that
it was a large, dark, log home with a wide porch on that
corner, at least. It appeared to be recently built.

"Well, I'll be," said Osborne softly. "If you weren't
looking for something, you'd never see that, would you?
Now, who on earth would want to live out here—on *this*
water?"

Suddenly, Ray whipped his paddle into the water and
yanked the canoe back into the brush with one rude thrust.

"Duck," he hissed as he grabbed branches and thrust
the boat deep under the brush hanging over the water.
Osborne bumped his head hard on a large branch as the
boat swung back, but he resisted the urge to curse. He
hunkered down in the boat, right behind Lew.

Within seconds, they heard a soft purring that all three
recognized instantly: the well-oiled motor of a small seaplane. They pulled the branches down around them to
further hide the boat, but all three eased their way up so
they could watch as the small craft cut its motor to land
quietly on pontoons. A soft purring was all that could be
heard as it motored toward the house to their right.

"Do you think the pilot saw us?" asked Lew softly.

"Hell, no," said Ray. "He flew in from behind, and I
had us deep under these trees in plenty of time. If this
was an aluminum canoe, we'd be seen, but we're nicely
camouflaged right now. I'm keen on who's arriving,
aren't you? Dinner at Dead Creek—now there's a social
event not to be missed."

They were too far away to identify who was in the
plane as it drifted gently toward the house, but they didn't
miss the narrow dock that suddenly, silently moved out
over the water as the plane got closer. As the dock was
electronically extended, a literal wall of trees and brush
opened up to reveal a boathouse, into which the plane
slipped with ease. The wall of brush slid back over the
boathouse, the dock retreated, and the shoreline was still.

"State of the art," commented Osborne. "I've never seen such a thing."

."Well, I'll be. . . ." Lew was puzzled.

"Saves on ice damage during the winter," said Ray, pulling at his beard. Then he chuckled. "And it's great for smuggling."

"Smuggling?" asked Osborne.

"Into Canada?" Lew added.

"And beyond," said Ray.

"I'm not sure what you're getting at," said Lew.

But Osborne's mind had started to race with what he knew from Kansas City. "Let's see what we hear from Bowers's lawyer tomorrow," he whispered. "Let's just see—and, Ray, let's get out of here."

"Hold on, hold on," said Lew, raising her arm as if to stop them from going anywhere. "Ray, can you get us out of here in the dark if we hang around a little longer to find out if we can't see more when they turn their lights on?"

"No problem," said Ray. "Here's something that might help." He handed a pair of binoculars to Osborne to pass to Lew.

"Where did these come from?" whispered Osborne.

"Here," said Ray, pointing behind him, "I had a little cabinet built in to hold a few things: the binoculars, a couple beers, and some extra lures."

For the next half hour, they sat silent in the canoe. No one even whispered. As it grew darker, a fog bank rolled in from behind them, and Ray eased the canoe into the fog, using it as a cover. They moved in close to shore right in front of the house. No one moved. Osborne knew they were all thinking the same thing: the slightest sound would carry, clear and sharp, straight to any accomodating ear in the house or on the property around it. And that was one thing no one wanted to happen, even if they were desperately curious to know who was inside.

But the trees were so close that even though they could

catch glimmers of light through the branches and between patches of fog, they could neither see nor hear much of anything. At one point an outside door slammed shut, sounding like a screen door. But then a loud motor went on and drowned out any hope of hearing slighter sounds. After five minutes of gentle rocking close to the shore and with no sign the motor would be turned off, Lew motioned to Ray to pull back.

sixteen

The best chum I ever had in fishing was a girl, and she tramped just as hard and fished quite as patiently as any man I ever knew.

Theodore Gordon (1890)

"**Jeez**, they got an air conditioner running in that place," said Lew about twenty minutes later as they were paddling upstream. "It's fifty-five degrees out."

"Or an air compressor," Osborne responded, "all my dental units ran on compressors that sounded like that. But what would they be doing with an air compressor?"

Though it was dark and the fog thick, in less than ten minutes Ray had run the canoe silently along the brush-lined lakeshore, swung expertly into the cove, and pointed them back up the now-narrowing stream. The forest underworld that had seemed so dark and muted during the day was now a deep, impenetrable black to Osborne. Ray, however, seemed to be able to see just fine.

Once they had found the stream and paddled in a good 500 feet, Lew spoke, keeping her voice low in the darkness, "Ray, I'd like to try down that road with the B-and-B sign as we head into town. Not too far, just enough to get an idea what's back there. We'll come back out tomorrow."

"Fine with me," said Ray. They paddled upstream in silence, finally reaching the point where they had put in. Hoisting the canoe onto their shoulders, they trudged back through the dense brush and down the rutted logging road past Ted Bronk's body to Osborne's car.

"I'm not letting the dog out," said Osborne as he reached up to help Ray lash the canoe onto the police boat. "That would be one big mistake."

"Damn," said Lew, stomping the mud off her boots before climbing into Osborne's car, "I forgot we didn't have my cruiser. I have to report that we found Ted right away. Let's skip going down that other road and hustle back to the main highway. I saw a tavern out there where I can call in."

"Lew," said Ray, a cautious tone in his voice. "I know it's important that you do that, but I'd like to drive down the road a bit while we know that plane and its pilot are there, which might not be the case in the morning."

"Good point," said Lew. "Okay with you, Doc?"

Osborne agreed with Ray and made a slow arcing left turn off Highway C onto the dirt road heading toward the B-and-B. About a mile in, they passed the little log cabin inn. The place had been one of the small family resorts that flourished in the forties and fifties, then fell on bad times when Americans decided they all had to go to Disneyland. These resorts were made up of a series of tiny cabins, each with about twelve feet of lake frontage for wading and swimming and one larger lodge that served as office, dining room, and recreation center. Tonight, lights were shining in the main lodge and a dark-green Volvo with Missouri plates was parked in front of one of the tiny cabins.

"So they're open for business already?" Lew turned her head in surprise.

"They probably stayed open all winter for snowmobilers," said Osborne. "I don't know who owns that place anymore. Emily Swanee used to own it, but she sold and moved to Chicago a few years back."

The car had hit a rough gravel road, barely one lane wide. Osborne slowed, uncomfortable with the loud grinding noise his wheels were making. They moved on in the dark. At one point an owl suddenly flew up from the right, thick and oblong like a large rock, and bounced hard off the windshield.

"There we go again," said Ray, "we're close."

And they were. The road ended abruptly at an old squat brick building fronted with an overgrown clearing infested with a few random rusted lumps of machinery. At first glance, the place looked abandoned. At second glance, tire tracks were clearly visible in the dirt.

"Well, well, one of the old Cantrell warehouses still standing. I was right. This *is* where they ran the paper mill once upon a time," said Ray. "Herman told me they tore the original plant down some time in the late forties. This is the one that piped into Dead Creek. Shall we check it out?"

Neither Lew nor Osborne said a word. If anything, Osborne felt like he sure didn't want to, but there was no choice.

Instead, he cut the car engine but left the lights on and opened his door very slowly, as did Lew and Ray. The three of them stepped into the dark and stood listening. Then Ray jogged up to the door of the old building. He ran the beam of his flashlight over it, then he walked back and forth across the front of the building and checked back along both sides to the rear. He turned and walked back to the car where Lew and Osborne stood waiting.

"Someone's working around here, all right. They're using the back way. See?" He aimed the beam of the flash, and they could see a well-worn track over the grass that led to the back of the building.

"This must be the road Erin found," said Lew. She had

already begun to walk forward with Ray. Osborne got the distinct feeling that he didn't want to stay by the car alone. He quickly caught up to the other two.

"Ray . . ." Lew stopped and pulled at Ray's sleeve, "shine that light through the windows here." She had stopped in front of the darkened building. Ray did as she asked. "That's interesting," said Lew. The flashlight illuminated a pile of cardboard boxes neatly stacked one upon the other. Beside the stack were several large wooden crates, each about six feet wide and four feet high. Steel wire gleamed in the beam of light. "These are not old boxes," said Lew.

"No, they're not," said Osborne.

"Maybe it's a new UPS drop site," said Ray. No one laughed.

The tire tracks meandered behind the old building then seemed to end in a garbage pit, heaped with old springs, a couple of car skeletons, and other debris. Ray walked around the pit to the right and stopped, then he walked to the left. A huge boulder, about six feet wide and four feet high blocked the way. He looked it over. Fifteen tons minimum. Lew and Osborne stood right behind him and followed the beam from Ray's flash as he ran it over the ruts in the track, obviously made by cars and maybe deep enough to be from trucks as well.

"This doesn't make sense." Ray's flash showed the tracks ran right under the boulder. "How dumb do they think we are? Hold this." He handed the flashlight to Lew. Then he bent his knees as he wrapped his arms around the boulder and lifted it lightly. "Whaddya say, about seven, eight pounds?" He set it aside. The tracks ran forward, past the dump and up a slight rise.

"Keeps hunters out," said Lew.

Lew, Ray, and Osborne moved forward as a threesome. When they neared the top, Ray put his arm out to stop them. The cloud cover overhead had broken, and a very bright moon was shining through.

"I think we've got a little too much light, folks. We may not want to broadcast our silhouettes," he whispered. "But I smell water. Let's get down on our knees to look over the top of this hill."

All three dropped for cover, and he was right. Just over the rise, the road curved slightly to the right, and there stood the same log house. No lights were shining, but the moonlight caught every detail of the full porch running around the outside.

"I'm sure this is the house that Erin found," whispered Osborne.

"Yeah, she drove in during the day, and that boulder was set aside," said Ray, his voice low. "I have no doubt we've located the same building we saw from the lake, too. Same color and frame, and the distance feels right."

"We can't go any farther," said Lew. "See?" She pointed the beam of her flashlight to a tree on which was posted a bright red No Trespassing sign. "I'm gonna check the fire number. That'll tell us something."

"There is no fire number," said Ray.

"I can tell you something else," said Osborne, his voice soft and grim. "See that car parked over to the left?" Lew and Ray looked to where the moon was illuminating a white Cadillac, just barely visible at the corner of the house. "I'd know that car anywhere. It's always parked behind mine at 6:30 Sunday Mass . . . Judith Benjamin."

Back in the car, Osborne pulled them onto the gravel road, and they headed out. "Lew," he asked, "you made the comment the other day that you knew a few things about Judith Benjamin you might tell me sometime. Is this a good time?"

Lew chuckled. "Sure. Ray, you may know this stuff already."

"I dunno," said Ray, "depends."

"Judith is what, forty-two, forty-three, now? This goes back a good twenty years," said Lew. "Long before I entered law enforcement. I was redoing some of our files a few years ago, and I found one on Miss Judith. Seems that in her teenage days, she specialized in leading certain prominent Loon Lake gentlemen into compromising situations, then blackmailing them."

"Oh really?" said Osborne, genuinely surprised. "Like who?"

"I'm not getting into that. Several are still around, and they learned their lesson the hard way," said Lew. "But she had a very nasty habit of enticing them into various infractions of statutory rape only to—literally—pull a knife or a gun on them."

"I'm not sure I might not be a little on her side," said Ray. "Sounds to me like some old geezers who deserved it, maybe?"

"Maybe," said Lew. "Except for the guy we found in the rest area on Highway 51 with his throat slit. She was never charged because there was no evidence linking her, but I am ninety-nine percent sure it was our Miss Judith."

"What made her stop?"

"We don't know, except that right around that time, she was able to buy her first tavern, and she's been legit, so to speak, since."

"Doc, I'm just letting you know that she has a way about her," said Lew. "She's pretty high on my list right now for questioning about Ted Bronk and the missing dancer. And now this business with the plane and the hidden house? What the hell is she up to?"

"What about me?" said Ray in mock dismay. "I thought we started out to find out who clonked me on the head."

"That's becoming obvious," said Lew. "You stumbled onto some property where you weren't welcome for all the reasons we're beginning to see here."

"But who hit me?" said Ray. "That's the weird part. See, now I remember going in to try to find the place where the babies where found, okay? I remember parking my truck and unloading my canoe—but that's all. Then you found me. So who hit me?"

"Maybe the creep that Erin saw at the house," said Osborne. "That could fit." Then the three of them fell silent.

Osborne mulled everything over as he drove. The news about Judith was particularly interesting. *And now that ass Brad Miller is hanging around her,* he thought. *That pompous, prententious mean little son of a bitch. Well, maybe this time he's picked the right friend. Maybe this time, Judith Benjamin has a real sucker on the line.* Osborne couldn't help enjoying a mildly homicidal wish that smart-ass Professor Bradford Miller would get his.

Osborne and Ray waited in the car at Mary's Tavern so Lew could call in news of Ted Bronk's body. Both were lost in their thoughts until she returned.

"The report is in from the Wausau boys," she said when she returned. Osborne and Ray waited expectantly. "They expect to ID all of them by tomorrow and this YPO lead is right on," said Lew. "One looks to be an executive, a company president, from Ames, Iowa, whose family finally reported him missing. They want the Bowers's lawyer to do an eyeball ID tomorrow, so we're gonna have to get her over to Wausau."

"Cause of death?" asked Osborne.

"Very curious," said Lew. "They found no marks, but the men were frozen before their bodies went into the water. They know they froze to death, but they did not have water in their lungs nor any indications that would mean freezing in water. The report is very specific, according to the way Roger read it to me. Also—that fourth body? Traces of a theatrical adhesive across the lower half of the face."

Lew took a deep breath then and sighed heavily.

"What's wrong?" asked Ray.

"You," said Lew. She had a succinct way of getting to the point that Osborne found rather startling. Most women he knew always hedged their way into confrontrations. Not Lew, she was straight on.

"Sloan called in from the hospital and insisted I take you off this case, Ray. He's complaining to the town board if I don't. He considers you a convicted felon and everything else!" She threw up her hands in frustration.

"From my high school days, he hasn't forgotten."

"C'mon, Ray," said Lew, "you're still a pothead. News travels. On the other hand, I'm getting very tired of John Sloan behaving like he's still in charge."

"He thinks you're a girl, Lew," said Ray.

They all sat silent for a long, long minute in the car. Osborne was sorry this was happening. Ray's presence when they were in the woods or on the water was the one thing that made Osborne feel a heck of a lot safer than he might if he were on his own. He knew Lew wasn't a skilled woodsman. They were already ahead on the case just because Ray knew which way to turn.

"Maybe I could talk to him," said Osborne finally. "This isn't good."

"No, it isn't," said Lew. "And I refuse to make an issue over the information from Shanley. I want to keep that under wraps. I know the board, and if I have to tell everyone, then the whole story will be all over town. The mayor is a different story. Him I can trust to keep his mouth shut, and his backing is all I need. I wish to heck I had something other than the Shanley connection to say in Ray's favor." She turned to look hard at Ray. "You know, it's your own fault."

"Okay, okay." Ray leaned forward. Now it was his turn to sigh deeply. "Lew, if there is ever the least hint, if any of my local buddies ever even suspects that there is a remote possibility that I'm undercover for the DNR, I'm going to lose a lot of business. You know what I mean? God forbid Sloan even hears such a rumor."

"That's a preposterous rumor."

"It's ridiculous," said Ray, "but if it gets out, you know

what'll happen to me. I'll never dig a grave in this town again."

"Trust me, Ray, I don't intend to destroy your livelihood."

"Thank you, Lew. Are we in business?"

Osborne noted that Lew simply reached over the car seat and shook Ray's hand. Nothing more was said about the DNR. Not then and not ever again.

seventeen

O give me the grace to catch a fish
So big that even I
When talking of it afterwards
May have no need to lie.

Anonymous, "A Fisherman's Prayer"

Osborne was surprised to see it was only 8:30 when he dropped off Lew and Ray at their cars in the jail parking lot. The day had seemed a month long. But as he started home past Saint Mary's Church, parked cars lining both sides of the street indicated the Sunday night Lenten service was still going on. He pulled the station wagon over, feeling a little too wound up to go back to the dark silence of his house quite yet.

As he entered and took his usual seat in the eighth pew on the far right, it calmed him to hear the familiar singsong phrases, the muted responses from the small crowd attending. Tonight he even savored the smell of incense in the air. It was all familiar, it was all safe, and it kept him from wondering what the hell he was getting himself into.

The ceremony was over in less than ten minutes, but

Osborne sat quietly until most of the parishioners had left. Then he rose and walked over to the nook under the statue of the Blessed Virgin, Mary Lee's favorite. He slipped two quarters into the scuffed tin box attached to the stand of vigil lights and heard them rattle loudly in the now-empty church. He picked up a taper and book of matches from the little tray beside the coin box and lit two candles. They would be the only two burning that night. Then he bent his knees and lowered himself slowly onto the kneeler before the statue of the Holy Mother.

The Virgin was hidden under a dark-purple Lenten shroud, and Osborne wondered if the churches in the big cities still followed that ritual. He closed his eyes, bowed his head, and mentally ran through a "Hail Mary" while trying to summon up a prayerful calm and an image of Mary Lee, but all he could see in his mind's eye were the twinkling dark-brown eyes of Lew. He clenched his eyes shut and tried to concentrate.

"Dr. Osborne?" A gentle hand touched his shoulder. Startled, Osborne jumped involuntarily and opened his eyes to see Father Vodicka studying him intently.

"Are you in a rush?" the elderly priest had an eager look in his eye.

"I have a few minutes. What's up?"

"Well, ah, we'd planned a demonstration for folks this evening, after the services, but, ah, well, no one has stayed, and I was wondering . . . well, it would be a little less embarrassing if you wouldn't mind . . . ?"

"Of course." Osborne got the picture instantly. The poor guy. Father Vodicka was taken for granted in the parish, even as he struggled to bring modern ways to the church with not a little resistance from his flock. "What are we demonstrating, Father?"

The relief on the priest's face was palpable as he shepherded Osborne toward the door to the adjoining offices.

"Oh, Dr. Osborne, this is quite impressive. We've had our first computer installed, and a computer sciences student from Nicolet College over in Rhinelander is inputting all the baptismal records onto a database."

The chapel office was brightly lit and a distinctly hip-looking young man with long hair and a semi-insolent look on his face was typing away on a keyboard. He looked up with some interest as Osborne entered the room.

Clearly, he and Father Vodicka had been looking forward to showing off their achievement to someone. Osborne was happy he was a professional man with the title Doctor. It would lend weight to the significance of their little meeting. It might even make the snub from the other parishioners a little easier to take. And Osborne was a past president of the church board, so that would help, too.

"I'm afraid I know nothing about these kinds of things," he said. "Please keep it as basic as you can."

"Don't worry about that, Dr. Osborne," said the priest, "but we thought you might like to see how Wally takes the original document, scans it with this penlike instrument, and—there—see all the information on the screen?"

"Very nice," said Osborne. "Now, why are you doing this?"

"Oh. people call all the time for their baptismal records," said Father Vodicka. "In some communities, you can't get married in a Catholic church if you can't furnish a copy of your baptismal records. Then, of course, years ago, many early residents never did file *birth* certificates. Often babies were born in the home, and they never thought too much about it, but they *always* had their children baptized. So we have calls from people looking for their baptismal certificate in lieu of a birth certificate. Very important, these. We used to have to spend hours looking through files, but now, if people give us a name or a date or even just the month, we can find the correct listing in seconds and print multiple copies instantly."

"Father," the student spoke up, "have you decided what you're going to do about the fancy ones?"

"Oh, those. Look at this, Doctor." The priest picked up a box from the floor and pulled open the flaps. "These are from the late 1800s." He pulled out a sheaf of papers, many on parchment, some with delicate hand drawings and elegant script. "People drew up their own baptismal records in those days. Some are works of art. I'm not sure what to do with them."

Osborne reached for one, but even as he looked at it, his mind was leaping ahead to a much more contemporary question.

"So, if I give you a date right now, maybe just a month, can you locate the records as we stand here?"

"If we have those years completed," said Father Vodicka.

Osborne reached into his jacket pocket. He had slipped the folded dental record for the Bowers boy into his pocket early that morning to show Ray. He pulled it out. Yes, it had a birth date. What if Shanley were right? What if the boy had been born in the area? What if Ray was right, and the victim was connected to those triplets born so many years ago? It was a long shot, but anything is possible in a small town.

"Okay," said Osborne, "let's see March twenty-fifth." Then he gave the year.

"Good," said Wally, "I've got that year all done."

His fingers danced over the keyboard and he punched lightly with his forefinger several times.

"March twenty-fifth?"

"Right," said Osborne. His fatigue had disappeared. He felt wound up if not tense.

"Nothing for the twenty-fifth."

"Oh." Osborne's disappointment was obvious.

"Now, wait," said Father Vodicka, "that was a birth date, correct? Most Catholic parents had their babies baptized three weeks after the birth. Let's move up two to three weeks. . . ."

"We're looking for triplets," said Osborne.

"Triplets?" The priest's head and the student's eyes swung toward Osborne simultaneously.

"I know who you want," said Wally. "Here it is."

And it was: names, date, family.

"Now . . ." the student shifted forward in his chair, "here's an interesting piece we added to this particular record. Father Vodicka and I decided that the entire file should be input. So see this box? I'll move my cursor here and click on this like so. Voilà! Now you have the entire record that was attached to their certificates. Here, take my chair and sit down so you can read it."

Osborne moved much faster to sit than he had twenty minutes earlier to kneel.

As he read, Father Vodicka leaned over his shoulder. "I thought everyone had forgotten about this," the priest said softly. "Mother Superior kept it all quiet, you know. Only a few of us in the parish knew that the convent had taken in those children under such circumstances, but Mother Superior prided herself on running an unofficial adoption service that kept Catholic babies in Catholic homes. That's why the records are here, she took responsibility for those youngsters."

Sure enough, it was all there, straight from the nuns who'd brought the children to the priest for baptism. First, Mother Superior's note stating the local superstition that these "poor babes were considered 'evil angels' by their late mother . . . because of that some rather outspoken and unkind members of the church are insisting they not be baptized because it can't be proven that the deceased parents were, indeed, Roman Catholic . . . however, given their French-Canadian heritage, I believe there is no doubt of Catholicism," the good nun had said.

In addition to the note from the nun, the parents' death certificates showed cause of death to be suicide. These were followed on the screen by medical records from the hospital detailing the health exams of fraternal triplets, two boys and one girl. The attending physician noted simply that the children were healthy and normal in every respect with the exception of both males having undescended testes.

Finally, the names of the adoptive parents. There were two family names—the Bowers took one of the triplets, a boy, and Ruth Minor took the other two.

"Ruth Minor?" Osborne was stunned. The names of the babies surprised him, too: Charles William Minor and Judith Benjamin Minor. "I never heard of Ruth having adopted a brother and sister," said Osborne. "Never. She raised Judith Benjamin, and that's the only child I ever knew her to have in her home. Whatever happened to the third child?"

"You know, I'm not sure," said the priest. "This was Mother Superior's responsibility, and she kept things very hush-hush always. Quite a few young women from the area were able to have babies placed after they got into trouble, thanks to the good nuns. It was a woman's thing, and they didn't share much with me. The last of the nuns in that group passed away a few years ago, I'm afraid."

Osborne remembered Mother Superior well. She ran the convent and the priests with an iron hand. Father Vodicka had probably dedicated himself to staying out of her way.

"Let me try . . ." said Wally, punching the keys of the computer. He waited for a few moments, "No . . . these are the only records we have on those names," he said.

"Now, the Bowers name . . ." said Father Vodicka, "I remember that well. Mother Superior was most pleased with that adoption. The Cantrell family felt quite badly about the situation. I'm not sure why, but Mrs. Cantrell inquired personally. As it turned out, her sister was eager to adopt one of the children. She was in her early forties, and in those days, you know, it was very difficult to adopt if you were older. That child went to a very good home— out of town, of course."

Osborne decided to say nothing more. He had to get this information to Lew as soon as possible.

"We also kept this," said Father Vodicka. From the box with the beautiful, handwritten records, he pulled a dingy envelope. It contained a scrawled note from Herman Ebeling.

"I know this man," said Osborne. "We call him Herman the German. He's a hermit, lives out past McNaughton. Hasn't come to town in years."

"Oh? He's still alive?" Father Vodicka looked quite surprised. "I told someone recently that I was sure that person must be dead."

"To whom did you say that?" asked Osborne. "Did you mention Herman's name?"

Father Vodicka looked alarmed as if the tone in Osborne's voice was alerting him to something amiss. He thought hard for a minute.

"Judith Benjamin asked about the old man," said the priest. "At the time, I was standing outside the church, telling some folks about this fascinating discovery, but I couldn't remember the old gentleman's name. She didn't seem to want to get in touch with him, it was more a question of whether or not anyone knew if he was still living. No one knew anything. She asked me to let her know if I heard anything. You know Judith Benjamin, Doctor. She's at Mass every Sunday."

"Yes, I know her." Osborne decided not to say more. He certainly wasn't going to say another word about Herman until he knew what was going on.

"Father, if you don't mind, I'd like to discuss this with someone—a friend of mine—in law enforcement before you say anything to Judith. I am not in a position to explain why that is, but could you extend this courtesy for a few days?"

"Of course," said the priest, now clearly taken aback. "That was several weeks ago, and she hasn't pursued the matter, so I feel no obligation."

"Wally?" Osborne had noticed that the young programmer was all ears. "This entire discussion is confidential.

Agreed?" Wally nodded, his eyes large and serious. Osborne patted him supportively on the shoulder.

The note from Herman said two things. It attested to the Catholicism of the parents, and it stated that Herman would accept the guardianship of the triplets' older sibling.

"Do you have a record for this other child?" asked Osborne after absorbing the meaning of Herman's note.

"We should," said the priest, "since the nuns took the children in, all their records were kept—birth and medical."

"Do you have a name or a date?" asked Wally.

"Let's try the family's name," said Osborne.

The computer could find no more family members with the same name.

"Wait," interrupted Father Vodicka. "Look under Ebeling. I'm guessing that Mr. Ebeling might have had the child baptized in his name."

"Good idea," said Osborne, somewhat doubtfully.

The name came up instantly: Marie Ebeling.

"I wonder if that child has a medical record?" asked Osborne out loud, though the question was really for himself.

"Let's check," said Wally, clicking on a small box again.

"Sure enough," said Osborne, his voice soft and wondering, "looks like they had all the children examined at the same time. This one is one year older, female. Isn't this just the darnedest thing?"

"That's not bad, Dr. Osborne," said Wally, flipping his long hair out of the way and looking up at Osborne with wide brown eyes. "You should see some of the weird stuff in these records, like—"

"Now, now," interrupted Father Vodicka, "we have to keep quite of bit of this confidential. Wally, you must remember that."

Osborne looked at the priest.

"Oh, you can imagine," said Father Vodicka, "we have illegitimate children, fathers with names different from the mothers—that kind of thing."

"What about the baby that looked like a fish?" asked Wally. "That's the weirdest. They even got a picture of it in the file!"

The priest tried to ignore his assistant. Osborne could see he was trying to avoid the impression that he and Wally had been more than a little taken aback with their discoveries. "I don't think all the people in Loon Lake know exactly who their ancestors or siblings are . . . in all cases. And it is not our job to tell them."

He was beginning to look a little flustered, and Osborne restrained a chuckle. The demonstration had gone further than good Father Vodicka had planned.

eighteen

See how he throws his baited lines about,
And plays his mean as anglers play their trout.

O. W. Holmes, *The Barber's Secret*

"What time *is* it?" said Lew to no one in particular as she glanced down at her watch. Osborne looked at the wall clock in the small Rhinelander airport. The morning sky was lightening with sun and it looked like a lovely day was on its way.

"Seven-thirty—that Northwest flight'll be landing any moment now," said an elderly man, leaning on his cane beside them at the windows. Lew, Osborne, and Ray were clustered together before the expanse of glass overlooking the landing strip.

Osborne noticed all three of them were inhaling strong black coffee from the hospitality pot. He set his down on the sill, aware his hand was beginning to shake. He'd started the day with a pot of his own that he'd drunk with relish, sitting on his porch, catching up with the Sunday paper as Mike curled up beside him. Constantly nosing his master, the trusty black Lab made it clear he felt neglected.

But that was two hours ago. Right now, the three of them were still digesting the news that Osborne had delivered over more coffee at McDonald's an hour earlier. The meeting was the result of Lew refusing to let him continue when he'd called her at home late the night before.

"We're not discussing this on your damn party line," she'd said before Osborne had had an opportunity to pass along his discovery at the church. Following that, both of them heard two light clicks signaling guilty listeners. "Why on earth do you have a party line anyway?" Lew demanded. "That's like having every one of your phone calls taped. Don't tell me those old biddies down the road from you don't eavesdrop all day long!"

Osborne sighed resignedly and repeated what he said to his daughters at least once a month: "The phone company won't spend the money to rewire our end of the lake until every single household approves it. Right now, we have three of the thirty-five homes holding out because it'll increase their phone bills by twenty bucks a month. Lew, that's a lot of money for some folks, especially the retirees in the mobile home park over on Moens Lake."

So instead, they'd arranged to meet early for coffee, and Osborne had walked next door to alert Ray.

McDonald's was bustling, even at six A.M., but they were able to get a table apart from the crowd. Osborne delivered his news. It was quickly agreed that Lew would drop in on Judith Benjamin later that day not only to question her about Ted Bronk but see if she knew anything about Ruth Minor's other adopted child.

"Not that she'll enjoy chatting about Ruth," Lew had chuckled. "There's a few of us in town still think it was Judith who did the old lady in, even if she was only nine years old."

"Judith Benjamin is the only woman who ever beat me up," said Ray between bites of an Egg McMuffin. "Boy, was she a vicious bully when we were kids. She jumped me on the way home from kindergarten one day and kicked the bejesus outta me." Ray sat up straight, his eyes wide over his beard that held crumbs from the muffin. "I was only five years old. I think she was eleven or twelve. Boy, she was big even then. Was my mother mad! Whew!"

"Now, Ray. Tell us the truth. You had a reputation even at age five. I'm sure you gave her good reason, didn't you?" Lew's eyes crinkled with the tease.

Ray thought about it, pulling gently at his beard, finally tipping his trout hat back on his head as he thought her question over quite seriously. "I really don't know. I think she did it for sport."

"This *is* the flight she said to expect her on," said Osborne, repeating himself for about the tenth time. They were all three very anxious to meet the lawyer, get over to Wausau, and get an official ID on the body.

Just then, from behind, an authoritative but feminine voice called out, "Dr. Osborne? Dr. Paul Osborne?"

The three spun around to see a young woman with a cap of naturally curly darkish blond hair, held back from her face by a dark green scarf. She wore no makeup. Loudly she repeated Osborne's name. "Dr. Paul Osborne?" She had wide cheekbones in a squarish face, the cheekbones all the more noticeable because of the dark, serious eyes they emphasized. She was wearing jeans, hiking boots, and a forest green cotton duck jacket that featured more leather and brass knobs than Osborne had seen at the taxidermist's.

"I'm Dr. Osborne." Osborne stepped forward quickly, more than a little anxious. The woman spoke as if she might be a physician, some kind of professional. Had something happened to Erin or one of his grandchildren?

"Gee, that was easy." The young woman relaxed and smiled broadly, reaching out a hand to pump his with firm enthusiasm. "I'm Julie Rehnquist—Robert Bowers's lawyer. I'm so pleased to meet you. The people at the *Kansas City Star* couldn't say enough good things about you."

"But . . . Miss Rehnquist . . . I thought you were due in on this flight?" Osborne took in her appearance again, the jeans, a T-shirt, and the heavy hunter's jacket. This young woman a lawyer? He guessed her to be in her thirties, though she had a brightness to her eyes and manner that made her look even younger.

"I flew to Mosinee and drove up late yesterday afternoon," said Julie, extending her hand to Ray and Lew in turn.

"Pleased," said Ray, ducking his head to ceremoniously remove his stuffed trout, bow slightly, return the hat to his head, and then, with a bashful grin on his face that Osborne had never seen before, say absolutely nothing. Ray without a quip and a bad joke on meeting a new person? Osborne raised an eyebrow.

Lew was not so restrained. "Quite a surprise, Miss Rehnquist—or is it Mrs.?" She fired her words off in what Osborne now recognized was her getting-down-to-business style. "But it's good you're here and we'll get the worst over quickly. But how did you get a flight so soon? Charter one? Those flights into Mosinee are always oversold."

If Julie was taken aback by Lew's directness, she didn't show it. She chuckled instead, a disarming chuckle that made her seem instantly likable.

"I'm sorry, I'm one of those terrible type A's that rise at the crack of dawn," said Julie. "I like to get an early start. After I heard from Dr. Osborne, I thought I'd like to get this investigation underway ASAP. And since the weather was so lovely yesterday, why not just get going? I said to myself, 'If they've got the nerve to call it God's country up there, then get your rear in gear and see it in all its glory! So I corralled my trusty travel agent at home on Sunday and demanded she book me or lose the firm's business." Osborne assumed she was kidding, but he wasn't sure.

As Julie talked, Lew marshaled the group out of the airport and down the road toward her car. The air outside was cool but continuing to turn into a sunny, crisply clear Monday morning.

"Oh, one other factor," said Julie, "I really wanted to get the lay of the land up here, and I thought you all might be pretty busy, so I just figured I'd do it on my own. I found the neatest little bed-and-breakfast place as I drove in yesterday—"

"We only have one close to Loon Lake," said Lew, still clipping her words, "you must be checked in at Cranberry Hill in Rhinelander?"

"No," said Julie, "I'm out on a lake at a place called Marjorie's Bed and Breakfast. It's rather . . . rustic . . . but cozy. I saw a sign on Highway 8 after I missed a turn coming into town and blew by Loon Lake. I was doubling back when I saw the sign. Maybe genteelly shabby would be a kinder description of the place, but I like it. I'm quite comfortable there."

"That's interesting," said Ray as he folded his lanky frame into the backseat of Lew's sedan alongside Osborne. "That place and the area around it always reminds me of something out of *Deliverance*." He looked at Osborne and Lew. "I know I'm repeating myself, but there is no better description of that lovely neighborhood. You know, Miss Rehnquist, we do have backwoods types that eat their own around here. Not rednecks, human mutants."

Before Julie could say anything, Ray went on in a kinder tone, "You wanted to get the lay of the land? Or you wanted to check things out without all of us leaning over your shoulder?" His point was unmistakable: He didn't believe her. And he wasn't going to let her off the hook.

"Is something wrong?" Julie looked from face to face.

"Who knows? Certainly something's very wrong when

you have four murder victims," said Lew with a shrug
and a very businesslike tone in her voice. Her eyes were
as hard as the twist she gave the key in the ignition.

Lew looked over at Julie in the seat beside her, "But
you're the one who said one thing and did another—so
you tell me." Without waiting for an answer, Lew said,
"We're heading over to the State Crime Lab in Wausau,
and we've got an hour's drive ahead of us. We'll leave
your car here and be back to pick it up later. That is," she
said with exaggerated politeness, "if that's all right with
you? On the other hand, maybe you'd prefer to drive
down alone."

To Osborne's ear, Lew's message was unmistakable: if
you think you're going to take the lead on this investigation, then go it alone, babe. Osborne felt like the odd
man out; his gut instinct was to like the young woman.
Right now, he felt a little sorry for her.

"Oh, no, I'm with you," said Julie, again with a smile.
Only this time Osborne noticed that her eyes stayed serious over the gently smiling lips. "So . . ." She turned
around from where she sat in the front seat to face Ray
sitting immediately behind her. "You're a detective with
the police department?"

"Not exactly," Lew interrupted as she swerved the car
onto Highway 17 and tromped her foot on the accelerator.
"Both Dr. Osborne and Ray are filling in as deputies on
this case. I'm the Loon Lake chief of police. We had a
big designer drug bust outside Wausau two weeks ago that
pulled two of my regular team off for duty on that, then
a senior deputy has been hospitalized with pneumonia for
a few days. Dr. Osborne's forensic skills have been *very*
appreciated, and no one knows this region like Ray. Ray's
a jack-of-all-trades and probably the best hunting and fishing guide you can find—when he's sober. Right, Ray?"

"Lew?" Ray made no effort to conceal his annoyance,
"I thought we had a deal. . . ."

Julie kept her eyes on the road straight ahead. Osborne

wondered if she felt like she was in the middle of an argument in a highly dysfunctional family.

"We do, Ray." It was Lew's turn to look back at him. "We do. Ray knows everybody who's anybody and everyone who's not. Do you want to let Julie in on your secret?"

There was a silence in the car. Finally, Ray leaned forward in the seat and lowered his voice behind Julie's head, "I dig graves on the side."

"You're kidding!" Julie spun around with a laugh.

"No, he's not," said Lew with a slight smile. "Between the three of us, we got 'em covered—the living and the dead." Then she chuckled. Later, Osborne thought that was the play that won the game: Lew's chuckle broke the tension and, for the first time, signaled that Lew might consider cooperation.

"What do you do in the winter when the ground is frozen?" asked Julie with genuine curiosity.

"Besides getting busted for smoking dope while ice fishing—" interjected Lew.

"Jeez, Lew, ease up! Now that's a go-o-od question," said Ray to Julie. "Very few people think ahead to ask me questions like that. Actually, I do quite a bit. I shovel snow for some of the commercial establishments in town—the bank, the pub. Other odd jobs—the outdoor stuff. Up here you can make a modest living shoveling snow off rooftops for three to four months."

"I see." Julie was thoughtful. "What did your father do?"

Now it was Ray's turn to look taken aback. "He was a surgeon."

She turned around to look at him again, her eyes shifted to Osborne and then to Lew. This time, the eyes stayed dark and the mouth didn't smile. "What we are really discussing here is that things are not always as they seem. Right? That Ray can track in the world of humans as easy as in the wilderness?"

Again there was silence in the car, and Osborne marveled at the communication that was taking place between the law officer, the undercover agent, and the lawyer who was making it clear she was no dummy. She knew that no one was being totally honest, including herself, but what little Lew and Ray were saying was, at least, true.

"I'm real curious," said Ray. "Why are you so convinced your client was murdered?"

Now Julie stared straight ahead, eyes glued to the highway. "Because I know exactly who did it. Don't underestimate me. I have a lot at stake in this case, and I am not bullshitting around. You're right, of course. I came up early to do some of my own checks. I'm staying at that weird little place because Robert Bowers stayed there once, and I want to know why. Why would a multimillionaire stay in such shabby little resort?

"I know it's close to property he inherited from the Cantrell side of his family. I like that proximity because I have a hunch that I have a better chance of running into someone who might know something." She was quiet for a moment, still watching the road ahead. "You know, it's too bad those other people had to die, because Robert was the real target."

"Really?" said Ray. "You're sure of that?"

"Oh quite. I'll tell you who did it, too. I was introduced to him as Brad Kirsch, an antique silver dealer," said Julie. "He also goes by the name Fred Shepard. Fred Shepard is a known silver thief who operates out of Las Vegas. He's very canny, and he always works with a woman. But . . ." Julie paused as if trying to remember something she'd forgotten, then she gave a shrug and smile. "I guess I'd rather talk about Robert, if you don't mind?"

"Shoot," said Lew. "Doc, since I'm driving, would you please take notes for me?" She handed him a long, narrow notebook, spiral-bound at the top. Osborne flipped it open, past pages filled with a neat, slightly slanted script. Random phrases or entire lines were sometimes highlighted in yellow. He could see that Lew was meticulously well-organized. A little unnerved by her careful attention to detail, he tried to write as quickly as Julie talked so as not to miss anything. Fortunately, Julie seemed more relaxed, and her story unfolded at an easy pace as the police car sped toward Wausau.

nineteen

Bait the hook well; this fish will bite.

Shakespeare, *Much Ado About Nothing*

"**My** father was a psychiatrist at Menninger's and old Mrs. Bowers brought Robert to Dad for therapy when he was fourteen. She trusted Dad, so when he wanted to bring Robert home to spend time with our family—there were five of us kids—that was fine.

"I was a little tyke and always thought of Robert as one of my big brothers. I never knew there was anything wrong with him. That was Dad's point: if Robert had a chance to build a sense of self-esteem before the social taboos set in, maybe he'd be strong enough to make it as a whole human being, even though his body was so different from everyone else's."

"What exactly was wrong with him?" asked Lew.

"As a young child, he had been absolutely beautiful. Delicate features, big eyes with long, long lashes, lovely, soft skin. A stunning-looking child, the kind that's always picked to play the angel in school plays. The problem was that at the age of fourteen he was *still a beautiful child.*

"Delayed puberty turned him into a Dresden doll instead of a growing boy. He went from being the perfect child and everyone's pet to the runt of the class—picked on, made fun of, everything that happens to you when you're so different from everyone else. I don't know if it was that or body chemistry or what, but Robert was suffering from severe clinical depression by the time Mrs. Bowers brought him to Dad.

"No one knew what to do. They tried giving him shots of testosterone to bring on puberty, but he had severe reactions to the medication, so they had to stop. I don't know all the details. I do know that in his late teens, they found something to work—at least he grew to normal height, but his body never developed the way a boy's should. Even as a grown man, for example, he never had to shave, and he put on weight like a woman does, in his hips and lower torso.

"But bright! Robert was smart and good and kind, a thoughtful, sensitive person. He was also a very pleasant-looking man. He never lost those lovely, gentle features.

"My older brothers and I, we all loved Robert. He'd come for weekends, and he came all one summer to stay with us. Then Mrs. Bowers did something that my father urged her not to do. She sent him to an elite prep school on the East Coast. I think it was Choate. Maybe he was there for a month. Not much longer. Dad got a call in the middle of the night and flew out there to get Robert. Something terrible had happened to him. I never knew what exactly, but I can imagine.

"Dad kept him at Menninger's through high school and, I believe, most of the college years. He came by the house sometimes, but I was all wrapped up in my own life and really didn't pay too much attention.

"I got married in college, divorced in law school, worked for a New York law firm for nearly ten years. I moved back to Kansas City three years ago. Mrs. Bowers was ninety-seven years old and fading fast. One afternoon, Dad gave me a call and asked me to meet with Robert.

"I hadn't seen him in nearly fifteen years. He asked me to meet him out south at the big house. Robert had never married and he lived there with Mrs. Bowers and a house-keeper. He wanted to see me for advice, relative to the effect on the estate, on whether to donate Mrs. Bowers's magnificent antique English silver collection to the Nelson-Atkins Museum in Kanas City or to Yale University. Mrs. Bowers had received a letter from an antiques dealer who bought for very wealthy collectors, and that individual was coming into Kansas City to meet with Robert.

"That's when I met Brad Kirsch. I thought he made a rather curious dealer. . . ."

"In what way?" asked Lew.

"To begin with, he had the social skills of a spider—at least with women," said Julie. "He would be so charming in a social scene, then bait you in a subtle way and thoroughly enjoy making you look like a fool. Always in front of a crowd. When it came to business, I couldn't get straight answers out of him on financial details. He was a master at putting me off. For weeks.

"Meanwhile, two things happened: Mrs. Bowers died, leaving Robert sole heir to a fortune worth seven hundred and fifty million dollars. Two weeks after her death, while Robert was off on a business trip, the house was robbed of almost the entire silver collection. Actually, he was on one of these YPO trips when it happened."

"How long ago was this?" asked Lew.

"I have a question—sorry to interrupt, Lew," said Ray. "This antique dealer—what did Robert think of him?"

"That's what was so difficult," said Julie. "Robert liked him. He trusted him. Apparently they had some soul-to-soul talks, and Brad had some elaborate story how he had been abused as a child, so Robert felt all this sympathy for him. I think it was a big fat lie, but at that point, I couldn't say so. Brad was gay, and he made like he'd been discriminated against for that, too.

"Anyway, Robert trusted him, and I didn't, but I couldn't come out and say so. It was so bad that when I called a few of his supposed clients and they had never heard of him—I couldn't tell Robert. I was going to be the bad guy for telling the truth. Get the picture? This had become an absurd situation and, I know now, a very dangerous one."

"Do you think that Robert and this Brad had a relationship?" asked Osborne.

"On the surface you might think so," said Julie. "Certainly Grant Moore thinks they did. But I don't."

"How can you be so sure?" asked Lew.

"I asked Robert, and he said no, and I believe him," said Julie. "He said he felt great affection for Brad, but not a sexual attraction."

"What does this Brad guy look like?" asked Ray.

"He's a small man. Pudgy, just short of being a real tub. He has a round face, white, white hair. Very thick and bushy. Too bushy—I think he wears a piece. He is exceptionally fair-skinned and always flushed in the cheeks. For lack of a better description, he looks like Santa Claus."

"So the silver was stolen. Anything else taken?" asked Lew.

"Well . . . I think so," said Julie. "Brad said he had a written approval from Robert to pack up all his art and send it to Brad. Supposedly, Brad was assembling an international art exhibit featuring works owned by YPO members. All very hoity-toity and very hush-hush. Not a public exhibit, you see, but one for YPO members *only*."

"Interesting," said Ray. "Was everything sent off?"

"Yes, it was," said Julie. "I think Brad has stolen the art. The Bowers family has . . . *had* . . ." Julie seemed to correct herself with effort, "some very fine pieces, about ten in total. A complete folio of original Audubon prints, which is priceless today. Several Impressionist paintings, including a Monet. Robert himself had two phenomenal early Georgia O'Keefe watercolors that are museum quality. Mrs. Bowers was given them by her uncle, who lived next to O'Keefe in New York years and years ago. He pulled them out of the trash."

"Serious capital gains on those babies," chuckled Ray.

"You know art?" Julie's voice did not disguise her complete surprise that Ray would have the vaguest idea what she was talking about.

"Just because I trap leeches doesn't mean I'm uncivilized," said Ray, ever so slightly petulant.

"Ray's older sister has one of the finest Japanese print collections in the country," said Osborne. "She and her husband also collect some large paintings—Ray, who's the artist?"

"Helen Frankenthaler."

"I see," said Julie. "Serious collectors."

Lew interrupted again. "What else was missing. Any other valuables?"

"I have a list," said Julie. "Robert and I had inventoried his mother's estate for probate purposes. I kept a separate list of Robert's properties so there would be no confusion. I would ballpark the value of the missing art and several pieces of jewelry to be well above five million dollars. Not the silver. It was an exceptional European collection, but the police and I agree that the pieces were probably melted down within hours of the heist."

"Have you run a check on Brad Kirsch?" asked Lew.

"Of course," said Julie, obviously pleased to be asked and quite willing to share her findings. "Yes. He is listed as a member of all the professional antique and art dealer associations, which is how he gets his leads on collections to rob. There were reports filed suspecting him of theft, but no one has ever nailed him.

"When I called the Las Vegas police to check the profile of the silver thief, Fred Shepard, I hit pay dirt. Shepard's photo matched Brad. No question. Unfortunately, I did not run these checks until after Robert was gone. By that time, Brad was gone. The only clue I had that he might be up this way was the new house."

"The new house?" Osborne, Lew, and Ray exclaimed simultaneously. "What new house?"

"Robert wrote me a lovely letter the day ... several weeks ago," said Julie, starting to say one thing and looking again as though she was trying to remember something. "I have it at home, but I'll send you a copy. In it, he describes a beautiful log home he was having built up here on property formerly owned by the Cantrell trust and part of his mother's estate. It has its own private lake. Did I tell you he had taken up fly-fishing? Brad was helping to design the interior. Robert planned to move his favorite paintings and art objects up here."

"Where is this?" asked Osborne, curious she hadn't mentioned the home earlier.

"I don't know," said Julie. "He said it was in a hidden wilderness area with trout streams nearby, but he never told me where exactly. When he left Kansas City the last time, he said that he would be at a YPO retreat, then stop to see how work was going on the house. The house was supposed to be a surprise of a certain sort."

Julie sighed deeply. "If I sound matter-of-fact about this, it's only because I have reached a point of complete despair. I just ... I see so many ways I might have been able to stop Robert had I just been more alert to what was happening." She sighed again and dropped her face into her hands.

Ray patted her on the shoulder. "What makes you think you sound matter-of-fact? You sound like someone who's lost a very close friend." Everyone in the car was silent for a few minutes as they sped toward Wausau.

Finally, Lew broke the silence. "I checked my fishing maps yesterday. Ray?" She didn't take her eyes off the road, but she made sure she had Ray's attention.

"My geographical surveys are from 1955, and I went over the area real carefully up behind Moen Lake, Stella

Lake, Angelo, looked over by the Nelson and Brown Landings; I followed the Gudegast way north and over to the right by Hutchinson Creek. I drew a triangle between Moen, Mud, and Shepard Lakes. Nothing. No lake. Totally different terrain from what we found yesterday. I don't understand. What do you think? The new surveys were just finished, and we won't have new maps for another six months."

"Could you see where the old Cantrell plant might have emptied into Crescent Creek, flushing down toward Lake Kecheewaishke?"

"Yep. On the maps. But that's not what we saw yesterday. The maps show swamp, some high ground—they don't show another lake."

"Beaver," said Ray. "Must be beavers."

"Explain to Julie what you mean by that," suggested Osborne.

"We have a bounty on beavers up here," said Ray, "because they'll go in, build their dams, and reroute the creeks and streams that feed the lakes. One dam can drown or parch several thousand acres, completely devastate entire forests and lakes. Lew, you know who remembers that area real well is old Herman the German. Let me talk to him about it. He might remember when the terrain changed."

"I sent one of my deputies over to the county clerk's to check deeds and titles," said Lew. "We might find something on file."

"I doubt it," offered Osborne. "If I were Bowers and I owned that land and I found I had a nice little unregistered lake on it, I wouldn't make waves. Hell, the DNR'll come in and tell you where and how to build. Whoever put that house in there—with a boathouse that big—has violated more than a few lakefront regulations. No need to register a building on property no one knows is lakefront unless you have to."

"I've been thinking about the building itself," said Ray.

"It reminds me of something, but I can't put my finger on it. Something strikes me as very familiar, but I'm not sure what exactly."

"What building are you all talking about?" asked Julie. "Do you mind my asking?"

"Well," said Lew thoughtfully as she drove, "I think we may have found Robert's surprise." Neither Osborne nor Ray contradicted her.

"Let me repeat this, and see if I read the coroner's report correctly," said Julie, three and a half hours later as they waited for their lunch orders at the Loon Lake Pub. "Those bodies sank like rocks in the icy water and didn't decompose because the temperature stayed below thirty-eight degrees, which is why they have no easy way to set time of death. But they do know that they didn't die in the water. They froze to death but not in the water. But . . . they can't explain *how* if not in the water. Right?"

"You've repeated that six times now," said Ray, tempering his words with a pull on his beard and a gentle grin. "Repetition does not lead to change."

"The Wausau lab doesn't have the staff and know-how to tell us more." Lew ignored Ray as Julie gave him a look of mock irritation. Osborne could see she was quite charmed by Ray's fishin'-huntin' old-man-of-the-forest persona. "I'm not sure we can't get some better results elsewhere," said Lew, "but I've gotta work the politics and the logistics, and this is a small town with a modest budget for these kinds of things."

"I understand," said Julie. Osborne was liking her more as the day went on. She was a direct, no-nonsense type of person. He noticed that Ray, too, was responding very seriously to her queries and, a first for Ray, not teasing her with the put-downs that he used on most women, including Donna. Ray had once told him that Donna wouldn't marry him because "she makes more money than me and she doesn't want to put up with my bullshit."

He wasn't even trying the latter on Julie. Lew, on the other hand, still seemed edgy, almost rude at times.

Julie excused herself from the table just then to use the ladies' room. With her gone, it was the first time since the airport that the three of them could talk alone.

"She's got quite an agenda," said Lew, bending low to take a sip of her coffee the minute Julie was out of earshot. "I'd sure like to know what it is."

"What makes you think it's any different from ours?" asked Ray, picking at the parsley that rested between his cheeseburger and the French fries. "Don't we all want the same thing?"

"Her reaction to the body was a little stronger than she wanted us to think," said Lew. "She's being very professionally casual, but I have to believe that we have something beyond the usual client/lawyer relationship here. She hid it well, but I saw it in her hands. She was trembling during that ID. She almost lost it.

"And why did she get up here early and not call us? That's very strange. Given that she's a lawyer and knows better—it's inexcusable. No, she's got something going on, and I want to know what it is before we share any more information."

"For all we know," said Ray thoughtfully, "she may have had something to do with the murders. I mean, we don't know who she is beyond what that reporter told you, Doc, right?"

"The reporter seemed to trust her," said Osborne, wiping his face with his napkin. He felt an unreasonable urge to support Julie. He paused, thinking over every word that had been said in the calls to Kansas City. "He described her as being quite feisty and very sure that Bowers had been murdered. You two may be judging her a little harshly."

"Sssh." Ray looked over Lew's shoulder. "Here she comes."

Julie slid into the booth beside Dr. Osborne. All she

had ordered was a bowl of chicken noodle soup, and it was steaming in front of her. But she made no move to pick up the spoon. Instead, keeping her eyes on the table and avoiding theirs, she crossed her arms and began to talk.

"I, um, I need to tell you something." She pressed her lips tightly together as if steeling herself. "It's very, very confidential and something that I haven't shared with people back in Kansas City."

She inhaled and exhaled deeply. "In fact, only my parents know. Robert and I were to be married." Even in the bustling little pub, her words managed to carve a huge circle of absolute silence in the air above their table.

Finally, Lew lifted her fork, cut into a canned peach resting on the plate in front of her, and asked softly, "That was going to be a little difficult to consummate, wouldn't you say?"

Osborne resisted shaking his head. Why did he always find himself around women who went straight to the point? He caught Ray's eye and saw a clear signal to keep his mouth shut. It was Lew's turn to pass or fumble.

"As I told you, I have known Robert for many years," said Julie. "In doing business together, we found our way back to the relationship we'd had as kids. We found that we shared a lot of the same ways of looking at things, that we really were the best of friends. That a deep, close friendship may be . . . what we all want most out of life.

"So . . ." She sighed again. "That may explain to you why I must know how and when he died and if he suffered. I must know these things."

Julie looked down, then away at the bustling room for a brief moment, then back to the three of them.

"To answer your question, Lew . . ." Her hands rested palms down on the table as she looked directly into Lew's eyes and Lew stared back at her. "I firmly believe, I know from experience, that marriage is about many things between two people. Sex may not always be first on the list." Her voice had faltered ever so slightly as she spoke.

"You see, Robert had all this money and no family. All he really wanted in this world was love and light and life—not money. He would gladly have traded every nickel of his wealth just to have family. He wanted children. We planned to adopt. Alone, he would find it difficult; together, we could have a real family. I wanted this, too. We had all these plans. . . . Then, when he disappeared, I thought maybe he'd just changed his mind and didn't have the heart to tell me."

Suddenly, the hands that had been resting on the table dove into her lap for her paper napkin and brought it swiftly to her eyes. Pressing the napkin against her eyes with both hands, she gave a soft sob.

What happened next just broke Osborne's heart. The sob gave way to weeping. A weeping from so deep inside the woman that he wondered if Julie had cried at all before this.

"I think she truly had hoped she might find him alive," he said to Ray later. Osborne knew he was right. He knew now that she had stayed at the B-and-B, hoping that Robert was hiding out close by.

But at that moment in the Loon Lake Pub, all that Osborne, Lew, and Ray could do was sit there dumbfounded. Five minutes passed. During that time, Lew would periodically tear a bunch of paper napkins from the metal container and pass them across the table to Julie. When people at a neighboring booth glanced over curiously, Lew returned their glances with a stony stare. Finally, the storm eased. Julie wiped her nose and smiled wanly. "I'll be okay," she said.

"All right, dear," said Lew, in a motherly tone. "You need to finish your soup. Everyone—eat lunch. We'll talk about all this later."

Relieved, Osborne bit into his first French fry and discovered he was famished.

twenty

A lake is the landscape's most beautiful and expressive feature. It is earth's eye; looking into which the beholder measures the depth of his own nature.

Henry David Thoreau

As the four of them walked out the front door of the pub after lunch, Osborne could feel his French dip sandwich hit his drowse button. That plus the fact it was nearly two, the usual time for his thirty-minute nap. Nor did it help that the April day had turned heavy and gray, a dismal bank of slate-hued clouds spreading their bad humor across Main Street, making the modest little shopping district look like a dingy used car lot.

They all paused, pulled their jackets tight to keep out the chill, thrust hands into pockets, and looked blankly at one another. Then Julie, whose color had improved one hundred percent since finishing her soup, piped up that she wanted to meet old Herman the German.

Ray immediately offered to drive her out to McNaughton to see him. "C'mon, Doc, you too."

"Okay, okay, I know I better join you." Osborne agreed reluctantly to go along, torn between the urge to nap or to see Herman and Marie, a sight much more significant now that he knew the history behind their relationship. He was curious to see if there was any physical resemblance between Marie and the corpse. "But I want to leave Mike in Erin's backyard. If you don't mind following me over there, I'll drop off my car and drive with you."

"Me, too," said Julie. "Shall we take my car out to Herman's?"

"I'd rather not," said Ray. "If you don't mind getting squashed in my pickup, I think Herman will be a little more relaxed if he thinks you two are with me and we just dropped in while scouting some good fishing spots. Whenever he thinks he's helping me make a good impression on future guiding customers, he's always a little more forthcoming."

"Ray's right," said Osborne. "We should keep everything looking as normal as possible. Not," he added, "that I think Ray's one-door special is normal." He winked at Julie. "You realize anyone who rides with Ray enters his truck through the window—unless he grants a special dispensation and lets you use his door."

Lew nodded in agreement with their plan and said she needed to get back to her office to return phone calls and prepare for the meeting with Judith Benjamin at four.

"I've got to call the mayor after that," she said. "We've got a board meeting this week, and I'm up to my ears in paperwork now that I have a confirmed ID on the Bowers body."

"I'm planning to stay in town for another few days," said Julie. "I have to set up some meetings with lawyers and bankers here to settle details of the estate properties located up here. How can we all best stay in touch?"

"Call me anytime," said Lew. "Lucy on the switchboard will patch you through to wherever I am. Let's all meet tomorrow morning back here at the pub . . . around eight?"

Lew motioned to Osborne as she started to walk away,

and he stepped over so she could talk to him privately. "Doc, I'd like to meet with you and Ray after I see Judith Benjamin. Think you two would mind stopping by my office around seven this evening?" Osborne nodded. He found it interesting that Lew was putting a few controls on how much she wanted Julie to know.

They pulled up in front of Erin's house, Julie and Ray following Osborne in their respective cars.

"Wow," said Julie, stepping out of her rental car, "what a house!" She stopped and looked up, exclaiming to no one in particular: "Look at the detail in those wooden arches above the front porch and along the roofline—it's so delicate."

Ray overheard her as he walked toward them. "I like all the shades of cream and white," he said, then pointed, "See how the lighter colors offset the shades of yellow and green lining the windows and the porch railings?"

Julie nodded admiringly.

"I'm glad you like it," said Ray. "I painted all that."

"Another one of your odd jobs? In between graves?" Julie grinned.

"Yep. Last spring. I painted all the trim, and I was personally responsible for gutting the three bathrooms," said Ray. "With some help from Erin and Mark," he hastily added, bowing to Osborne who was about to protest, remembering well the long hours all three had put in on the project. Ray did have a talent for exaggeration, thought Osborne with some irritation. But Ray seemed to sense Osborne's criticism, as he also said quickly, lest Julie think he was taking any other credit for the loveliness of the house, "I may not be the best carpenter, mason, or plumber around, but I can sure take a place apart."

"I'm impressed," said Julie. "This home is as authentic and as pretty as any I've ever seen in San Francisco!"

Osborne's fatherly heart warmed at her praise but, at the same time, he was finding it a little odd that Erin had left her front door wide open. Leaving Julie and Ray to wait on the sidewalk, Osborne locked Mike into the side yard and ran up the front porch stairs. He knocked on the open door, saying loudly, "Hel-l-o-o, anybody home?"

He stepped into the living room. Cool afternoon breezes had chilled the house. But neither Erin nor the baby responded. His two elder grandchildren were in school, he knew. Their father was sure to be at his office.

"Erin?" he called again, but there was no answer. Osborne gave up. He ran back down the stairs, made sure the gate in the fence was secure, and left the dog barking in the backyard, confident Mike would quiet down after they drove off.

Julie asked about Lew as the truck bounced the back roads toward Herman's place. Since Osborne was sitting against the door and had closed his eyes in obedience to the overwhelming sense of drowsiness that had crept over him again, Julie's questions were directed to Ray.

"She's one smart cookie and a hell of a fly-fisherman, not bad when it comes to muskies either," he said to Julie. "Tough to get much past old Lew. She may know more than I do about everyone in Loon Lake."

"I didn't know Lew was that good a muskie fisherman," said Osborne, surprised, even in his semialert state, at the compliment Ray paid the older woman.

"Oh-h, yes!" Ray's eyebrows went up four notches. "She won the Hodag Muskie Festival over in Rhinelander about eight, maybe ten, years ago. Doc, you didn't know that? Hey, she's the one talked me into that surface Bobbie Bait doctored up with red nail polish. She swears by it! I've been disappointed she's been so into fly-fishing for the last couple years. Jeez, Doc, I never told you but three, four years ago, she was one of my best leech customers for walleye. Don't you ever tell her I said so, but Lew may be one of the best bait fishermen I've come across."

"And you're the expert," offered Osborne with a wink at Julie.

"Damn right," said Ray. With that, he reached behind Julie's head for his trout hat and crammed it on his head, the top of it grazing the roof of the cramped cab.

"Ray's the name, muskie's my game," he said to Julie. Osborne recognized Ray's lead into a lengthy discourse on muskellunge and its kin, so he closed his eyes again and tried to nestle into the lumpy truck door for a quick, hopefully unnoticed, snooze.

"I know a little about fly-fishing, but muskie?" he heard Julie ask. "Aren't those pretty big fish? What's the biggest *you've* caught, Ray?"

"Fifty-two inches, thirty-three pounds. Nice fish. Mounted and manages the household."

Julie laughed. "If I'm up here for a few days, think you'd have the time to take me out to try it?"

"How 'bout tonight?"

"Oh. Isn't it a little too cool and wet?" Julie's enthusiasm suddenly grew tentative.

"This is quintessential muskie weather," said Ray. "A little coolness in the air up top pulls the mothers up from the thermocline."

"The what?" asked Julie.

"The thermocline—the band of water sandwiched between the upper layer, which warms during the day, and the very bottom of the lake, which remains quite cold and dark," explained Ray. "That middle layer, the thermocline, that's where the big boys hang out."

"Do muskies attack people?" asked Julie.

"Once in a while," said Ray, leading her on.

"Not in twenty years," offered Osborne dryly from his snooze position. "Even then, the story they tell of some woman tourist dangling her toes over a diving raft and getting pulled under is an urban legend. Never happened."

Osborne looked over Julie's head toward Ray's smiling, relaxed face. He wondered if this little tease over big fish could be the start of something between the two.

And then he thought of Lew's nut-brown, intense eyes and imagined her standing tall in his fishing boat, flipping her wrist expertly as her lure arced high and far, cutting sweetly through the air, then landing with a whisper on the water.

How very interesting that she didn't tell him she was an experienced muskie fisherman. Was this her way of letting him lead for a change? He hoped so. It was a dance he knew he would enjoy. Now he would make sure to take her out in his boat—and soon.

He wondered if she had such expert control that she could be reeling in even before that lure hit. Now, that would be something. A woman with that kind of control? He doubted she was *that* good. On the other hand, given Ray's opinion and her fly casting technique . . . you never know. He'd better get some practice in before he got her in the boat. Getting upstaged in the trout stream was one thing, he'd grant her the edge there. But over his own weed bed? No sirree.

The truck sped toward Herman's. Osborne closed his eyes against the glare of the late afternoon sun, letting the murmur of Julie's and Ray's voices lull him into a hazy daydream of Lew on a lake, casting, reeling, and casting again.

In the dream, Lew's bait is taken suddenly and pulled deep, deep into the water. He watches her play the line out, then jerk her rod to set the hooks deep in the muskie's jaw. She shifts her feet and hunches her shoulders for the fight. He's in the boat with her, gaff and net ready. They work together: he steadying the boat as she plays the big fish. When the fish is close enough to thrash along the side of the boat, he readies the gaff to hook it with his left arm, net it with the right. "Yours!" cries Lew. The moment is right, and he stands to reach forward—

"Well, I'll be, Herman's expecting us." Ray's voice shook Osborne from his daydream as they pulled into the ruts beside Herman's cabin. The old man was indeed standing out in the grassy area that passed for a yard. The clouds and the towering white pines that hung over Herman's beat-up old shack made the day seem darker and later than it was. Hunks of fabric hung in his windows, and a rusted old bicycle rested against the outside wall near the front door. Osborne had first seen this shack thirty years ago, and he didn't think a single detail had changed. Same old bike, same old raggedy curtains in the windows. Same old Herman.

Herman waved and walked slowly toward them as they piled out of the truck. It always struck Osborne whenever he first saw the old man that his skin was as black brown as the tree trunks around him. Black brown and creased even blacker.

Herman's wasn't a dirt like the soiled, grimy surfaces caused by food and lack of cleanliness. His was the black dirt of tilled soil from his vast truck garden. It was the dark dust that floated up from ditches that he drove through on his ancient tractor. It was a dirt permanently imbedded in his skin, maybe even his veins. Mary Lee used to threaten their kids saying, "If you don't rub that washcloth hard, you'll stay as dirty as old Herman the German." It never occurred to her that Herman seemed rather happy in his dirt.

And he looked happy today, though hunching and shuffling toward them under the weight of the blackened old brown tweed overcoat he wore winter and summer, it struck Osborne the odd figure might fit Julie's image of Rumplestilskin—or an overdressed crab. Under the grimy, green plaid Scottish golfer's hat that he'd worn for all the years that Osborne had known him, the grizzled, rough-bearded face parted in a smile. Of course, he wasn't wearing his teeth. Osborne grimaced and said what he always said when he greeted Herman: "All that time and money, Herman, all that time and money."

Julie was charmed. She extended her hand to shake

Herman's and gave him a warm smile. Then she stepped back as Ray leaned down to put his arm around the old man's shoulders.

"Herman, you old coot. You never told me you adopted Marie. I thought she was your natural daughter."

"Hmm, ymmm."

Ray could understand him, but Osborne couldn't. As Herman and Ray exchanged friendly mumbles, Osborne walked Julie over to Herman's vegetable garden. The long, raised beds had been freshly tilled, and the soil was a deep, deep black. Osborne whistled at the sight.

"You don't see rich loam like this very often, Julie." He knelt to grab a handful and rubbed it between his fingers. "See how fine it crumbles? Herman's been working leaf mold into this for fifty years, I'll bet. A number of years ago, back when I made his bridges for him, he offered to pay me in fresh corn, tomatoes, raspberries, little tiny new potatoes, and pumpkins for five years. Best deal I ever made," said Osborne, keeping an eye on the conversation between Ray and Herman. He reached for another handful. "I'll tell ya, this soil is pure gold."

"This is good country, isn't it," said Julie quietly. Then the two of them stood and waited in silence, their hands thrust into their pockets and a crisp wind blowing against their faces.

Finally, Ray turned toward them and hollered, "C'mon, he's gonna take us out to Marie's place so Julie can meet her."

They followed the old man down a well-worn path that took them west across his front yard where they passed a decrepit shed with its roof caved in. On the far side of the shed, a wooden canoe, turned upside down, rested on sawhorses. That struck Osborne as a little strange: He knew of no water close by, and the old man's battered truck wasn't going to pull a trailer of any kind. Someone appeared to be working on the canoe. It looked as though it had been hand-sanded and given several coats of varnish. Now, that was very interesting: Osborne could see the boat was an antique. *Antique and valuable,* he thought, keeping his opinion to himself.

"Well, hey, this could turn into something nice," said Ray, stopping to look over the canoe. He gave the boat an affectionate pat. "Is this Marie's work?" he shouted at Herman who was a little hard of hearing. The old man nodded. "Marie's one talented carpenter," said Ray to his friends. "She made my kitchen cabinets, y'know."

The path continued through a field a brief distance, then meandered into a stand of pine, and then suddenly, to Osborne's great surprise, emerged along the bank of a tiny lake.

"Herman!" he said. "I've hunted this region for years, and I never knew there was a lake here!"

The little lake, maybe a half mile long and less than a quarter mile wide, was nestled beneath the shadows of elegant, loopy-branched tamarack. Lily pads were just sprouting around a huge boulder not far from shore. Across the lake was another boulder where a duck was currently resting against a backdrop of cattails.

Even Julie was struck by the pristine beauty of the place. "I wish I had my camera," she said softly.

"I thought you'd like it back here," said Ray. It was clear the lake was no surprise to him.

A small cabin stood off to their right. Less than ten feet from shore, it stood sturdily on a dark-green cement foundation. That plus the rough shingles covering the sides, which had also been painted a deep, dark green, combined to make the cabin blend into the pine forest. What caught Osborne's eye was a chimney made of river rock, each rock carefully chosen and set into place. He whistled. Someone had taken a great deal of time to put that work of art together, rock by rock.

Osborne touched Julie's arm and pointed. "You don't see stonework like this anymore," he said. She nodded. The three of them stopped and watched as Herman walked haltingly up to the door and knocked. The door opened. He was muttering and gesturing, and then he stepped inside so they couldn't see him. A few minutes passed.

"Now, you know about Marie, right?" Ray asked Osborne in a low voice.

"I haven't seen her in years," said Osborne. He turned to Julie, "Marie's a hermit. A true hermit. She attended the same grade school as my daughters but I don't think she graduated from eighth grade even. As a child, she was absolutely beautiful. Blond hair, white skin and these angel-like tiny features. But she never went to junior high or high school. As far as I know, she's always hid back here in the woods. She and Herman pretty much just live off the land."

"Berries, veggies, and fish," said Ray. "I stocked that lake with walleye and trout for Marie a few years ago. I always bring the old man some venison. He gives me tomatoes and fresh corn—"

Just then, Herman stepped out of the cabin, followed by a short, thickbodied woman in washed-out denim overalls and a dingy gray sweatshirt. For an absurd moment, the sight of her made Osborne think of a squat concrete silo with a black dome. Like Herman, she wore an old wool golf hat. Hers was black tweed flecked with white. It sat on her square head over stringy white hair that hung around her ears and down her back. Her face, much broader than Herman's, was weatherbeaten, sun-spotted, and heavily freckled. The delicate features of childhood were gone, coarsened by weather and weight. She had short, stumpy, strong arms, and her stride was ponderous with her legs far apart as if to balance the bulky upper body. If they hadn't been expecting a woman, Osborne would have guessed her to be a man.

As Marie neared them, she grunted several times in response to something Herman was saying to her. Then, looking at Julie and Osborne, burst into a giggle. She kept giggling and started to nod her head up and down.

In spite of the giggle and the nodding, her eyes, wide-set under a high forehead, struck Osborne as glowing with intelligence and good cheer. She seemed genuinely pleased to see Ray, and as she grinned broadly to greet him, Osborne noted she practiced Herman's mode of preventive dental care: she was missing a number of teeth.

"Marie, it's been awhile." Ray stepped forward and put a friendly arm around her shoulders, as if oblivious to the giggling and nodding that Osborne figured was some kind of involuntary tic. "I'm afraid we have some disturbing news for you. Our friend here is a lawyer from Kansas City, and she's come to Loon Lake to investigate the murder of a man who might have been your natural brother."

Osborne thought later that it should have dawned on him right then, when Marie's giggling and nodding never broke its rhythm, when she registered no surprise at the mention of a sibling—a *murdered* sibling, no less—that his life was about to change. Ray described the finding of the bodies, then he introduced Julie. Julie told Marie of her legal relationship with Bowers, briefly mentioned the adoption history, and then, Osborne noted with surprise, told Marie of her engagement to Bowers.

"So," she said at last in gentle tones, "you and I might have been family if this hadn't happened."

"Oh? Yeth? Heh, heh, heh, heh. . . ."

Ray's eye caught Osborne's: That was one weird concept—the idea that these two women could be remotely related.

Meanwhile, Marie, who had taken a seat with the rest of them at a wooden, beaten-up old picnic table by the lake's edge, continued to grin as the staccato-like giggle repeated at a low hum. The nodding, once she sat down, turned into a full-body rocking motion. She didn't seem to notice anything unusual in her behavior, her eyes eagerly observing each of them. Herman said nothing. Then Herman mumbled something to Ray.

"Excuse us for a minute, folks," Ray said, standing up,

"Herman's got some blackberry bushes he wants me to see." As the two men stood, Marie pulled out a pack of Marlboros and a lighter. She lit a cigarette and inhaled with satisfaction.

Osborne suddenly wished he still smoked. This was the perfect time to fiddle with a cigarette and have an excuse to turn away from the strange scene, if only to think over what to do next. But he didn't smoke, so he decided to sit still and observe the next few minutes. He figured Julie must be finding the entire scene even more surreal. But he should have been prepared. Hang around with Ray long enough and you discover that life exists on planes you never knew about.

As he sat quietly, an overwhelming sense of déjà vu swept over him: He inhaled the cool late afternoon air into his nostrils, he felt the breezes blow across his fingers where they rested on the table before him, he looked at the color of the lake surface behind Marie's rocking head directly in front of him—and he felt he had been here before, seen this scene, felt this space, heard this silence. He felt strange and light and disconnected from everything around him.

As the two men walked off, Julie looked at Osborne with an expression of helplessness. She didn't know what to do or say.

"So . . . Marie, how do you know Ray?" she finally asked Marie, her voice loud enough to be heard over the giggle.

"Rayth's a good friend," said Marie, blowing smoke through her nostrils. She spoke with a lisp due to the lack of teeth but was otherwise rather matter-of-fact. From all the cigarette butts Osborne had seen as they walked along the path, he figured she smoked as heavily as Herman.

"Have you been friends a long time?" prompted Julie.

"Um-hmm. Since Saint Mary's—I think twenty, twenty-five years maybe?"

"Same class?" asked Julie.

"He'th much younger," said Marie softly. She'd stopped giggling and spoke so softly that it seemed like a spell was cast around the three of them as they sat there. Julie told Osborne later, she felt the same way. Both of them were wise enough not to say another word. Marie sat silent but rocking steadily back and forth for a few more moments. Finally, she inhaled deeply, tossed the cigarette down at her feet, and ground it out with her heel. Then she spoke. Her voice was firm and reedy now.

"Hmm, in them days, Herman was pretty bad, y'know. He's drunk as a skunk most of the time. He sure didn't know how to take care of a little kid, y'know. Heh, heh, heh. So's I didn't have nice clothes or nothin'. He got me to school 'cause the sheriff made 'im take me, but that's 'bout as much as he did." Marie smiled sweetly. "He isn't mean or nothin', he jes didn't know no better, heh, heh, heh, heh. . . ." The giggle rattled on for a while.

"It was okay at first, but pretty soon the other kids could see that I was funny, y'know. I started to look funny. I've always looked funny. My hair? See, it's all over me. I, heh, heh, heh, I had too much hair since I was maybe seven years old, heh, heh, heh. . . . That's why I like living back here . . . y'know?" With that, Marie rocked harder and giggled a long spell, as if angry about something she'd just said or thought about.

Then the giggling stopped again. She rocked as she spoke. "One summer day I was at the park by Ray's house, watchin' kids fly kites. Herman'd come to town and brung me along. I didn't have no kite, of course. I was jes watchin' and tryin' to stay out of the way so no one'd pick on me. Then Ray came over and asked me if I would like to fly his kite."

Marie's eyes were soft and friendly as she spoke. "He gave me his kite 'cause he said he had to go home for lunch. He jus gave it to me—this beautiful kite. Heh, heh, heh. . . . That was very nice. He was my first friend."

Marie stopped rocking and stood up, reaching into her

overalls pocket for the pack of cigarettes again, shook one out, reached into her other pocket for the lighter, and flicked. She inhaled deeply, then exhaled, giggling as she sat down again. The air had grown cooler around them, and the sky was starting to darken, but it seemed very calm and peaceful to Osborne. Julie was sitting in silence, her elbows on the table, her chin resting in her hands. She had not taken her eyes off Marie.

Marie took another deep drag on the cigarette, and then she repeated her earlier words, "Ray is a good friend. I have two good friends. Ray is one." She resumed her rocking.

"Who's the other?" asked Julie.

"Herman. Heh, heh, heh, heh. . . . Come on, let me show you something." Marie stood and motioned for them to follow her back toward her cabin. Then she motioned for them to stop before the front door. She went inside, walking through a small outer porch, then through another heavier door into the interior of what must be a two-room cabin. Julie watched her go inside, then she stepped to the left and craned her neck to look through the outside window at something on the small porch. Osborne noticed Julie had tensed and moved forward, her nose literally pressed against the window pane.

Osborne cleared his throat. She was pushing the bounds of etiquette. Marie had made it clear she wanted them to remain outside. Then, from where he stood, outside one of the main cabin's windows, Osborne saw a light go on in the dim interior. Marie bent down toward the light to reach for something. As she did so, her hat fell off, exposing knots of hair growing in clumps from her skull. The light caught the shadows of her cheekbones and eye sockets, offering an effect identical to that of a flashlight aimed from the chin up. Osborne froze, the image setting off a flash in his memory. The interior light went off, and he looked away quickly. The shock of what he saw had so stunned him that he didn't even notice the strange, tight look on Julie's face.

Just then, Marie stepped out of the door. Her head was tipped down, but her eyes were watching theirs as she held in both hands what looked like a rolled-up old map. "Heh, heh, heh. . . ." The staccato giggle ran on like a low-toned motor.

Gently, gently, she unfolded her paper treasure: the kite. The vivid colors of the old Japanese kite had faded, but its support sticks had been tucked inside, and all the strings were still attached. With two deft moves, Marie held the delicate paper in one hand and snapped the support sticks into place.

"I bet it can still fly," said Julie.

"I wouldn't want to rip it or nothin'," said Marie. Then she unsnapped the supports and very, very carefully rolled it back up. She gave them both a sweet smile of pride, then shrugged and giggled. She walked back to open the porch door and set the kite down inside, then she returned, her hands thrust deep into the pockets of her overalls.

Osborne didn't know what to say, so he said nothing. Julie, too, seemed at a loss for words. Marie had seemed so vulnerable, standing between them with her talisman of friendship. Osborne knew then why she had been in the woods that night. Just as the three of them started slowly back to the picnic table, they heard voices and looked up to see Herman and Ray coming toward them. Osborne was anxious to get moving. He signaled to Ray.

"Oh, Herman, sorry," said Ray. "Looks like I gotta get the good dentist back to his dog."

"I left him at my daughter's house," apologized Osborne, "and I must pick him up before five." The three men started back toward Herman's house and the truck. Julie hung behind, deep in conversation with Marie for about five minutes before she ran to catch up.

Once in the cab of the truck and down the road far enough to be out of earshot of Herman and Marie, Julie spoke. "Can we pull over and talk for a minute? I'm quite upset."

Ray did as she asked. He kept the truck idling as both men looked at her.

"Marie has one of Robert's paintings hanging on the wall of her porch," said Julie evenly. "It is an early Georgia O'Keefe watercolor, and it is worth at least three hundred thousand dollars."

"Are you sure?" Ray asked, his voice very, very even.

"No doubt whatsover. I told her I admired it and asked where she got it."

"And—"

"At first she made like she didn't know what I was talking about. Then she said her sister gave it to her—"

"Her sister?" Ray asked.

"Her sister, Judy, was all I could get out of her."

"Has to be Judith Benjamin," said Osborne. "Has to be. But why would Judith give Marie an expensive painting?"

"Marie said she saw it at her sister's new house and loved it, and Judith said she could have it in payment for work Marie's been doing for her. I asked what kind of work. She's making cabinets and furniture. Then—and she volunteered this—she's also making crates and boxes. Large crates and boxes out of wood and steel mesh, she said, for fish. She said Judy sends fish to Japan."

"Crayfish, is probably what she means," said Ray. "Ron Hubbard's got a huge business going exporting crayfish from this area. Maybe Judith Benjamin is horning in on his business. She's the type."

"Ray," Osborne interrupted, "Marie is the woman I saw in the woods that night. When she leaned over the lamp in her cabin, her hat fell off, and I recognized the head and the shadows in her face. That's who was there when we found you. Marie is the mushroom woman!"

"You're kidding," said Ray, looking hard at Osborne. "You're sure?" He wrinkled his brow as if thinking back over what few sensations he could remember. "I know I had this intuitive sense of being held by my mother, which sounds crazy, but now it makes sense. I would trust Marie with my life. . . .

"Yeah, I guess I'm not surprised," Ray said, putting the truck into gear. "I have news, too. Herman told me he knows the beavers went to work about ten years ago around the old Cantrell land. They dammed up a creek that used to flow into the Gudegast. He figures that's good water in that lake. I was wrong when I thought we were on Dead Creek yesterday. That was the Guddy.

"He's been back and forth in there a lot recently. He said it's Judith Benjamin building in there, all right. She's put up one of the log houses that come in a kit and has Marie doing finish work on it. Herman drives Marie over to work every day and picks her up. Except Saturday, he couldn't find her. Worried sick about it, but she showed up yesterday just fine."

"Did he mention if he saw Ted Bronk hanging around?" asked Osborne.

"Yep. That's why he was worried about Marie. Herman doesn't trust Bronk. Didn't know he's dead, either, till I just told him. He was worried the guy might go after Marie in his slimy way. He knows Marie's intelligent, but he knows her limits, too."

"But she was okay when he found her?"

"She was okay, but she wouldn't tell Herman where she'd been."

"Jeesh," said Osborne. "Wait'll Lew hears this."

"We have got to reach her as soon as possible," Julie interrupted. "Now that I saw that painting, we can get a search warrant—"

"Whoa, whoa, slow down there." Ray looked at Julie. "Don't get frantic, okay? Marie is not going anywhere. We've got time. We've got to find the linchpin here. We've got too many unanswered questions."

"He's right," said Osborne. "For one thing, we haven't looked closely at the responses from the families of the other victims—they may have information that could put an entirely different spin on this. We have been so focused on Robert Bowers that we could be overlooking something quite important."

"You may have Marie in possession of the painting," said Ray, "but I swear to you Marie did not mastermind a multiple murder that involved siphoning assets out of the Bowers estate. Not Marie."

"How do you know?" said Julie, a grim tone to her voice. "How do you know she's not scamming?"

"What!" Ray's voice didn't hide an edge of anger.

"Sorry, forget it, I take it back," said Julie. "I'm really sorry. That was unkind."

"Then why did you say it?" asked Ray. "Now, Julie, I'm not mad, but I'm curious as to why you would say that. I've known Marie for years—years—and she's always been this way."

"I just feel . . . well, now this is strictly intuition. I don't think Marie is retarded. And please remember I grew up with a father who treated disturbed people. I don't think she's even learning disabled. If you ask me, odd behavior patterns aside, I think Marie is every bit as bright as the three of us. Maybe brighter."

"What makes you so sure?" asked Ray.

"Because when I put her on the spot with questions about the painting, she stopped all the nervous tics," said Julie. "I caught her off guard. If she had a real physical problem, there wouldn't have been a blip in her movements. If she was slow mentally, she wouldn't have answered the way she did: she dodged all my questions quite neatly. I'm a lawyer, Ray. Questions are my craft, and judging answers is my talent."

Ray heaved a sigh. "This complicates things."

"That depends," said Julie. "You don't seem all that surprised."

"Well . . . I've seen some things that have made me wonder, too," said Ray.

"Personally, I'm with you, Ray," said Julie. "I don't think Marie is who we're after. But what's with this Judy person?" said Julie. "Isn't she the one who set up the party with the dancers for the YPO group?"

"Not exactly," said Osborne. "She provided dancers at the request of a professor from the university branch over in Rhinelander who was offering some sort of bonehead art class. Ted Bronk was to drive them over and back from the resort or wherever this party was supposed to be."

"I can't wait to see this Judith person," said Julie. "Maybe something will jibe. Hey, guys, we need to get in touch with Lew as soon as possible."

"Yep." Ray put the truck in gear and pulled onto the highway. "Let's go by Thunder Bay and see if Lew's still there." He looked over at Julie. "Be prepared. This is a joint, a raunchy roadhouse. It is not *your* kind of place—"

"But a lot of fishermen?"

"Yeah, bait and spinner guys. Hunting season, you get the bear guys, deer hunters. But class, it ain't, kiddo."

"Don't worry about it," said Julie absentmindedly. Osborne noticed she was staring out the truck window as if she had something on her mind other than listening to Ray.

"Drop me off at Erin's, will you, Ray?" Osborne asked. "I'll pick up my car and the dog and follow you out to Thunder Bay."

"Still worried?"

"Not really. I'm sure Erin's back by now. But, you know? I've been thinking about that Judith. Remember how she shuts that bar down every Labor Day and goes away until March? Do you know where she goes, Ray?"

"Nope. Now that you mention it—no, I don't."

"Ah," said Julie, turning away from the window as if another puzzle piece had fallen into place.

twenty-one

But Death is sure to kill all he can get,
And all is fish to him that comes to net.

Anonymous

Erin was not home. Nor the baby. But Osborne's son-in-law was, and he looked tense. He was waiting on the front porch as they pulled up.

"Dad, isn't Erin with you?" Mark came running down the stairs to the truck as Osborne was climbing out.

"No, I haven't seen her all day. She isn't back yet?"

"What do you mean, yet?" asked Mark.

"I dropped the dog off two hours ago, and she wasn't here."

"I don't understand," said Mark. "Our car is in the garage, she didn't leave a note, and there is no sign of her and the baby. I just sent the girls over to the neighbors. I thought I'd go out and drive around a little in case she's walking back from downtown or something."

"Who saw her last?" asked Ray from inside the cab of the truck.

"The girls when they left for school at nine this morning," said Mark. "Even her coffee cup is half full and sitting by the sink. She always finishes her coffee. And the wash was half-stuffed into the washing machine, none of the beds are made. It's like she left in a rush hours ago."

Osborne saw his son-in-law's eyes tear up suddenly. He resisted a rush of panic himself. "Ray, why don't you and Julie come on into the house. Let's call the station from here and locate Lew. I—we—"

"Good idea." Ray waited to get out of the truck on the passenger side after Julie. "Erin first. Then we can see how Lew wants to handle this other."

The four of them hurried into the tall Victorian home. Mark picked up the phone. He reached the police station and asked for Lew.

"She's not there and they don't know where she is." He looked at Osborne.

"Let me talk to them," Osborne reached for the phone. Lucy Olson was on the line. "Lucy? This is an emergency," said Osborne. "We'll get in the car and go find Lew if we have to."

"Good luck, Dr. Osborne," said Lucy. The older woman had a decidedly stressed-out tone to her voice. "She said she had a meeting with Judith Benjamin at four but she's not there now. Neither is Judith Benjamin. No one knows where they are."

"She never showed up?" Osborne was incredulous.

"I don't know. I've got two cars out looking for her because I can't get no response from her on the radio either," said Lucy. "This is not like her. The mayor is demanding to talk to her right this minute. I've got him screaming on the other line."

Osborne exhaled deeply, "Lucy, my daughter Erin is missing. Can we get someone to help us look for her?"

"Erin is missing?" This time it was Lucy's turn to sound incredulous. "Well, I don't know. You want me to call someone in from Rhinelander? I've got our guys out after Lew."

"Yes, I want someone from Rhinelander. As soon as possible," said Osborne. He set down the phone.

Ray stepped forward and put a hand on Osborne's shoulder. "Okay, Doc, you stay right here with Mark until the Rhinelander cops come. Julie, you come with me."

"Where are you going?" asked Osborne.

"We'll drive up to Thunder Bay and see what the story is," said Ray. "I'll call from up there and tell you what I find."

"Good, good." Ray and Julie hurried from the house.

"Did she tell you about seeing that guy the other day?" Mark asked Osborne.

"Yes, but I can't imagine that is related to this," said Osborne.

"Well, she was worried about it," said Mark. "She must've told me five or six times she couldn't get over this look of intense fury on the guy's face. I think she felt like he might come after her."

"That doesn't make sense," said Osborne, wondering and doubting his own words even as he said them.

He walked over to where Mark stood, a look of great worry and helplessness on his face. At first, Osborne started to reach for his son-in-law's shoulder to give a reassuring squeeze, but he found himself putting both arms around the younger man instead. As he looked over his son-in-law's shoulder, his eyes caught the gleam of a bottle on the top shelf of a half-open cupboard.

He remembered his solution to the despair he felt right after Mary Lee died. One night, in fact, it had been Erin and Mark who found him passed out in his own kitchen, tucked him into bed, and called the rehab center at Hazelden for him the next morning. It was Erin who volunteered to take the role of the family in confronting Osborne with his alcoholism. He couldn't bear to lose Erin, too. If she was lost, he was lost.

"Mark, I know we'll find her. I'm sure everything is all right," whispered Osborne hoarsely. The two men clung to each other for a brief moment. This was so unlike anything Erin had ever done. They both knew something was very, very wrong.

"Mark, I'm going to take a walk over to Saint Mary's. If anyone calls, I'll be back in ten minutes." Osborne walked quickly toward the front door. He needed a few minutes alone.

twenty-two

It's no fish ye're buying; it's men's lives.

Sir Water Scott, *The Antiquary*

Osborne didn't even nod to Mike's plaintive bark as he ran down the front stairs and hurried along the sidewalk toward the church. Erin and Mark lived exactly one and a half blocks from Saint Mary's. In less than three minutes, Osborne had turned the corner, walked another hundred yards rapidly, and tried the side door of the church. It was open.

He slipped inside. The interior was dark and empty, with enough of the fading sun still glowing through the stained glass windows that Osborne could find his way to his usual pew. He sank to his knees and buried his face in his hands. First, he prayed. Then he began to think. He let his mind move back and forth over the scenes of the week. What kept crowding back in was a trio of images led by Lew's dark, penetrating, emphathetic eyes. Eyes that watched his to see if he could see.

Suddenly he remembered the boots, the boots on the dead body in the road. Ted Bronk's boots.

He had this very strong image of the boots stomping

across the porch of the house where Erin saw him. Stomping after her and the baby . . .

And with that, Osborne realized why Erin could be a target: *She can place Bronk out in the woods at that strange house. She is a witness to his dealings with someone who may have killed him. And if that's true,* thought Osborne, *could her disappearance be directly tied to the other murders?*

His head still in his hands while he was thinking, Osborne had not seen the door from the sacristy open. Nor had he heard the young man approach. Osborne jerked his head up at the soft pat on his shoulder.

"Oh! I'm sorry, Doctor." Wally, the young student who'd been helping with the baptismal database, stood in front of him. "I saw you walk in a little while ago, and I thought you'd like to know I found some more records with the names of the two babies that Mrs. Minor had adopted."

Osborne sat back on the seat of the pew. "You did?"

"She gave one up to another family," said Wally. "That family had the baby's baptismal records changed because they changed the baby's name. It's a very confusing set of records, but I think I got it right. Father Vodicka found some more information in the convent files about how it all happened because Mrs. Minor said two children were too expensive and too much work for her, so she brought one back to the sisters. Then the second family made a big deal that no one should know their child was one of the triplets. I guess that mother wanted everyone to think her baby came from Rhinelander. Anyway, it was kept pretty quiet by the nuns." And with that, he offered up the names.

Osborne felt his entire body begin to vibrate.

"Thank you, Wally," he said quickly. "That's very good to know. Thank you." He thought later the kid must have thought he was berserk the way he ran from the church.

Ran out and all the way back to Erin's in a minute or less.

"Mark! Mark!" He was shouting as he neared the house. Mark came running out the front door. "C'mon. I think I know what's going on." said Osborne. "I've got to find Lew. I've got to get her." He pushed past Mark into the house and to the phone. Frantically, he dialed the police station and got Lucy again. "Lucy, any luck locating Lew?"

"No. Doc." said Lucy. "I am so sorry—nothing. I was going to call you. The Rhinelander police are on their way. They said they'll be there in about twenty minutes."

Osborne and Mark heard footsteps running up the front porch even as Osborne put the phone down. But the faces that burst through the front door weren't cops. it was Ray and Julie, both looking grim.

"Doc. I've got some interesting news." said Ray. The easygoing. laconic Ray had disappeared. replaced by the rapid-action. no-nonsense guy whom Osborne had only ever witnessed during the landing of a very large muskie. The man in front of him was "business Ray." all the way. in spite of the trout hat.

"No Lew at Thunder Bay. But the bartender said he passed a couple cars on his way out to clock in this afternoon and he was pretty sure one was Judith. For sure one was a cop car because he slowed down when he saw it." said Ray. his words firing in staccato. "but Julie and I stopped at Guptill's Grocery for gas and the bathroom. and we're walking in past the community bulletin board when Julie sees a poster for the Northwoods Regional Art Show. curated by—guess who?" Ray paused for one brief instant. "*Professor Bradford Miller*. with his picture front and center—"

"That's Brad Kirsch!" interrupted Julie. her voice loud and insistent. "That's him. That's the dealer I've been telling you about—and he's the silver thief! He's the same guy that goes by Fred Shepard. too. He always works with a woman, remember? I'll bet my life I'll recognize Judith Benjamin. Doc, these are the two. I'm just sure they killed Robert. I'm sure." Julie was shaking.

"It fits," said Osborne, his voice very calm in spite of the feeling that his entire body was one raw nerve. "I just learned Brad Miller is the third of the triplets found by old Herman. Ruth Minor adopted him originally but gave him up within three months to another Loon Lake family—"

"When did you hear all this?" asked Julie.

"About ten minutes ago. I ran into the college kid inputting the baptismal database over at Saint Mary's. He finally found all the documents from the baptisms that followed the adoptions. The whole thing was confused because one of the babies was baptized twice. My old friend, Joe Miller, and his wife—they adopted that third baby."

"Jeez. . . ." Ray raised his eyebrows as he looked at Osborne and Julie, each in turn, his eyes questioning theirs. Osborne didn't find his spirit helped by the deepening concern evident in Ray's expression and his uncharacteristically subdued manner.

He could see Ray was worried, and that *really* worried Osborne. In fact, it pushed him to the brink of panic. He forced himself into calmness, if only to fortify his son-in-law, who was standing off to the side, listening and watching the three of them, his arms crossed, his body tense.

"Erin and the baby are still missing," said Osborne abruptly. "I think I know why." His heart pounded as he spoke. "I think the angry, crazy man she saw when she was delivering those brochures was Ted Bronk. She told a lot of people about that encounter. I'll bet Brad and Judith heard about it and realized she knows about the house in the woods. If they killed Ted because he knew what they were up to, maybe they think she saw something or he said something or . . ." Osborne stopped. He couldn't finish thinking what was on his mind, much less putting it in words. "I—we've got to find Lew! We need her help."

"You're right, Doc," said Julie, putting a hand on Osborne's arm, "but you need to settle down. Lew is right where you want her: interrogating Judith Benjamin. Just hold on until she's back in touch with the office—"

"But they think she's missing!" Osborne insisted.

"I think they're wrong," said Julie firmly, so firmly he believed her. "Doc, how often do you have criminal interrogations up here? A session can go on for hours. Lucy is just a switchboard operator. She's overreacting. Okay? Relax."

At least he *wanted* to believe her.

"I think Lew found a way to work on Benjamin and is taking her time to get everything she needs," said Julie. "The bartender told us he saw Lew's cruiser pull into the lot at Thunder Bay. He saw Judith go out the door to see her, and then they both drove off in their own cars. I figure Lew was successful at getting Benjamin off her own turf for the interrogation, which is critical to gaining an advantage. I know that from my own experience."

"Julie's right," said Ray. "We both know Lew can take care of herself. Doc, I think it's time we go to the source. We should be talking to the good professor. The man with the answers."

Osborne took a deep breath. The logic was sound, but something felt wrong. It was just a feeling. He kept his mouth shut.

"The last I heard, the professor was living at home with his mother," said Ray. He glanced at his watch: "Teatime. Let's pay a call on the Miller household."

"Where are we going?" said Julie.

"Right up the street," said Osborne. "Mark, you stay here. Give me a call at the Millers' when you hear from Lew."

"Tell her to meet us there," added Ray as the three of them walked toward the front door.

"No. Stop," said Osborne, balking in the hallway near the door. "I don't think this is right. I think we should get out to that log house. Someone who knows something is there. I'm sure of it!"

"You may be right," said Ray, tipping his hat back on his head and looking hard into Osborne's face. "But even if you are right, we don't know exactly who that is. We can't just barge in and accuse somebody of murder. We can't just barge in period. We need to know if we're dealing with people carrying weapons. If we aren't careful, someone could get killed—"

"Or sued," said Julie. "Ray's got a point. Before we drive out there, we need more information. We need to be very, very careful."

"Look," said Ray to Osborne, his voice sympathetic, "Ten minutes with the professor or with Peggy and we'll have a much better read on the situation. Are you with me, Doc?"

"Fine. Okay. But let's hurry. We're running out of time."

"Yes, we are," said Ray. "But look at it this way. It is either too late already or we've got enough time to make sure of what we're doing."

Mark looked stunned at his words. "Please go," he said. "I'll keep checking with the station."

Osborne, Ray, and Julie raced for the cars. "Take mine," shouted Osborne. "I've got plenty of gas."

Peggy Miller lived seven houses away, up six doors and around the corner, in an elegant red brick home with white shutters on black-trimmed windows. Osborne had always thought the house unspeakably pretentious for Loon Lake.

"Well," said Julie dryly, unable to resist a chuckle in spite of the tension as she tipped her head to look past Ray at the house, "Do I see a Williamsburg mansion set down in a Yankee town? Correct me if I'm wrong: This woman loves money?" The men nodded. Then she briefed them on her approach to Brad's mother.

Oh, Peggy loved her house, all right, thought Osborne as he listened to Julie's plan. And Peggy loved Joe's money. Just like she'd loved the little bridge parties with tea sandwiches and weak coffee that she and Mary Lee had hosted for years, always being sure to leave out some young wife that the two of them didn't care for at the time, making sure that woman knew she wasn't invited—and giggling over it later. They had wielded enough social clout that Osborne had felt its effects on his practice from time to time.

No, Peggy loved the money and the house, but she never loved Joe. She made that clear when she left him to die alone in the hospital. Alone with his lymphoma, a difficult death from a cancer probably brought on by the stress of working at the mill to pay Peggy's bills. Osborne had arrived at the hospital to visit his friend, only to find Joe had passed away just thirty minutes earlier. The nurses told Osborne it had been two days since either Peggy or Brad had been in to see the man, even though he was conscious to the end, and they had placed numerous phone calls to the home. The nurses had been disgusted with the family.

As Osborne parked his truck, he realized for the first time how much he disliked Peggy and how he had hated that Mary Lee was a partner in her little schemes. Now he wondered if that twisted side of the woman had coalesced in Brad, the adopted son that she had indulged and cooed over, even when he was a grown man. Brad, a killer? Brad holding Erin and the baby somewhere? Osborne took a deep breath as Ray and Julie gave him instructions.

It was 5:30 when they rang Peggy's doorbell. She cracked the door open so quickly after the ring, Osborne figured she'd been watching from behind the curtains as his car pulled up and the three of them got out.

"Yes? Who is it?" Peggy peered out. She was a slight, stiff woman with a long, horsey face. Her distinguishing feature was a jaw that thrust forward and appeared to be elongating with age. Above the jaw was a pointy nose and two close-set and intense black eyes. When he first met her, many years ago, Osborne had made a mental note that she was one of those women who was always watching.

Today her hair was neatly fluffed in a beauty parlor pageboy, and she was wearing trim navy blue wool slacks, a pale pink blouse, and a navy blue cardigan sweater. A small brooch secured the neck of her blouse. She wasn't pretty, but she wasn't homely, and she had a crisp, tailored style. Perhaps it was the style that had made her hate Joe for locking her away in little old Loon Lake.

"Well, my goodness, Paul Osborne." She opened the door wide. "What are you doing here at this time of day? And Ray Pradt? Gracious, what brings you folks out?"

"Mrs. Miller?" Julie extended her hand and stepped forward with authority. "I'm Julie Rehnquist from Kansas City. I'm the lawyer Brad is expecting to discuss his inheritance. Is he here?"

"No. He isn't."

"I don't understand," said Julie graciously. "I asked his office to make an appointment for us to meet at this time, but maybe I misunderstood. You aren't expecting us?"

"Julie is the daughter of an old school friend of mine," volunteered Osborne. "Ray and I met her at the Mosinee airport earlier today. We thought we'd just drop her off for the meeting with Brad and come by later to pick her up."

Peggy looked very confused. She stepped back and opened the door wide. "Come in, everyone. I don't understand. Brad didn't say anything about your appointment. But, please, come in and sit down."

She beckoned them into the front hall and on into her living room. The room was filled with reproduction English furniture: ornate mahogany tables and overstuffed chairs and sofas. It was formal, not comfortable. Ray and Osborne sat side by side on a small sofa, Julie picked an armchair. Peggy excused herself for a minute, saying she would put some coffee on to brew. She was back quickly and seated herself primly in a small rocking chair.

"Now, tell me about this inheritance?"

"Brad hasn't told you?" Julie looked strained, as if to convey that if he hadn't brought it up then perhaps she shouldn't be saying anything.

"Oh, he did!" said Peggy quickly. "He just didn't tell me you were coming *today*. That's all."

Julie let herself look relieved. "Good. Then, as you know, the initial bequest was for twenty million, but we found more paperwork last week. It seems Mrs. Bowers had two safe-deposit boxes in yet another bank, and the trust officers there were late informing us of the contents. Most of the assets are in real estate, and then there's five million in cash that should be put in an interest-bearing investment or account somewhere. I brought the paperwork with me so we can execute a wire transfer in the morning."

"Ah," said Peggy. "I imagine he'll do exactly what he did with the other."

"Oh?" Julie sounded surprised. "I'll strongly advise against that! He has two million dollars in cash already, I can't imagine he wants to lose interest on this money."

Something happened to Peggy's face with that remark from Julie. Her eyes darted down and up again and the jaw slackened. Then her features tightened and she stood up, "Let me get the coffee. Does everyone take cream and sugar?" Osborne thought she hurried out of the room.

They sat perfectly silent, listening. Osborne expected a rattle of cups, maybe even a murmur of a voice on the telephone. They heard nothing. Ray pointed a finger at Osborne, and Osborne rose to walk toward the kitchen. He pushed open the swinging door. Peggy stood still at a kitchen window, her back to him, her arms wrapped tightly around her body as if she was holding herself together.

Osborne walked up and placed his hands on her shoulders. "Peggy? Is anything wrong?"

The face she turned to him was the real Peggy. Her mouth and jaw were twisted with hate. Her eyes were black and cold.

"The little shit," she spat. "The little shit. He took every dime Joe and I had and made me mortgage this house up to the hilt last year. When Joe was so sick, we gave him power of attorney. Joe was always so conservative, we just had savings accounts, so I asked Brad to invest it for me, but he put it all in his name. He said it would save on taxes.

"Before I knew it, he had all our assets in his name. Even this house! And he hasn't talked to me in six months. He said I depress him. He said I make him sick to his stomach. He lives here, Paul. He lives right upstairs but I'm not allowed to go up there. Do you know—all he gives me is two hundred and twenty-two dollars a month. I barely eat on that."

"How did this happen, Peggy?" Osborne asked her softly. "I don't understand what you're saying."

"He's mean, Paul. He's bone mean. When he was a baby, he would bite until you bled. When he was in high school, he would say the nastiest things about people— the things he said about you and Mary Lee. It was disgusting." She dropped her face into her hands.

"Oh my God, it's all my fault. I never could figure out what he needed."

"Peggy . . ." Osborne actually felt some sympathy for the woman. Why, he didn't really know.

"He . . . um . . ." her voice was shaking as she raised her head. Osborne sensed she was on the verge of hysteria. "Just last week he told me I could leave if I didn't like it . . . but he controls my whole life. Oh, Paul, this is all so humiliating. And now I find out that he's got all this money? Oh, I'm going to kill myself."

"Hold off on that action," said a woman's voice suddenly. Julie had entered the kitchen with Ray right behind her. "Brad has a few questions to answer before any funds are signed over. Peggy, I think it's time we tell you the truth. Yes, he's an heir to a massive fortune, but only because I believe he murdered his brother."

As the expression on Peggy's face turned into bewilderment, Osborne let her down gently into a kitchen chair. "Peggy," he said, "we'd like to take a look at Brad's room. Would that be all right with you?"

"We don't have a search warrant," said Ray. "You don't have to let us do this, but Dr. Osborne and myself—we're working on the investigation as deputies for Chief Ferris."

"You can do anything you want up there if you can get in," said Peggy. "He's kept the place locked up tight for months. I don't know—I'm afraid of what you'll find up there.

"Here, over here, is the back stairway. See the lock on that door?"

"Sure do," said Ray, pulling a Swiss Army knife from his back pocket. "Where's your screwdriver?"

"Joe's workbench in the basement," said Peggy.

The lock was expertly jimmied in less than five minutes. "Another notch in the belt for the exit expert," said Ray with a slight grin, pulling the door open.

Just then the phone rang. Osborne picked up the nearby kitchen wall phone.

It was Mark. "I called Lucy. No sign of Lew yet. I've tried every one of Erin's friends. No one has seen her!" Mark sounded like he was going to cry.

"Mark, hold on," said Osborne. "Let me call you back in five minutes. Just hold on, okay?" He set the phone down and raced up the stairs behind Ray and Julie.

They found three bedrooms and a bathroom on the upper level. In one room, the furniture had all been pushed to the side as if to make room for storage.

"Looks to me like he had boxes in here," said Ray, pointing to dust patterns on the floor. He smeared his finger through a footprint. "They were recently moved, within the last few days."

The next room had served as an office. A desk in the corner held envelopes and papers littered across it. Julie ran over and shuffled through a few. "Nothing here. Some college staff memos and stuff. Old, a couple years old."

The third room had definitely been used as a bedroom. Dirty sheets and an old quilt lay loosely across the double bed. Otherwise, Brad appeared to have packed up and left. Two dingy white towels lay on the floor in the closet. A small dresser was empty.

At the end of the hall, the last door, the bathroom door, was closed. They paused before pushing it open. More towels on the floor, trash overflowed out of a wastebasket just inside the door, and a discarded travel kit lay on its side beside the toilet.

"Get a load of the mirror." Ray pointed and they crowded around. Across the top of the oak-framed mirror Brad had tacked a series of photos. From left to right, three shots, taken from the waist up, showed Brad Miller in different stages of weight loss.

In the first shot, his face was pudgy, eyes bulbous and staring at the camera, mouth grim, head bald. The next shot was of a slightly thinner Brad, while the third was of a startlingly slim man. It was still Brad, but this shot showed him standing alongside another person: Robert Bowers.

"My God, look at the resemblance," whispered Osborne. He was right. Having lost weight, the facial structures were uncannily similar, although Robert's neatly trimmed beard provided a sharp contrast to Brad's smooth-shaven face. Both were bald and the shapes of their skulls identical.

Tacked to the right of the three photos, grainy as if it had been enlarged from a much smaller picture, was a head shot of Judith Benjamin. Her face was much thinner than the two men, even though the basic bone structure was similar. On her, the flat, fishlike eyes were tempered with makeup. The blond hair that was so neatly pulled back into a French twist now looked quite obviously like a wig. Osborne was surprised. It had never occurred to him that she might be bald. He knew, of course, why the line of her jaw was so different.

"Check out the five o'clock shadow around Judith's mouth," said Ray. "She shaves."

Osborne looked back at the shot of Robert Bowers. The face looked robust and healthy above the crisply tailored beard. His eyes, under his gleaming bald head, were alert and smiling, with natural crinkles of humor at his temples and at the edges of his gentle grin that made him look happy and attractive, in sharp contrast to Brad's hostile stare. And yet, in all three, the noses, the eyes, and the mouths were almost identical.

"My God, it is amazing how much they look alike, yet the differences in expressions and their body weight makes the similarities tough to catch," said Julie softly. "Maybe that's why I didn't notice how much they looked alike when I met Brad." She studied the photo closely. "Like I said earlier, I thought he was wearing a piece. The man I knew in Kansas City was not bald.

"And the police drawings of the silver thief—they show a man with hair and a beard—but pudgy. I remember thinking it was odd that Brad and Robert shared some mannerisms, in their speech patterns especially, but I didn't really think they looked that much alike. Brad was such a prissy guy, always wearing his pants pulled up to his nipples. Robert was an athlete and very trim. He always. . . ." Her voice caught suddenly and trailed off. Osborne put his arm around her to give her a hug.

"Well, well," said Ray softly, "we may have something

here." He had reached behind him to open a linen closet. Towels were neatly stacked on the two shelves. The third and fourth shelves, the shelves at eye level, held a complete studio's worth of stage makeup.

On the floor was a large black case. Ray pulled it forward and opened it. Trays slid out on hinges, a fully stocked makeup artist's case. He lifted a plastic box from the bottom section of the case and tipped the lid open. Inside was a soft chamois pouch. He shook it and out fell a beard. A neatly trimmed, straight, grayish blond beard.

"Robert's beard," whispered Julie.

"He must have big plans if he doesn't need this stuff anymore," said Ray, "*big* plans."

Just then, Peggy called up to them from downstairs. "I just talked to his secretary from the college at home," she said. "I thought it might be worth the chance she would know where he was going. Brad has always loved ordering other people to do his work for him. I was right. She ordered his tickets. He's booked on a flight to Japan early tomorrow morning, first class out of Vancouver."

"That means he's gone already," said Julie, turning around anxiously.

"He only had tickets from Vancouver," said Peggy. "He wouldn't tell Linda how he was going to get to Vancouver."

"Lemme call Mark," said Osborne, scrambling down the stairs. He picked up the phone and punched in Erin's number.

"Mark, any news?"

The answer was negative.

"Now, don't worry. We think we know where they are. I need you to call the police station and tell them to tell Lew where we're going. If she isn't there yet, give these directions to Lucy. Tell her we need backup as soon as possible.

"This is tricky, but Lew knows the way: Take K toward Shepard Lake. Take the right at the sign for Marjorie's

Bed and Breakfast off Old Highway C onto a gravel road, go back a good five or six miles. At the old Cantrell warehouse, drive right back behind it, drive around a landfill and a berm, just keep going. The road dips down to a new log house set way back. That's the place.

"Got it? Good, we're on our way." He hung up before Mark could answer.

"Paul," Peggy stood before him, "I want you to know something I've never told anyone in Loon Lake. Brad got kicked out of Princeton after his first semester. He never worked at Yale. He's been lying to everyone. He falsified documents about his graduate schools and teaching career and made me swear to secrecy. I want you to know in case it helps."

"It sure does, Peggy. Thanks." Osborne gave her a quick pat on the shoulder. "I'll call you when we know more."

"Thanks so much for your help," called Julie as the three of them walked rapidly through the house and out the front door.

Osborne's car was rolling down Pelham Street before Ray and Julie had shut their doors.

"Back to Erin's," said Ray. "We'll take my truck. I've got a goddam arsenal in the back. We may need it."

"This is one time he's not kidding," said Osborne in response to Julie's raised eyebrows.

"Do you always drive around with loaded guns?" she asked.

"No," said Ray, "but I just had all my rifles and my shotguns cleaned and oiled by a gunsmith up in Eagle River last week. I picked them up Thursday and then I got bonked on the head before I had a chance to put 'em back in the gun racks. They aren't loaded—yet."

twenty-three

You can't catch a fish if you don't dare go where they are.

Norman Maclean

Ray cut the engine and the lights as he turned off the gravel road. He let the truck roll down the grassy ruts toward the old Cantrell warehouse. A cloud bank cut off any light from the moon, but once their eyes adjusted to the dark, they could make out the familiar shape of a car parked in front and to the right of the brick building.

"Lew's cruiser! That's a good sign," said Osborne. His confidence level shot up a hundred percent. His entire body unclenched ever so slightly as, for the first time in hours he began to think that Erin and the baby might be okay. He realized he'd spent the entire drive out from Loon Lake hunched forward in his seat. He sat back and tried to relax his shoulders as he moved his hand to grip the door handle, ready for a signal from Ray.

"I hope you're right," said Ray under his breath as he sat motionless behind the wheel. He gave no sign for anyone to move. Instead, he scrutinized what landscape was visible in the deepening blackness around them: the sky faint behind the tree line, the forest hiding anything that might be lurking along the outside walls of the brick structure.

Ray cranked his window down and motioned to Osborne to do the same. He listened. Osborne and Julie sat perfectly still, listening and waiting.

Not a hint of light came from inside the old warehouse. The clouds did not move to unveil the moon. The woods were silent. Finally, in the distance, a great horned owl hooted.

"Do you think anyone's in the building?" asked Julie softly.

"Nah. I'd be very surprised," said Ray, his voice low, "but we better take a look."

The three of them climbed out of the truck on the driver's side. Ray left the door slightly ajar to avoid making a loud noise. As he walked to the back of his truck, Osborne noticed that the easy, casual lope had disappeared, replaced with the quick step and the deft movements of a man with every muscle on alert.

Ray leaned over the truck bed to unlock the padlock on the beat-up old metal chest he kept in the back of his truck. He opened the lid and reached inside for a black Maglite flashlight, which he handed back to Julie. Then he pulled out his deer rifle, checked the action and the sight, and handed it back to Osborne. "Hold this for me, Doc." Osborne heard the clink of bullets as he stuffed them into his jacket pockets.

"I don't know how to use a gun," said Julie lamely, as if apologizing.

"We'll certainly have to change that, won't we," said Ray briskly, glancing at her with a quick smile. Seeing the anxious look on her face, he amended his words. "Not tonight. Don't worry. If one gun isn't enough, then even a dozen guns won't do it.

"What do you think, Doc? You want the twenty-gauge?"

"No, Ray. My eyesight in the dark—God help us if I made a mistake."

"Not a problem. We know Lew is armed."

Ray reached through the driver's seat window for his trout hat. He set it carefully onto his head, tipping it slightly to one side. "Mandatory for good luck." He winked as he reached for the rifle.

"Ready?" Ray sprinted toward Lew's cruiser.

"Oh, boy," he said softly. The front door of the car was ajar, the keys in the ignition. "No interior light may mean the battery is dead, and that means she didn't expect to be gone long," whispered Ray. He swung the door wider. No light went on. He checked the keys. "She left the ignition running, too. Out of gas. Looks like she got out to check on the place and never came back. Not a good sign."

He turned and moved toward the front of the old building. Julie followed right behind, waving the flashlight so the beam bounced through the front windows. Osborne peered over her shoulder. The boxes that had been piled high earlier were gone.

"Aim for the corner to the right," said Ray. The light picked up a haphazard pile of silver candlesticks, bowls, and other odd-shaped items that glinted under the beam.

"Looks like they dumped the small stuff," said Julie.

"Or didn't have time to smelt it," said Osborne. "Ray, remember the smoke I remarked on yesterday? They've definitely been smelting something with a high silver content."

"We'll check the house, but I want us to stay back in the trees as we come around that boulder and the berm," Ray cautioned as the three of them started toward the corner of the building. He shifted his gun to his left hand and reached for the flashlight.

"I'll go first. Doc, you behind me. Julie, you follow last. Try to stay on grass so we're not heard. With the cloud cover and no moon, we should be able to get pretty darn close. But keep low and stay behind me."

Ray adjusted the flash to a low beam, aiming it right at his feet. He started forward slowly. They moved across the ground behind the warehouse and toward the fake boulder that hid the road to the house. As they came around the berm to the point where the road dipped, Osborne was surprised to see that the house was clearly visible and brightly lit, top to bottom. He glimpsed a flash of color and movement on the main floor.

"Looks like a party," whispered Julie.

"You two stay here," said Ray. He handed Osborne the flashlight. "I'll go around to the front, check it out, then come back. Don't move from here. I'll be just a few minutes." His lanky form vanished into the night blackness without a sound.

Osborne took a deep breath. His entire being had switched on a familiar, intense concentration, a mind-set that he remembered from the many times he'd stalked a deer. Every sense tuned, every muscle tensed, his peripheral vision alert to the tiniest motion.

He wished like hell he had his own rifle with the sight adjusted to his eye and vision, the familiar checkering on the stock that fit his hand like a glove and the trigger through which he could slip his finger without thinking. That gun was like an extension of his arm, and how he wanted it right now.

This was no deer approaching. This was the enemy. These were people who threatened what he loved most in the whole world. For an instant, he felt hot tears press against his eyelids, but he blinked them back. He clenched his jaw and forced the fear and worry over Erin and the baby to pump his adrenaline.

The minutes passed slowly, incredibly slowly. He could hear himself and Julie breathing. Then Julie nudged him and whispered, "I see him!" Ray reappeared, as silently as he had left.

"The boathouse doors are wide open," he whispered.

"The boat is outside, tied to the far side of the dock, and a two-engine seaplane is floating in the boathouse. It's a pretty spacious little four-seater. Looks like they took out the seats. The doors on both sides are open. I could see several wooden crates. Hard to tell from a distance, but I thought I saw Judith sitting in the pilot's seat with interior lights on, studying something."

"No sign of Brad?" asked Osborne.

"No. The lake-side windows on the house have their shutters closed tight, so I couldn't see a thing. Let's try this back window to the right."

They crept forward. The house had been situated against a thick stand of evergreens fronted by arbor vitae, which made it easy to get within five feet of the windows yet remain hidden. If the builder had deliberately tucked the house under the towering pines in order to hide it, the opposite had also been accomplished: a visitor could approach and remain hidden until nose-close to the back windows.

They looked directly into a kitchen. Fully lit and empty. Even as they peered in, Brad entered the room from the left. He was dressed for a business trip in a dark suit with a pale-colored shirt and a tie. His jacket was open, and Osborne could see he wore his pants, as usual, belted primly up and over his potbelly. Slung around his neck was a long red silk scarf. He looked less like a criminal than a pretentious fop.

He walked rapidly straight across the room, crossing in front of them to a closed door opposite the window. He stopped and crooked his head as if to listen. For a long moment, he stood quite still. He must have heard something because he lingered. Then Osborne heard something, too, and grabbed Ray's arm. He heard the distant, muffled sound of a baby crying. Osborne recognized the cry of his grandson.

"They're here!" He almost spoke out loud.

"Steady, Doc," Ray whispered. He laid a reassuring hand on Osborne's shoulder.

They watched as Brad shrugged and started to walk away from the door. As he started to move, an outdoor air compressor, not far from where they were standing, clicked on with a loud, sharp whir. Julie yelped in surprise. Brad twisted toward the window, his eyes wide and alert.

Osborne backed quickly into the brush with Ray and Julie right beside him. He wasn't sure if they'd been seen. Brad hurried to the back door. An outside light clicked on, but the pool of light that it threw over the stoop and stairs fell a good ten feet short of where the three of them huddled.

Brad stepped out into the night, peering into the dark around him. Osborne was reminded again of how serpentine the man looked: Brad seemed to hold his head perfectly still with only the flat fish eyes moving in their sockets.

"Jude?" he called into the crisp night air. "Is that you?"

No one answered. He listened for a few seconds. Not even a breeze rustled a branch. Only the faint calls of young peepers down at the water's edge broke the silence. An owl hooted, soft but piercing. It hooted again, this time a shriek—the aggressive cry of an owl striking prey. Brad jumped back into the doorway.

What he couldn't see was that the owl was six foot four, wore a stuffed trout on its head, and happened to be standing right beside Osborne. Startled but satisfied, Brad stepped back in the house and closed the door. Ray waited a few beats and hooted again. Then he moved up toward the window. Osborne and Julie followed. The kitchen was empty.

"Where's Lew?" asked Julie. "This doesn't look good, Ray."

"Okay, I'm going in," said Ray softly. "I want you two to wait here. If I have any trouble, I'll fire the rifle. That means you head for the truck and get help. Doc, here's the key."

He moved swiftly to the back door, which opened silently. He disappeared inside.

Osborne took a deep breath and shifted his feet. Julie reached over to give his arm a squeeze. "He knows what he's doing," she whispered.

Suddenly, the air compressor kicked off as quickly as it had come on. An instant of silence followed and then a shrill cry that seemed to come from underground. A baby's cry.

Osborne was through the back door without even thinking. He ran down a short hall, turned sharply to his right, and crossed the kitchen toward the door he had glimpsed through the window. If the sounds had come from below, he figured this must be the door to a basement.

Curiously, instead of a knob, it had large silver handle in the shape of an airborne eagle. The right wing was designed to lock down into a steel hook on the wall, but it wasn't in place at the moment. Instead, the door stood slightly ajar. He grabbed the wing, the door swung open toward him, and he found himself staring down at rows of wine bottles. He ran down a short stairwell into a fully stocked wine cellar.

Osborne stopped and looked around. He could hear a voice off to his right. He recognized Brad's. At that moment, the baby wailed again, the sound still muffled but closer—definitely off to his right. But Osborne couldn't see where the noise was coming from. He looked frantically to his left and to his right, along a wall of bottles. The baby had begun to cry hard. Osborne walked quickly between six-foot-high stacks of bottles in the direction of the noise. Sure enough, at the far right end of the wine cellar, set back so it was nearly hidden by shelving, was another door. This one was steel and it, too, was ajar. Osborne stepped through. Cold, cold air hit him in the face.

At first, all he could see was another short hallway. He crept down the hallway to peer around the corner. At the end of a room about five feet wide and fifteen feet long were three chairs. In the chair farthest to his right, tied hand and foot with cord and with clear packing tape twisted around her head and over her mouth, was Lew.

Beside Lew, her son tied to her chest with a bath towel so his little head and body faced her, was Erin. The baby was banging his head against his mother's collarbone and screaming. She was also tied hand and foot and gagged with the tape. If Lew and Erin had worn jackets earlier, they didn't have them on now, and the room was absolutely frigid. Osborne could see his breath in the air.

Beside Erin, tied into a chair, was a third woman, a blond wearing jeans and a short-sleeved T-shirt, whose head drooped down against her chest so Osborne couldn't see her face. The exposed skin of her arms looked dead white. In front of the three, his back to Osborne, stood Brad. He was rocking back and forth on his heels with his arms tightly crossed and chattering at his victims, a condescending tone to his voice.

Lew's eyes caught Osborne's, but she looked away quickly, focusing on Brad. Erin didn't see him. Her face was turned up toward Brad with a pleading look in her eyes. Tears were streaming down her cheeks. She was making guttural noises in her throat.

"Oh, hush that disgusting child! And wipe that look off your face, you stupid woman." If Brad Miller had ever attempted to hide his whining, effeminate mannerisms, he certainly didn't any longer. "I'm sick of that idiot child crying," Brad shook a threatening finger at her. "I'm doing you a favor, you know. It doesn't hurt to freeze to death. Just ask dear departed Miss England here. See? No pain on this face."

From behind, Osborne saw him step forward and reach to yank back the head of the frozen corpse beside Erin. "Oops, sorry—ha, ha, ha," he laughed his flat, humorless laugh, "I forgot, frozen solid." Brad blocked his field of vision so Osborne couldn't see his daughter's face. Whatever her reaction may have been, she was silent.

The baby wailed again.

Brad took a step toward Erin, raising his right arm. Osborne saw he had a little Colt .25 automatic in his hand, holding it so the butt gleamed in the light. "I think I'll just clock that little sucker and put him to sleep early." Brad walked forward, the pistol raised. Osborne heard Erin scream from low and inside her chest. Now he could see her frantically wresting her body back and forth as if she thought she could jerk herself and the baby out of Brad's way.

Brad laughed louder at the sight of her twisting and raised his arm higher. Time suddenly stood still for Osborne as Brad's arm came slowly, slowly down. Osborne felt himself airborne, and as he traveled in space, an image flashed into his mind of a woman he'd watched years ago, a young mother in her twenties, who had had no trouble lifting a Ford Thunderbird off the broken body of her seven-year-old who lay pinned beneath the vehicle. He felt that strength. He knew he could tear Brad's arms from their sockets with his bare hands.

As Osborne dove, he saw a burst of movement in front of Brad. Lew heaved up from the floor, chair and all. She thrust her body across Erin and the baby. The arm and the pistol butt cracked down hard on Lew's head, the gun going off just as Osborne tackled Brad's knees from behind.

Brad stumbled back over Osborne but caught himself even as he sprawled off to the right. He yanked his legs and kicked hard at Osborne's head, connecting solidly with Osborne's nose and right eye. Osborne slipped into red flashes and blackness for an instant. When his vision cleared, Brad was scrambling to his feet with the gun in his hand.

"I got more bullets here, stay right there, you stay right

there, don't you move." Brad's voice cracked, and he waved the gun like a schoolteacher frightened by a class out of control. On his hands and knees but fiercely alert, Osborne stared up at him.

Another irrational memory flashed into his brain: Brad had the same petulant look of anger on his face that he'd had the day he threw the brand-new hundred-dollar muskie rod that Joe had bought him for his birthday into Loon Lake. The little shit hadn't owned that rod more than twenty minutes before he threw it overboard, ruining the expensive reel. Osborne remembered that moment keenly, and he didn't like seeing the identical look on the face of the person holding the gun.

He shook off the searing pain across the bridge of his nose. He was more worried about Lew, lying beside him in a pool of blood. She had taken a blow to the back of her head that smashed her face into the floor, knocking her unconscious. Automatically, he reached to loosen the tape around her face and mouth. It pulled down easily, the tape loosened by the blood running out of her mouth.

"Take your hands off her!" shouted Brad.

"She's unconscious, she's going to choke on that blood—"

"So? One less fat cow to worry about," said Brad. "Get up, you old fool." He kicked at Osborne, who let himself up slowly and backed off against a row of freezer doors that ran along the inside wall. As he stood up, Osborne could see Lew had hit hard enough that an incisor had jammed into her lower lip. He was relieved to see the blood was flowing out of her mouth and not back down her throat. The blood made the wound look worse than it was.

He looked up to see the shock and fear in Erin's eyes just as the sound of footsteps grabbed his attention. He turned to see Ray and Julie rushing toward them.

"Doc? Doc? Are you all right?" Ray's voice rang out loudly as the two of them rounded the corner into the freezer room. They skidded to a halt at the sight of Brad waving his gun.

"Stop! Stop right there. Put the rifle down very slowly." Brad's eyes widened, and Osborne saw he was shocked at the sight of Julie. The pistol shook in his trembling hand.

Ray set his rifle down carefully to one side, moved away from it, and raised his hands. "Fine, Brad. You see the gun. We're not armed. It's okay. We're not armed." His voice was calm, almost soft.

Brad waved the pistol at Ray and Julie. "Down on your knees, both of you—no, not there—over by Doc." Ray and Julie, their hands up, walked slowly toward Osborne.

As they passed Brad, he grabbed the trout hat off Ray's head and threw it in the corner. "Ha, ha, ha," Brad cackled, though his eyes didn't smile. They stayed flat and mean. "I've wanted to do that for years, you hick. You think you're so cute. You must be one of most ridiculous idiots ever spawned in this shithole."

Ray watched the hat sail through the air and shrugged. "Gee, Brad, I'm sorry if I offended you," he said evenly.

Brad's turtlelike eyes closed to slits as he spoke. "Offend? You make me want to puke. Wait, stop, empty your pockets, Ray."

Ray did as he was told.

"Kick that knife this way," said Brad. He scooped up Ray's Swiss Army knife and slipped it into his pocket.

Osborne kept an eye on Brad's trigger finger. The guy kept waving the damn thing, using it to punctuate his remarks. Chances were good he might pull the trigger by accident again.

"Offend?" Brad wasn't letting go of the word. "Actually *appalled* is more like it," he sniffed. "Do you—? Ha, ha, ha," he paused midsentence to laugh, "Do you have *any* idea how dumb-shit that hat makes you look?" He waved his hand archly.

"And you get away with it, see." He shook his finger

at Ray. "*That's* what I can't stand. People here think you're clever. They think your idiot act is *funny*. But hell—why do I care?" He shook his head, "In less than an hour, I will be out of here forever. Away from all you stupid, crude idiots."

"You're holding a gun on us because we're crude?" asked Ray.

Osborne almost rolled his eyes. This was no time for Ray to get cute.

"You're right, Ray. I have understated the case. Truth is, I'm gonna kill you because I hate your fucking guts," said Brad. "I don't even like looking at you. Turn around and face the wall. Good." No break in his voice this time. He looked cool, too, thought Osborne. He looked tense but controlled and very satisfied that this moment had come.

The three of them, Osborne, Ray, and Julie, now stood along the side wall, Ray with his back to the group. To their immediate left were Erin and the dead woman, Lew was on the floor at their feet, and Brad had moved to the center of the room. The baby had stopped screaming and slumped, exhausted, against his mother's chest, his eyes closed.

Above Erin's head, a cooling unit in the wall kicked on with a loud whir. Osborne recognized the air compresser they had heard outside. The temperature in the room felt close to zero already, thought Osborne. He wondered how much colder it could get. The baby's hands looked a little blue to Osborne. He felt okay, but he knew the tension was keeping him from feeling the full force of the cold.

"Now, all three of you on your knees. Hurry!"

As he knelt, Ray looked down at Lew on the floor, then at Osborne. "Is she—?"

"He stunned her with the pistol on the back of the head—"

"Hey, shut up! Everyone shut up," said Brad.

"I don't want to shut up, Brad," said Julie, her voice strident and slightly shrill. "If I'm going to die, I want to know why, and I want to know why you murdered Robert. I'm not going to shut up until you give me some goddamn answers."

Brad tipped his big head and swung his eyes toward her. "You're right, Julie, it is indeed time we talked." A nasty edge creeped into his soft voice. "I—well, ha, ha, ha—I do have some explaining to do, don't I?" He chortled and flipped the silk scarf up and around his neck.

"You can skip your ten years as a traveling silver thief," said Julie. "I've got the documentation on all the hits you and Judith made out of Vegas."

"Every one?"

"All sixty-seven."

"Ooh, that's close—seventy-eight, actually. Well, three were art thefts that *included* silver."

"Why did you wait so long to come after Robert?"

"We wanted the entire estate, and we sure couldn't get that until the old lady passed away, could we? If you're wondering how I found him, that was easy. Every time I misbehaved as a kid, old Potty Peggy would tell me that she was going to call up Mrs. Bowers in Kansas City and ask to trade for the 'good boy.' She made Robert into this mythical angel child whom I grew up hating. By the time we finally met, I'm afraid I couldn't get past all the hatred and envy old Peggy had inspired over the years. Robert the good one, the lucky one. Brad the brat."

Osborne heard the soft padding of steps behind Brad. They stopped at the corner. No one entered the room. He couldn't tell if Brad had heard or not, he was so focused on Julie. He was focused and he was preening. He was loving the moment.

"If you're so smart, Bradford, why didn't you hasten *her* departure?" challenged Julie.

"Believe me, I thought about it. But that old crone had too many people around her all the time. The damn house-

keeper for one. I never had the chance. Speaking of
chance—why *did* she pick Robert to adopt? To be her
heir? She could've just as easily picked me—or Jude—
why not all three of us? Julie, do you see why I am *en-
titled* to everything Robert had? Only by some quirk of
fate did he get chosen instead of me. At least in my hum-
ble opinion. And . . . right now . . . *my* opinion counts."

He drew out his words, enjoying center stage. He
looked around at the three of them, then at Erin and Lew.
He raised his right hand and waved the gun with a delicate
gesture as if tipping a tea cup with his little finger lifted:
"I just realized something. This is so perfect: my most
despised people in the world are all here today. Dr. Osborne, Julie Rehnquist, Ray the fish freak. Only Potty
Peggy is missing. This is truly my day. And they say
revenge is best served cold. Try frozen, huh?" And his
high-pitched laughter filled the room.

Osborne had inched closer to Erin until he could reach
out to put his hand on her shoulder. Mercifully, the baby
was still quiet.

"No, no, Dr. Osborne," warned Brad, waving his gun,
"don't try to help your little girl. It's too late for that.

"Tell me," Brad set one hand on his hip and leaned
forward with a smirk on his face. "Does your lovely
daughter know what a stupid man you are? That you practiced in Loon Lake because you were too incompetent to
get accepted into a practice in Wausau? Or Madison?
Peggy told me that you barely made it out of dental
school. I often wonder, why are stupid people like you
happy? Maybe you're happy because you're stupid?"

"Brad," said Osborne, speaking slowly. "Have I—has
my family hurt you in some way?"

"Hurt me?" With that, Brad trilled a shrill laugh and
waved his hands. "Hurt me? Think back thirty years, old
man! What about you and idiot Joe laughing at me in the
boat? Forcing me to feel stupid because I couldn't fish

and hunt like all the other boys. God, how I hated the two of you.

"I'll never forget how you'd make me cast and cast and cast, pretending like you were teaching me and then snickering. You think I didn't know? I know how you made fun of me. You and Joe and all your ignorant friends at the hunting shack. You think I didn't know? You two made me sit in that goddam deer stand all alone, for hours, freezing. The worst stand, the one no one else wanted. At night you made me go to bed early, then everyone told stories about me and laughed."

He lowered his voice and narrowed his eyes. "You think I wasn't aware of you making fun of me all these years? I saw it in your face at the bar the other day."

Right then, Osborne knew Brad lived in a world of his own. The truth was that he and Joe had bent over backward to teach the kid. They didn't snicker, they despaired. They had felt helpless trying to help the boy who wouldn't even try. They ended those afternoons almost in tears, not laughter. Then Peggy would rail at Joe for not trying harder. Joe felt inept. Many times he told Osborne what a failure he felt he had been as a father.

For several years in Brad's early teens, until it was clear that the boy hated it, Joe would try to include him in the warmth and camaraderie of deer season, bringing him to the hunting shack for the weeklong hunt. The other men's sons lived for the day they got the invitation: their ticket to manhood. But Brad turned up his nose, making it clear that he considered it a waste of his time. Finally, Joe had given up. But where the rest of the anger came from, Osborne couldn't even begin to imagine. Laughed at him? They never even talked about him. At least, not when Joe was around.

"But why hurt Erin and my little grandson?" Osborne asked, pleading. He held his arms out toward his daughter. "They haven't hurt you, Brad. Please, please let them go."

"Oh, no, no," said Brad, lively and happy. "I watched

you at the grocery store last Christmas, Doc. You were standing in line with Erin. I could see she's the most important thing in your life. Isn't she?" he demanded.

"That's what I like about this little mise-en-scène. Not only do you die, but you die *miserable*. You'll have to watch your daughter die. And your grandson. That's touching." He smiled. "Of course, the baby will die sooner. At least I think so."

"Brad!" Julie interrupted. "Okay, Brad. You've pulled this off quite nicely, I must say. I underestimated you." Julie was shivering hard.

"Really, Julie? So you are impressed with my fish locker?" Brad waved the pistol at the walls of the room. But he kept his eyes riveted on them, suspicious as to what Julie was up to. Osborne took a good look around him for the first time. It was the most elaborate fish freezer he'd ever seen with varied sizes of lockers and racks, some closed, some open.

"Quite Martha Stewart—all this just for fish? Or is it double-duty: fish locker and designer morgue?" asked Julie.

"Cute," said Brad. "You are very cute. Fish locker is the operative term. That's what I told Robert, of course. He was so stupid. Who would ever believe you could catch so many fish, you'd need a locker like this? My goodness, no. Jude and I keep the paintings here. Not quite this chilly, of course. See that state-of-the-art freezing unit? Perfect humidity and temperature control. This is where we keep the larger paintings until we trade them in Chicago for the tiny wonders that we're taking to Japan."

"Tiny wonders?" Julie asked. "What do you mean?"

"My stroke of brilliance, dear," bragged Brad. "It is just too ridiculous to ship or travel with huge, clunky works of art, I don't care how much they are worth." Brad waved a fussy hand. "No, I said, no, no. So instead, I traded in all Robert's monumental junk like that Bacon that I couldn't stand, the Frankenthalers, those impossible Diebenkorns. Out the door! I kept the small O'Keefe's, Chagalls, several Monets. Then I picked up some Corots, two *exceptional* Vermeers, one stolen, of course. My dear Julie—do you believe it?! I've got *a hundred thirty million bucks* in small paintings to unload in Japan two days from now. Unload and sell. Even my buyers are all lined up."

"No silver?"

"A little, only a few special items. Why do you ask?"

"Oh . . ." Julie sighed. "Mrs. Bowers had those lovely silver pitchers from her family, pre–Civil War. Are those gone?"

"Melted down, dear. Sorry," said Brad. "I have ingots up the wazoo. That's the only thing I liked about you, by the way. You do have taste."

"Thank you," said Julie sweetly. "But you're leaving behind the other six hundred million dollars that belonged to Robert. What's so brilliant about that?"

"Ha, ha, ha—" Brad made an attempt to laugh. "What are you talking about? Are you calling me a fool?"

"Why not?" said Julie. Her agreeable tone vanished. "My percentage on getting out of here isn't exactly great. Why not exit leaving you a little unhappy, too?" She paused and took a deep breath. Brad watched her, his eyes shifting ever so slightly as though he was worried about what he might hear.

"For the record, Brad, Robert was planning to give you the goddam money."

Julie's voice cracked like she was close to tears. "He didn't want it. All he wanted was this house for the two of us and the children. That's all. His plan was to give me this house with this little lake for a wedding gift, set up a small trust for us to live on . . . and give you the rest. He told me he loved you . . . like a brother."

Julie's words seemed to stun Brad, who was staring at her.

"I told him I thought he was crazy. I told him I thought

you were a real weasel, but he wouldn't hear any criticism of you. He genuinely cared for you."

Brad stood speechless. Julie, pleased with the impact she was having, continued. "He didn't know you were natural siblings. Don't misunderstand. But he told me he felt you were kindred spirits—if you know what I mean. He told me that he knew what you'd been through, and he would forgive you anything because no human being should have to fight through life the way the two of you had had to in your own separate situations.

"He wasn't rational, Brad, but maybe that's a family trait. What I do know is this: he was planning to give all the Bowers money away—after he let you have as much as you wanted."

Suddenly a deep, almost musical voice rang out from behind Brad. It was a voice with a low timbre and a bell-like edge.

"Brad baby? Did I hear we've had a six-hundred-million-dollar oversight?" Judith Benjamin came around the corner and stopped in surprise at the sight of Ray's deer rifle. Brad jumped at the sound of her voice.

"I've been listening," said Judith, answering the question on his face. "Thought I heard a pop a few minutes ago and came up to see if you dropped something."

twenty-four

An excellent angler, and now with God.

Isaak Walton, *The Compleat Angler*

"**What** the hell is this?" Her eyes took in the room full of people, widening just slightly on spotting Julie.

Osborne was shocked at the sight of her. Gone was the trench coat and the French twist. Instead, stopped short behind Brad and dressed in a tailored charcoal-gray suit stood an individual whose appearance—tall, broad-shouldered, and dignified—suddenly made sense. What had been a too-tall, too-stout, too-burly female had metamorphosed into a stalwart, muscular male.

The head was bald with a light fringe of white-blond hair at the temples and ears and around the back of the head. The lower face sported a neat grayish blond beard and mustache, probably attached with theatrical adhesive. But it was unmistakably Judith. Osborne recognized the signature horn-rimmed glasses.

"Brad! Hey—we don't have time for any foolishness. I want us in the air in fifteen minutes." There was an imperious edge to her voice, and Brad's hand wobbled with the gun in it as if he was apologizing for bad behavior. Judith's eyes, flat and wide as her brother's, seemed even larger in the thin, strong-boned face. No makeup lightened their effect now. She let them play over the sight of Osborne, Ray still standing with his back to the room, and Julie. The ice in her eyes seem to drop the temperature in the freezer another ten or twenty degrees.

"Brad, give me that gun." Judith reached for the pistol, and her hand grasped it expertly. She pulled the lapels of her jacket close around her neck. "Brrr—what the hell do you have this set at?"

"As low as it can go—the flash-freeze temp."

"Good. We're out of here." She started to leave, then she stopped and turned, her eyes on Osborne. "I am sorry that Brad insisted on including you, Dr. Osborne. But it does make good business sense. Now that we have you and Ray, the good chief here, little orphan Annie, and Erin, this makes for a more efficient exit. Who's left to know any details? No one in Loon Lake. Right? If it took six weeks to find the other bodies, how long will it take until they find their way to a house that's not even on a map?"

"Judith?" Ray spoke up, his voice slightly muffled against the wall.

"I made him turn around," said Brad. "I hate his idiot face."

"Oh, Brad, stop it," Judith said mockingly. "You hate him because he's my buddy. You hate him because sometimes I think he's kinda cute."

It was becoming clear that Judith was running the show. "Ray, I do hate to leave you like this—I've always thought you'd make a great bartender. If I could leave you alive, I'd give you Thunder Bay. I really would. I know you'd clean it up, which is too bad, but you could do good things with that place."

"I could do that," said Ray. "I guess for the moment, it doesn't sound like a viable option."

"It isn't. Sorry, sonny."

"She's leading you on," said Brad, "payback for your lousy jokes."

"Mind your own business, Brad," said Judith sharply. "We'll talk payback all right—for your six-hundred-million-dollar mistake."

"Like what? What do you mean?" Brad whirled around to face his partner. Osborne heard fear in his voice.

"That isn't my fault—"

"It's never your fault. Forget it. Get down to the plane and check—"

"But—"

"But nothing, Brad. Just do it. Okay? Just follow my directions this one time."

"Judith?" Ray turned to face her. "I'd like to raise a nonhumorous subject if I may?"

Judith checked her watch. Brad still stood before her. He had planted his feet like a stubborn child. "I'm not going. I want to hear what he has to say."

"Brad . . ." Judith raised her hand and leveled the pistol at her brother. "Move. Get down to that plane. Count the boxes in the back, and make sure that fool Marie packed every one. We should have seven, not including the suitcases. We got about thirteen minutes to takeoff and I want no delays. My customs connections work tonight and tomorrow only. If we miss them, we can't get out of Canada. Do I make myself clear?"

Brad gave Judith a sullen look, then shrugged and walked slowly out of the room.

"Why did you kill all those men? Why not just Robert Bowers?" Ray asked.

"Oh, that's a good question," said Judith, shaking her finger. She chuckled.

"That was another one of Bradford's little schemes that went askew. He thought he could take over Robert's identity. Have you noticed how he lost weight? He had a special beard designed, he practiced speech patterns. He was going to impersonate Robert and return to Kansas City with the YPO guys, then transfer all the assets of the Bowers estate abroad, but he forgot one thing: those YPO assholes have these ridiculous secret handshakes and signs—a small detail that Brad overlooked.

"So we have them out here for an artsy-fartsy party, give them an artistic excuse to watch one of my girls dance and plenty of booze, then Brad gets in the car to drive back with them, and the asshole from Des Moines asks him some dumb question in code, some philosophical bullshit question. He blows it, of course.

"I was standing there watching it happen. I saw this look pass between the three of them. I knew right away they were suspicious. That was it. I couldn't risk blowing this deal that way. We had to kill 'em all. Too bad, too. Can you imagine if Brad had made it back to KC unde-tected and got—what did you say, Julie—another six hun-dred million bucks? That's real money. But we got a hundred 'n' thirty mil out of the art, and that's not to sneeze at. Of course . . ." She winked at them. "It counts for even more when you don't have to share."

"What about me?" asked Julie. "I would have known he wasn't Robert. You could never fool me!"

"You were the least of our worries," said Judith. "He could just say he broke off the relationship, and you were a spurned lover making up stories."

"I don't think so. I'm respected in Kansas City."

"Respect isn't worth shit when someone's looking at making a few million bucks off a deal, honey." Judith's eyes through her horn-rimmed glasses looked amused. She started to back out of the room.

"Remember Billy Spencer?" Ray interrupted as if anx-ious to keep her talking. Osborne felt a flash of anger and tried to get Ray's attention with an angry look.

What on earth was Ray thinking? What's with this in-ane topic of conversation? Who the hell cares about Billy Spencer, for God's sake! Time was running out for them.

The baby was looking bad. Where earlier the little guy had appeared to have fallen asleep, now it looked like he'd lost consciousness in the cold. Erin's eyes above her gag caught and held Osborne's in panic. She thought so, too.

Tears filled Osborne's eyes. He felt his heart breaking. He felt everything he'd done in life worth absolutely nothing in this moment: He was helpless to help his children. Helpless to help the woman who was in his thoughts almost every hour of every day, a woman who might have been the finest fishing pal he could ever wish for.

But he might have time to tell Erin how he loved her—if they could get Brad and Judith out of the freezer. He wanted time to put an arm around Lew and tell her that she had changed his life—and he hoped he had made some small difference in hers. It wasn't the worst way to go, he decided, with your arms around the ones you love most. But he needed time to do that. Time alone together. Thirty minutes from now, and he knew he'd be close to unconscious himself. If Ray would just shut up, they could have a few precious moments together before death.

Osborne tuned back into the words that were passing like an endless slow dance between Ray and Judith.

Judith had stopped and turned. "Yes. I knew Billy. He lived next door to Ruth Minor when I was living there. Why?"

"I was in Billy's backyard that Sunday morning." Ray's voice had taken on a slow, deliberate cadence, and Judith stood frozen, her flat, wide eyes fixed on Ray's. "I was watching through a hole in the fence, and I saw old Ruth working on her roses, and I saw you come up behind her. . . ."

"Shut up," said Judith. "Just shut up."

"I saw you push her," continued Ray. "I watched you swing at her with the shovel. She was crawling into the house and you . . ." He paused. Judith said nothing.

"She was a grown woman, Judith, and you were . . . what . . . nine or ten years old?"

"Hate makes it easy," said Judith. "You'd be surprised. It makes many acts easy. Remember," she snorted, "I was big for my age. So you saw it all, and you never told anyone? Well, Ray, that perturbs me," said Judith, sarcasm in her voice. "Now, why would you keep your mouth shut all these years? Waiting to blackmail?"

"Before that terrible day, I had been spending the night at Billy's a lot that summer," said Ray. "One night we snuck out to catch nightcrawlers, and we saw a man going into Mrs. Minor's store real late. We snuck up to the window. . . ." Ray paused. "Do you want me to continue?"

Judith nodded, but her eyes looked glassy. As Ray's low voice went on, Osborne remembered the small Minor house with its one-room little grocery store, its shelves of gums and candies by the cash register, and the short aisles with boxes of saltines and cereals and cans of soup. And old Ruth, heavy, ponderous, and mean. When little kids tried to swipe a piece of bubble gum, she didn't call a parent, she just grabbed the kid by the shirt, pulled him back to the cash register, made him put his hands on the counter, and whomped his fingers with an old wooden ruler as hard as she could.

"We watched Mrs. Minor take money from him and then we saw her pull you into the room. . . ."

"Go on." Judith's voice was steely.

"We started to watch, but Billy got scared and ran off. I watched everything. I shouldn't have. I lost my innocence that night. I knew why you killed her. I knew that I would have, too. When I was in high school, I learned that the statute of limitations never runs out on murder, so . . . I've never told anyone."

Judith took a deep breath. She gave a slight smile and shook her head, "You know, Ray, if you're trying to soften me up, it's too late."

"I wanted you to know because I want just one favor

in return, Judith. I want you to let Erin and her baby out of here. Doc and Lew and I—hey, we know the world is oversupplied with muskie hunters. But these two, please. Whatever Brad's feelings are toward the rest of us—they have not hurt anyone. Please?"

Judith looked over at Osborne. "Dr. Osborne?"

"Yes?"

"You have daughters. . . ."

"Yes."

"Do you remember a certain October night after a football game in the early sixties?"

Osborne did not think he could possibly feel any colder, but he did at this moment. He felt the ice deep in his gut.

"Do you mean the night that you were beat up?"

Judith looked at him and gave a wide, deliberate grin. "I mean the night that I made the mistake of thinking that a boy really liked me and was taking me to a beer party with all the rest of the kids. The one night that I let my guard down and began to think that I might have a life with some happiness like everyone else. The night when I went in to the woods to pee, they followed me. They all followed me . . . the boys and . . . the girls. You know the rest, don't you, Doc?"

Osborne did indeed. He first heard the story from Mary Lee who had heard the news from a close friend whose daughter was at the party. It started with about seven of the high school boys watching one pull Judith into a clearing and tear off her clothes. They'd crowded around to poke and look at her. Then one of the boys raped her. Two others followed. The rest said they found her body too disgusting. Then one swung a fist, and others followed. Toward the end, the girls had crowded around watching, too. They left her there, naked and bleeding.

Weeks later, Judith was brought to Osborne by her foster family for a final round of reconstructive work on her face. The injury to the jaw had been so severe than a portion of bone had been removed, necessitating dental surgery. That's why her face appeared so much thinner than her siblings: as a result of the beating, she lost an inch on each side of her jaw.

But she lost much, much more. That was the night the town learned exactly how she was different from other women. Hair grew down from her navel in a pattern familiar to boys her age. It grew between her breasts, across her back, and along the insides of her upper thighs, just enough to make her different.

But that wasn't all. Puberty had been cruel, arriving earlier than normal and causing her to have overdeveloped in every way. She grew too tall and too big, filling in with muscle when the other girls were turning soft and curvy. She had the shoulders of a linebacker but breasts that stopped traffic. She was more than a woman and armored like a man. No one understood. From that time on, she was the object of ridicule and an absurd, humiliating sympathy. If Judith had been excluded before, now she was shunned. Jokes were cracked that if she hadn't inherited her old man's looks, she wouldn't have had a problem.

"No one helped me, Doc. No one has ever said they were sorry. No parent ever stepped forward to say to me or anyone that a terrible thing had happened. Did they, Doc? Did *you*, Doc?"

She paused and looked hard at Osborne. "Do you know I lay in that field until dark *the next day*? I was unconscious, my right arm was broken. I went to the police station. They never did a thing. No one cared.

"So guess what—I sure as hell don't care either." Backing up as she spoke, Judith grabbed Ray's rifle, then turned abruptly around the corner and slammed shut the door to the freezer. Osborne heard the lock catch, then seconds later, the door to the wine cellar slammed shut.

twenty-five

The man that weds for greedy wealth,
He goes a fishing fair,
But often times he gets a frog,
Or very little share.

Anonymous, circa 1629

"**Lew**, are you okay?"

"I'm fine, just bit a chunk out of my lip. I'll live. Can you untie me?" Lew asked from where she lay on the floor. Ray bent over to untie Lew while Julie wiped the blood from her face. Osborne rushed to untie Erin.

"Oh, Dad," Erin blurted and burst into tears when he took off the gag. "I'm so cold, I think I'm going to faint. I'm so worried about the baby." She cradled her son close in her arms. Osborne pulled off his jacket and doubled it over to wrap around the baby just as Julie did the same with hers.

"Here, bundle him in this." The three of them huddled around Erin and the baby, while Ray bent over to pick up his hat.

"Who is that poor person?" said Julie, glancing over the body of the woman in the chair.

"That's the dancer from Thunder Bay," said Lew. "You can't do much to help her. She's been in here a good six weeks." Julie stepped back from the frozen figure.

"Everyone listen to me," Ray said, yanking at the lure that had been stitched onto his hat. "There!" He took the lure and twisted it. "Here's one of the unsung virtures of the mud-puppy surface lure." In his fingers, he held one of the metal disks that turn like propellers in the water when reeled back to the boat. He pointed to the freezer unit set high in the wall behind them. "If I can unscrew the casings around that unit, we should be able to push this right through and out. Say a prayer this is a Harvey unit out of Wausau. I worked for them one summer, and I know how they install these mothers."

Ray jumped up on one of the chairs and worked quickly. The disk was a good, hard metal, and the screws loosened easily. He pulled the screws and washers out. The metal casing on the front of the unit slipped off to expose the coiled wires of the motor right behind.

"Yes," said Ray with serious relief in his voice, "it's a Harvey—customized, but the basics are the same—we're outta here." With one hand he yanked the wires loose, then he shoved at the edge of the metal case that held the motor. With one heave, the entire freezer unit was pushed through to the outside. They heard it fall to the ground with a large thump. No one took a breath. No sound. No one coming. No one heard. They waited a full minute.

"Okay," said Ray. "Me first. I want to be sure it's safe for the rest of you. Brad or Judith may still be in the house so stay very, very quiet. If we can, let's move everyone through and into the woods as quickly and quietly as possible."

With a boost from Osborne, he was through the opening, and he rolled onto the ground outside. "It's clear," he whispered back. "Erin next, then hand up the baby." They all worked quickly. Osborne was the last one through. Lew stood waiting with Ray.

"Julie's rushing Erin and the baby to the hospital in Ray's truck," said Lew quickly before he could even ask. "I need you here, Doc."

The three of them rubbed their arms and tried to quietly stomp their feet in the air that now seemed almost hot compared to the freezer. "Jeez, I've got to get my blood moving," said Lew.

Just then, they heard an outboard motor kick on somewhere on the other side of the house. They ran to the corner. It was dark, but lights near the boathouse were brightly lit. The plane, its headlights off, was being pulled away from the dock by a small boat lit with a single headlight. They ran down toward the dock but stopped safely within the darkness of the trees. With the clouds still obscuring the moon, Osborne found it impossible to make out who was in the boat. Then his eye caught something glinting on the deck of the fully lit boathouse.

"Ray," said Osborne, "I see your rifle—right beside the boathouse door," but even as he whispered, Ray had already spotted it and was on his way toward the boathouse. The door was wide open, the gun resting in an area that was brightly lit and visible from the lake. Even so, Ray moved swiftly to grab it. He paused by the open door for a brief moment. Suddenly he dropped to the deck and lay still.

"Someone's in there." Lew's hand suddenly clutched Osborne's. "My God, I hope he's . . ." She didn't finish, but Osborne had the same panicked thought: don't let Ray get shot full face by someone waiting for him in the boathouse. Ray stayed where he was for a full minute or more before quickly scrambling to his knees and jumping back into the blackness of the pines. If anyone saw him, there was no reaction from the plane or the boat. Within seconds, Ray was back with Osborne and Lew.

"Little surprise down there, folks," he said, his whisper matter-of-fact but so low that Osborne and Lew bumped heads trying to hear him. "The good professor has his legacy all right—a bullet hole in the head."

"Dead?" asked Lew.

"I didn't see any movement," said Ray. "I had a pretty good angle, and looks like he got it right through the temple." He looked up at the sky and out toward where the small light from the boat was bobbing in place.

"Let's move down to the water's edge. These clouds are breaking up. Pray for moonlight. My only chance to get a shot off is when or if I can see the damn plane." They started forward, slipping on the pine needles that covered the ground. Shards of moonlight were starting to break through the dense clouds. Osborne thought he could make out a figure standing in the boat and reaching toward the door into the plane.

Suddenly, Lew grabbed both Osborne and Ray and yanked them to a stop. She put her finger first to her lips, then she pointed off to their right. Bobbing silently on the water, hiding in the branches of a fallen Norway pine but outlined off and on by the moon as it moved between the clouds, was a long, dark shape.

"That's a canoe," whispered Ray. "Now who the hell—?"

The cloud cover was definitely breaking up. With nearly a full moon about to break through, Osborne realized Ray would have an excellent opportunity to see his target. As if the pilot knew this, the plane's motor suddenly hummed, two bright headlights went on, pinpointing its location as it started to move across the lake. The clouds broke, and Ray raised his gun to his shoulder. The plane lifted off.

But just as Ray took aim at the aircraft, a shot rang out. From under the fallen pine, the canoe had moved out onto the lake. Though they could make out only the outline of a figure in the boat, they could see a rifle raised against the sky.

Boom! The gun went off. *Boom!* It fired again.

The plane poised in midair, then dropped straight down

toward the water. It hit at an angle with one pontoon, then appeared in the moonlight to tip forward and sideways.

Osborne, Lew, and Ray looked at each other.

"Holy shit," said Ray on behalf of all three. They ran for the dock. With no boat however, they were marooned. There was no way they could get out to the plane. The moon was bright now, but Osborne still could not make out the face on the figure in the canoe, even though it was only about three hundred yards away.

"Hey! Who's there?" shouted Lew, "Police here! Put that damn gun down and tell me who you are!"

Silence. Then the canoe turned slowly, pointed its bow toward them and, with a delicate motion, the canoist dipped a paddle into the black surface of the lake. Osborne watched the boat move silently toward them. Ray gripped Osborne's arm above the elbow, signaling he had recognized the figure, but he said nothing.

Meanwhile, not a sound came from the plane, but even if it had, they wouldn't have noticed. About fifty feet from the dock, Osborne recognized the figure holding the paddle: Marie.

She brought her boat close in and smiled up at them in the light, squinting into the glare. "Don't ask me to paddle out there, 'cause I'm not going, and you aren't either," was all she said. Her voice was sure and strong. Then she turned and looked out into the dark. Strange black angles jutting against the moon was all they could see of the plane. The angles were drifting lower and lower into the water. "No one goes anywhere until that plane is ten minutes underwater."

"Marie!" Lew was clearly stunned.

"They don't swim," said Marie, ignoring Lew as she rested her paddle in her lap and reached down for her gun. "Lew? Did you hear me? I said no one goes near that plane until I say so." The canoe floated about four feet from the dock.

"Marie, only Judith is in that plane," said Ray. "She

put a bullet in Brad. His body's in the boathouse."

"That doesn't surprise me," said Marie. Osborne was amazed at the transformed woman before him. All her strange mannerisms, her staccato chuckle, her silly smile, had disappeared. This Marie was very still and very strong.

"Marie, will you give me your gun, please?" asked Lew. "I refuse to allow you to hold that rifle on us. Not if you want to avoid arrest."

"If you promise me you won't take my canoe and go rushing out there."

"I promise," said Lew without hesitation. "I promise. Believe me, it's the last thing I plan to do, even though I should. She left us all locked in the freezer to die. This is self-defense."

Marie looked at Lew for a long moment. "Ray," she said finally, "pull me over to the dock." With those words, Ray knelt to grab the edge of the canoe. He pulled the wooden boat toward them, and Osborne recognized it. It was the very same one that had been resting on sawhorses at Herman's place.

Marie handed up her rifle. Then she got to her feet, holding to the sides of the canoe to steady herself, and let Ray give her a hand up beside them. Osborne noticed she even moved faster than she had earlier that day. She stood tall and straight.

"How did you get involved in all this?" Ray put his arm around her shoulder.

"They're family. You know that, don't you?" She looked around at the three of them, and all three nodded. "Some folks don't, but you do know that they were my baby brother and sister?"

"Yes," said Ray softly, "when did you first know?"

"Herman told me two years ago when they first looked me up and asked me to do some work for them," said Marie. "They weren't particularly nice, but I decided to do it anyway for the money. They promised to pay me," said Marie. "They promised me a lot of money. That's why I built that house for them. That's why I built cases for their art. Judith promised me.

"She promised . . ." Marie took a deep breath. "But I acted dumb like I always do, and pretty soon they started talking in front of me. I knew when they killed those men, and I knew when they killed Ted Bronk. But when I heard 'em planning to kill Ray, I decided someone had to put a stop to it. Look at me—no one in Loon Lake was going to believe me, you know? So I took care of it myself."

She drew herself up tall for a long moment and then, almost instantly, she sagged. She stood there all alone on the dock, her arms limp at her sides and looking to Osborne for all the world like a person deserted. Ray opened his arms like a welcoming big brother and stepped toward her, folding Marie's short, stocky body into his. He pressed her head to his chest and patted her shoulders.

"Hey, Marie, you did the right thing," he said. "If it weren't for you . . . well, if I'd known what you were up to, I would have asked Lew if you couldn't be deputized today to help me and Doc out."

"What are you talking about?" Lew's voice cut in crisply, "I thought you did."

"That's right, I did. Didn't I, Doc? When we were out to Herman's."

"We'll have to ask Julie," said Osborne. "I'm sure she remembers."

Marie stepped away from Ray's comforting arms. "I decided to do this when I heard them planning this trip to Japan. I knew what they were up to."

She looked back out to the lake, which had a still, unbroken surface now, gleaming quite beautifully, Osborne thought, under the moonlight. "I packed that plane so that it would be more than a little unbalanced. Know what I mean? I figured if I could bring it down, the weight would do the rest."

"But they could have escaped through the windows and the door," said Lew.

"I rigged it," said Marie. "The door and windows are locked shut so they won't open after Judith set the interior lock. I cut a hole near the engine so the body of the plane would fill with water pretty fast."

"Marie," Lew spoke, "were you involved in killing the men whose bodies we found?"

"No," said Marie. "Ted Bronk helped 'em. That's why they killed him—so they'd have no witnesses."

"But you knew. Why didn't they kill you?"

"They didn't really know that I knew," said Marie. "See, I'd work all day and act the fool, you know. They didn't know that I would come back here at night. I came to fish at first. Beautiful walleye in this lake. And then I found that I could hear what they were saying inside the house because they always had windows open. So I started to watch them. That's how I knew they were going after Ray that night."

She looked at Ray. "After you and Doc found those bodies, Brad tapped into the phone line and recorded all your calls. When he knew you were going to see Herman, he figured Herman might send you this way. They were waiting. Ted's the one who hit you from behind."

"Why didn't they kill me?" asked Ray.

"They were trying to," said Marie, "but they wanted it to look like you'd been drinking and got lost. They were pretty surprised that Doc found you, y'know. They thought Ted had dragged you way back in the woods to die."

"Marie, you were in the woods that night, weren't you?" asked Osborne.

"Yes."

"Why?" Lew jumped in with the question.

"I was going to move Ray before they could come back," said Marie softly. "I wasn't going to let them kill Ray, too."

"Marie . . ." Lew took a deep breath. "I think I can work this out so you won't be charged with the murder of Judith Benjamin. Our lives were at risk. All our lives. You made the difference."

twenty-six

The muskie is one fish that is hard to catch, whether you are rich or poor. It makes fools out of professional muskie fisherman as well as novices.

Tony Rizzo, *Secrets of a Muskie Guide*

It was three-thirty the next morning when Osborne found himself ecstatic that the Loon Lake Pub was open twenty-four hours, seven days a week. He'd never been so hungry in his life. From the looks on the faces of Ray, Julie, and Lew, the sentiment was exactly the same.

"Poor Sloan's not doing well at all," said Lew as she got out of Osborne's car after he'd parked at the curb outside the pub. "I checked with the nurses while you were in the emergency room with the baby."

They had just dropped Erin and the baby at the hospital for twenty-four hours of observation. Mark was there to meet them. Osborne wasn't too worried. The prognosis from the two physicians who examined them were excellent. Though the baby had slipped into unconsciousness, he revived quickly under treatment for hypothermia.

"If he had to suffer a trauma," said the pediatrician who'd rushed to the emergency room to meet Erin, the baby, and Julie, "this is the one to choose. The lower temperatures are the least likely to cause brain damage, and I see no evidence of frostbite. He's still chubby enough with baby fat that his appendages aren't long enough to be endangered. Nothing on his little body is too far from his heart."

Erin herself was still shaken, but she'd be okay. Osborne was worried she might have frostbite on her fingers and toes, but the trauma doc told Osborne she looked pretty good. The adrenaline rush spurred by her determination to save herself and her baby had kept the blood flowing in spite of the freezing temperatures. Once she had warmed up, the numbness in her fingers and toes was gone. They checked her over carefully to be sure she might not have a late reaction and slip into shock, but she had calmed down after finally getting to nurse the baby.

Lew had gone straight to the police department where she taped statements from Julie, Ray, and Marie. Then she'd hurried over to the emergency room to see how the baby and Erin were doing. She told Osborne that Ray and Julie had gone ahead to hold a table for them at the pub while she ran by John Sloan's room for a quick check on her ex-boss.

"If he hadn't smoked so heavily all these years, he'd have been out in a few days, but this pneumonia is hanging on. The nurse said he still has fluid on the lungs."

"I'm glad," said Osborne. "I mean, I'm not glad the poor man is so ill, but I'm glad that we were able to do what we did. I'm not sure we'd have had the same results if John had been around. He would have made it difficult to include Ray."

"Yep, Ray forces you to play your hunches, y'know, Doc," said Lew briskly. She looked up at him as he held the door to the pub open for her. Their glance held for an instant. Long enough for Osborne to make up his mind.

Ray and Julie had snagged a comfortable booth for the foursome. "I can't believe how busy this place is," said

Julie as a harried waitress arrived with glasses of water.

"The bars just closed," said Ray. "The tradition around here, if you've closed down the bar, is to hit the Loon Lake Pub for a double cheeseburger, fries, and a root beer float."

"Or a bowl of Marilyn's homemade chicken noodle soup," added Lew with one of her few quick smiles.

"I'll take both," said Julie. "I can't remember the last time I ate!" She turned to the waitress and gave her order.

"Save room for their lemon meringue pie," said Osborne. "Joanne from Eagle River makes it—may be the best you'll ever eat. Lew said Sloan's not looking so good," he added, handing the menus around the table.

"Speaking of looking good," said Ray, "I'm still trying to figure out why Judith Benjamin decked herself out like a man. I mean, what difference would it have made? I don't think the woman is gay or a closet transsexual, do you?"

"Insurance," said Lew. "Marie said she's got Robert Bowers's passport on her. The facial resemblance is close enough, given how bad those passport photos are."

"But her height and weight?"

"Doubtful they'd even check that," said Lew. "She probably wouldn't have needed the disguise, anyway. She and Brad had done this many times before. They had their contacts—and their bribes—all in place. But if anything happened to upset the timing, if just one official asked any questions, she would be covered. She could pass for Bowers, and even if they ran a check on the artworks, everything was registered in his name. She had a fail-safe setup. Now, if only our friend Doc here hadn't jumped the gun on opening day for muskie fishing . . ."

"Now, Lew, I was scouting. Just scouting."

"And if you believe that one . . ." said Ray. Osborne kicked him under the table.

"Right," said Lew. She opened her menu, looked quickly, and closed it, putting it down on her plate. Then she leaned forward and crossed her arms on the table in front of her. The swelling on her lower lip was barely noticeable, and she had the no-nonsense, intense look on her face that Osborne now knew meant business. She did not look like a person who'd gone too many hours without sleep. Osborne wondered where on earth she found the energy. But she did, and she made him feel wide awake and twenty years younger, too.

"Y'know, Ray, try taking it easy on the controlled substances, if you would. Because if and when I have an opening—and I know I will eventually—I would like to talk to you and the good dentist here about working together in the future—on a project-by-project basis maybe?"

Osborne looked over at Ray. He liked the sound of that. He liked the idea of working around Lew. And life was always interesting around Ray.

"I'd like to keep my family out of it, but I could handle a career change," said Osborne.

"Yeah," said Ray, "I'll have to run it by Shanley and make sure he has no problems with that, but our project is pretty low-key with a five-year timeline on it. I can probably work something out."

"When did you start working with Shanley?"

"Oh . . . right around two years ago."

"Is that why you went into rehab?"

"No." Ray sat up straight and reached for his cup of coffee. Now it was his turn to lean forward and look around the table. His eyes stopped at Julie. "These folks know that I was a serious pothead and an alcoholic up until—well, two years ago. I always had problems measuring up in a family where all my siblings became doctors and lawyers and I just wanted to go fishin'. To make a long story short, I hit bottom just after I turned thirty-five. Donna found me unconscious one day and drove me to the mental health ward at the hospital and checked me in. I was up there, still resisting, when my good buddy, Dick Harvey, lost his oldest son in a freak accident."

"I remember that," said Lew. "He was terrific kid. Dropped dead from a heart attack playing soccer. He was only thirteen years old."

"Right," said Ray. "It happened in the morning, and that afternoon Dick came to see me at the hospital and demanded that they let him in. You know how many rules they have over there. But he found me and he grabbed me and he looked me in the eye and he said, 'Ray, you gotta help me. You're the only one that can help me.' Well . . ." Ray looked around the booth at Lew and Osborne and Julie. "I never thought I had anything to give to anybody up to that moment."

"What did you do?" asked Julie softly.

"Not much, really. I put my arms around him and I said, 'Dick, what's God gonna do? He needs a new angel.'" Ray took another slow sip of his coffee. "That's all. But it helped. So when I learned Rick Shanley's group was looking for someone to do this, I gave them a call. The money's not great, but it gets me through the slow season."

"And you're doing something pretty darn important," said Julie. She reached over and squeezed Ray's arm.

Ray put his hand over hers and kept it there. "Thanks."

"Is that why you put in your septic system?" asked Osborne.

Julie and Lew swung their heads toward Osborne in disbelief.

"Hey!" Osborne put his hands up defensively. "He was piping his raw sewage into my rose garden," said Osborne. "I never did know why he stopped."

"Actually, Doc, you nailed it," said Ray. "The institute crowd made me do it. They went over my record and inspected my trailer. They want to make sure you aren't violating any codes or stuff if you're working for them. Their inspector caught that, and he helped me get a good deal on a septic. I didn't mention it because my deal with Shanley is confidential."

"How's Marie?" Osborne asked.

Ray had dropped him at the hospital to check on Erin and the baby immediately after the powerful spotlights on the police boat confirmed that the plane was in seven feet of ice-cold water with Judith Benjamin strapped tightly into the pilot's seat. Not only did the spots pick up the plane, but it had sunk at an angle so they could make out Judith's head against the window. Her head was tipped back and up, the eyes open. Even in death she appeared to be casting a baleful stare at the crowd.

Marie's gunfire had scored twice, hitting the plane's engine and also shattering the door on the pilot's side. A bullet may have hit Judith, but no one knew for sure. A crew would raise the plane sometime the next day.

Meanwhile, Marie assured everyone, the precious paintings still on board were quite safe. Airtight and watertight. No moisture was going to seep onto those canvases. Judith had insisted on special packing, concerned that the freight compartments on the international flight might not allow for the necessary humidity control. Little did she suspect why Marie had followed instructions so carefully this time.

"Marie seems okay," said Ray. "Lew had me take her to the station for a statement. I asked her to join us here, but she wanted to get home to Herman."

"You gave her a ride?"

"Nope. Wouldn't take one. She had that old truck of Herman's, and she insisted on getting herself back. They're very close, those two."

Just then their waitress reappeared with a full tray of soup and burgers and began to set steaming bowls in front of each of them. Then she crowded plates of burgers and fries between the bowls as they all watched in hungry silence.

"Marie sure can pick and choose who she wants to do

carpentry for from now on," added Julie between bites.

"How so?" asked Lew, when the waitress had left.

"She's Robert Bowers's next of kin," said Julie, her eyes smiling mischievously over her cheeseburger.

"My God, I forgot about that," said Ray. He set his burger down and wiped his lips and beard carefully with his napkin. "How much is she worth?"

"Close to a billion dollars, counting the insurance on Robert that gets paid now that we know how he died," said Julie. "That oughta rock this town."

Osborne raised his eyebrows and glanced up to see Lew doing the same.

"Whoa, that'll buy her a good lawyer if she needs one," said Ray, and they were all quiet for solemn moment. "Does she know it yet?"

"I thought I'd stop out to Herman's place sometime later today—after I get some sleep—and have a little chat with her," said Julie. She looked at Ray, and it was a look both questioning and ever so slightly demure. "I was wondering if you'd go with me."

"Sure. Let me take you up the Loon Lake Chain afterward. In my boat. We'll get that fishing lesson in before you have to go back to Kansas City. . . ."

"I was thinking of staying an extra day or two," said Julie, her eyes on Ray.

"That would be loverly," said Ray, his eyes on Julie. "And perhaps I can recommend a rod or two—in case this becomes a habit?"

Before Julie could answer, Lew interrupted. "Oh—Ray. I almost forgot." She unzipped the small black leather bag she wore strapped to her waist near her revolver and pulled out the muskie lure that had once graced Ray's hat.

"We've got your hat at the station, but I was afraid this might get lost. You may want it as a souvenir."

"Thank you, Lew." Ray reached out his hand.

"Have you ever caught anything with that or you just

wear it on your hat?" asked Lew with a dubious tone in her voice.

"I know you don't believe in surface lures," said Ray, his eyes earnest and persuasive as he looked at Lew, "but I've caught four big ones with this lure and raised, maybe, fifteen or twenty more over the past few years."

"Me, too," said Osborne. "That surface mud puppy is one of the best damn lures."

"I dunno," said Lew in disbelief. "I like the deep-water lure myself. I really believe you've got a better shot fishing the thermocline. Over the last ten years, I've hooked three big ones fishing deep with a Striker. Granted, I've only gotten three, but they're plenty big fish, guys."

"What is everyone talking about?" asked Julie. "This sounds too technical for so early in the morning."

"Dueling muskie hunters," said Ray with a grin. "This debate could go on for hours. Once you start to fish muskie, you have to commit—deep water or surface—there's no middle ground."

"Sure there is," said Osborne. "She can fish her side of the boat and I'll fish mine. But Lew," said Osborne, setting his fork carefully into his slice of lemon meringue pie, then raising his eyes to hers, "have you ever given the surface mud puppy a chance?"

"No."

Osborne sensed a challenge. He was more than up to the effort. He knew this woman's habits in the streambeds, in the rivers—he would like to know her better on the lake. "Perhaps it's time."

"Doc, are you *finally* inviting me to share your boat?" Lew chuckled. God, he loved her laugh.

"What do you mean 'finally,' " said Osborne. "I've been trying to get you on the lake for months. You just refuse to let go of that damn fly rod of yours. Of course, now Ray tells me you're an expert with a spinning rod, too." He was very surprised to feel his heart pounding.

He also caught a flash of amusement between Julie and Ray. He felt a little foolish.

"O-o-h, I doubt that," said Lew. She gave him a sideways look. "I'm sure there's a lot I can learn from you."

"I didn't hear that," said Ray, winking at Julie.

"You bet you didn't." Osborne waved a fork at Ray. "You keep your big mouth shut." That was hopeless. He knew Ray would be regaling the McDonald's crowd with every detail of his love life. But for some reason, he just didn't care.

"Doc . . ." Lew looked down at her plate and neatly set her fork to wedge out a small bite of pie, then she looked up at him. "I'll try the mud puppy if you'll try my Striker." Her alert, good-natured eyes held his.

"On one condition," said Osborne. "You let me take you to dinner afterward."

She never flinched, and he realized she'd been waiting. "Deal."

"I'm so glad you're okay, Lew."

Lew looked at him in surprise. Her eyes softened, and she reached over to lay her hand on his. "I'm glad you're okay, Doc." Ray and Julie were suddenly very busy chewing.

Osborne savored the last lemony bite of his pie. Some days life just didn't get much better.